The Wrong Box

Robert Louis Stevenson was born in Edinburgh the only child of Thomas Stevenson, a distinguis engineer, and Margaret Balfour, daughter of a Sco ter. Educated at various schools in the city, in 18(tered Edinburgh University to study for a science but, four years later, opted to read law. He was call Scottish Bar in 1874, but never practised in earnest, and from 1876 he followed a full-time literary career, beginning as an essayist and travel writer with the publication of *An Inland Voyage* (1878), *Travels With a Donkey in the Cevennes* (1879), and then graduating to the stories published in *New Arabian Nights* (1882). In 1880 Stevenson married Fanny Vandegrift, but because of his ill-health, he and his new family led a nomadic existence in Davos, on the French Riviera, and in Bournemouth. During these years he published some of his most famous works: *Treasure Island* (1883), *Kidnapped* (1886), and *Dr Jekyll and Mr Hyde* (1886). In August 1887 he left Europe for America, never to return, and in November 1890 settled in Samoa, where he died on 3 December 1894.

Lloyd Osbourne, born in San Francisco in 1868, was the son of Fanny Vandegrift, by her first husband, Sam Osbourne, whom she divorced in order to marry Stevenson. Lloyd and his stepfather soon became close, and the young man accompanied the author on his travels in Europe, North America, and the South Seas. He collaborated with Stevenson on *The Wrong Box* (1889), *The Wrecker* (1892), and *The Ebb-Tide* (1894). The Stevenson Estate passed to him in 1914, and he edited the Vailima Edition of Stevenson's work (1922–3). He wrote novels and motoring books, with varying success, and his last book, *Peril*, was published in 1929. He died in California in 1947.

David Pascoe is Lecturer in English at Oriel College, Oxford.

The Wrong Box

Robert Louis Stevenson
and Lloyd Osbourne

Introduced by

David Pascoe

Oxford   New York
OXFORD UNIVERSITY PRESS
1995

Oxford University Press, Walton Street, Oxford OX2 6DP

Oxford New York
Athens Auckland Bangkok Bombay
Calcutta Cape Town Dar es Salaam Delhi
Florence Hong Kong Istanbul Karachi
Kuala Lumpur Madras Madrid Melbourne
Mexico City Nairobi Paris Singapore
Taipei Tokyo Toronto
and associated companies in
Berlin Ibadan

Oxford is a trade mark of Oxford University Press

Published in the United States
by Oxford University Press Inc., New York

British Library Cataloguing in Publication Data
Data available

Library of Congress Cataloging-in-Publication Data
Stevenson, Robert Louis, 1850–1894.
The wrong box / Robert Louis Stevenson and Lloyd Osbourne;
introduced by David Pascoe.
p. cm. — (Oxford popular fiction)
Includes bibliographical references (p.   ).
I. Osbourne, Lloyd, 1868–1947. II. Title. III. Series.
PR5487.W8 1995 823'.8—dc20 95-11741
ISBN 0–19–282426–0

1 3 5 7 9 10 8 6 4 2

Typeset by Best-set Typesetter Ltd., Hong Kong
Printed in Great Britain by
Biddles Ltd

OXFORD POPULAR FICTION

General Editor Professor David Trotter
Associate Editor Professor John Sutherland
Department of English, University College London

Amongst the many works of fiction that have become bestsellers and have then sunk into oblivion a significant number live on in popular consciousness, achieving almost folkloric status. Such books possess, as George Orwell observed, 'native grace' and have often articulated the collective aspirations and anxieties of their time more directly than so-called serious literature.

The aim of the Oxford Popular Fiction series is to introduce, or reintroduce, some of the most influential literary myth-makers of the last 150 years—bestselling works of British and American fiction that have helped define a new style or genre and that continue to resonate in popular memory. From crime and historical fiction to romance, adventure, and social comedy, the series will build up into a library of books that lie at the heart of British and American popular culture.

CONTENTS

INTRODUCTION

'I believe in an ultimate decency of things', wrote Robert Louis Stevenson to Sidney Colvin in August 1893; but the actions of many of the characters he had created during the previous decade demonstrate that decency can often emerge from error; and that rightness and wrongness depend on each other for their survival.[1] Dr Jekyll, appalled by Hyde's murderousness, kills himself to prevent further carnage, but the last words of his confession are oddly egotistical: 'Will Hyde die upon the scaffold? or will he find the courage to release himself at the last moment? God knows; I am careless; this is my true hour of death, and what is to follow concerns another than myself.' A similar moral buck is passed in Stevenson's miniature version of *Crime and Punishment*, 'Markheim' (1885), whose protagonist murders an antiques dealer. In the minutes after this motiveless deed, the killer confronts a mysterious visitant to the shop, who, it soon becomes clear, is either a product of his deranged mind, or a representative of his conscience. After this eerie encounter, when Markheim sees the dead man's housemaid, he tells her 'You had better go for the police. I have killed your master.' Surrendering himself to the wheels of justice, he is finally careless. In *Prince Otto* (1885) the irresponsible ruler of a German statelet, hearing home truths about the way he has governed his kingdom, is galvanized into action to save it. His actions come too late, however, for the revolution has begun and, fleeing the new Republic, he ends up in a forest, happy at being released from the cares of state. 'The Misadventures of John Nicholson' (1888), portrays a prodigal son who returns for Christmas to the Edinburgh of his youth, and, finding a corpse in the house of his best friend, feels doomed, convinced that he—the wrong man—will swing for the murder: 'here was a new Judicial Error in the very making. It was not so plain where he must go, for the old Judicial Error, vague as a cloud, appeared to fill the habitable world.' It could have meant his death, but, facing up to and living through this error—his *mis*adventure—Nicholson is eventually reconciled with his family. There is a corollary, of course, in 'The Body-Snatcher' (1884), a

---

[1] *The Letters of Robert Louis Stevenson*, ed. Sidney Colvin, 4 vols. (1911), iv. 210.

pot-boiler which tells of Fettes's involvement, years earlier as a medical student, in a hideous series of grave robberies. In his depiction of this tormented old man, Stevenson is keen to show that behind the façade of 'a good, old, decent Christian' there may lurk some recollection of not just the decencies, but also the terrible 'things' that sometimes emerge from error.

G. K. Chesterton, one of the shrewdest critics of Stevenson, expressed surprise that the same author who was involved in 'the radiant harlequinade' of *The Wrong Box* (1889) could have written these last two works, since 'there is something very specially sordid and squalid about the glimpses of low-life given in the dissipations of John Nicholson; and something of the same kind comes to us like gusts of gas from the medical students of *The Body Snatcher*'.[2] Set against these narratives of moral carelessness, the action of the novel Stevenson and his stepson, Lloyd Osbourne, completed in late 1888, may, at first sight, seem to present an indecently careful situation. *The Wrong Box* concerns two penurious nephews, Morris and John Finsbury who take the utmost care of their aged uncle Joseph, but only because if he lives a little longer he may well inherit a Tontine, an annuity which increases in value as each subscriber dies, until the last surviving member of the scheme enjoys a lump sum—the proceeds of which the brothers expect to inherit in due course. This is their first mistake; others follow. Returning from Bournemouth (where Stevenson and his entourage lived from 1884 to 1887), the train carrying the Finsbury party is involved in a dreadful accident. Emerging unscathed from the wreckage, the brothers find a body which they mistakenly believe to be that of their uncle; but, to safeguard the Tontine, they determine that no-one shall suspect his death. In fact, the old man is uninjured, and, with some presence of mind, has seized the opportunity to break free from the clutches of his scheming nephews. The unfortunate victim of the crash is never identified, but his corpse, concealed first in a water-butt and then in a locked Broadway piano, is sent from address to address in London, by train, delivery van, and carrier's cart, in complete defiance of all probability, as well as of Victorian canons of funereal decency, until at last the cart is stolen, together with its incriminating cargo, and never seen again.

[2] G. K. Chesterton, *Robert Louis Stevenson* (1927), 61.

Chesterton, however, was wrong to single out *The Wrong Box* as a special case, since it is in keeping with so many of Stevenson's narratives. Because the plot turns on the various attempts made by those who find the body in their possession to palm it off on their acquaintances it is as farcical as 'John Nicholson'; but the final disappearance of the corpse carries us into the territory of 'The Body-Snatcher', where a gig, whose sole occupant is a 'dead and long-dissected' body, is last seen heading for Edinburgh. Nor is *The Wrong Box* far from one of Stevenson's earliest stories, 'The Suicide Club', first published in *New Arabian Nights* (1882).[3] Here a body is discovered in a hotel room by an innocent young man, Silas, who wishes to inform the police, but the physician Dr Noel persuades him to follow an alternative scheme. Looking on Silas's Saratoga trunk, he muses: 'the object of such a box is to contain a human body.' Poor Silas replies, disbelievingly: ' "surely this is not a time for jesting" ', but the good doctor is deadly serious, and so

The body of the murdered man was carried from the bed, and, after some difficulty, doubled up and inserted whole into the empty box. With an effort on the part of both, the lid was forced down upon this unusual baggage.

The finishing touch here is 'after some difficulty' which delicately suggests the onset of rigor mortis. That hint of physical, and moral, decay is followed up when, two days later, Silas, alone with the trunk in another hotel room, 'nosed all the cracks and openings with the most passionate attention. But the weather was cool, and the trunk still managed to contain his shocking secret.' The distinction is in the verb which both accommodates the body and stifles a bad smell.

Since the publication of *The Wrong Box*, many critics have sniffed the cracks and openings of its narrative as uneasily as Silas. An anonymous notice in 1889 sought 'to protest against the funereal fun of a story which has, as the pivot on which the whole plot turns, the buffeting from pillar to post of a corpse'; the reviewer continued by observing, with relief, that the story rattles through 'with sufficient rapidity to prevent the olfactory nerve discovering the whereabouts of the concealed carcase'. Indeed, the novel caused quite a stink among Stevenson's adoring and expectant public. E. T. Cook ob-

---

[3] Of *The Wrong Box*, Stevenson told J. A. Symonds that Osbourne 'would not have written it but for the New Arabian Nights' (*Letters*, iii. 26).

served that it would 'try the faith of his most ardent admirers'; while
J. M. Barrie complained of a 'fourth-rate book' which those same
devotees should 'drop behind the piano'. The venerable Mrs
Oliphant called the novel 'a very wrong box indeed', and argued
that while Stevenson's versatility might be admirable, it was going
too far when he attempted 'to show us how far he can climb a greased
pole and grin through a horse-collar'. The *Illustrated London News*
fulminated against this 'disagreeable story' and described Michael
Finsbury, the mischievous lawyer, and Pitman, the hapless artist,
as 'an idiotic couple' who should have contacted the police instead
of undertaking 'a series of disgusting tricks' to get rid of the body.[4]
The trenchant criticism has continued to this day, and two of
Stevenson's most recent biographers have little time for the merits of
the book: to Jenni Calder's eye 'it is clumsy and heavy-handed'; while
Frank McLynn splutters: 'This attempt to make a comedy of errors
out of a Victorian tontine and a misidentified corpse should never
have seen the light of day—it is a truly calamitous apology for a
novel.'[5]

Writing in 1892 about the state of the author's reputation, J. St. Loe
Strachey observed that 'Mr Stevenson's admirers may be divided into
two classes—those who like and those who do not like *The Wrong
Box*'; and from the outset its champions have been as vociferous as its
detractors. *The Times* described it as a 'romping farce' whose 'literary
grace . . . preserves it from the least suspicion of vulgarity'. To E. F.
Benson, it was 'perhaps the most superb extravaganza in the language', while V. S. Pritchett termed it 'a farce that slips down the
throat with the nicety of an oyster'. Max Beerbohm was animated by
the way in which 'the jewelled elaboration of the manner becomes an
integral part of the fun, and keeps us laughing the more irresistibly
and the more loudly'.[6] Between 1958 and 1971 a group of *Wrong Box
aficionados* held five dinners at the Athenaeum in order to consume

[4] *Pall Mall Gazette*, 19 June 1889; E. T. Cook, *The Athenaeum*, 27 July 1889; J. M.
Barrie ('Gavin Ogilvy'), *British Weekly*, 28 June 1889; Mrs Oliphant, *Blackwood's*,
Aug. 1889; *Illustrated London News*, Aug. 1889.

[5] Jenni Calder, *RLS: A Life Study* (1980), 179; Frank McLynn, *Robert Louis
Stevenson* (1993), 284.

[6] J. St. Loe Strachey, *Spectator*, lxix, 23 July 1892; *The Times*, 7 Aug. 1889; E. F.
Benson, 'The Myth of Robert Louis Stevenson', *London Mercury* (Aug. 1928), 378;
V. S. Pritchett, 'Introduction' to RLS, *Novels and Stories* (London, 1945); M.
Beerbohm, 'Lytton Strachey', *Mainly on the Air* (1957), 192.

the 'solidly British meal' set out before John in Chapter XV, and to read learned papers on the minutiae of the book. No doubt Rudyard Kipling's own experience of the novel was untypical of the enthusiasts' dinners: 'I read it first in a small hotel in Boston in '89 when the negro waiter nearly turned me out of the dining-room for spluttering over my meal.'[7] Like Kipling, Stevenson was a great giggler—once he began he could not be stopped unless (or until) someone bent his fingers back and pain interjected—and there are accounts of the paroxysms of laughter which occurred during the composition: 'Lloyd and I have finished a story, *The Wrong Box*. If it is not funny, I am sure I do not know what is. I have split over writing it' (*Letters*, iii. 102).

Yet for many, both in and beyond the novel, the laughter is tiresome rather than side-splitting. Writing in the *Athenaeum* (27 July 1889) E. T. Cook sounds off pompously: 'To have aided in the production of a book three-fourths of which consist of tedious levity, is indeed, not a thing to be proud of.' If this assessment misses the acuity with which *The Wrong Box* shows how some people find levity difficult to accept in serious situations, it is because the journal for which Cook was writing had been ridiculed by John Finsbury as 'the kind of thing that nobody could read out of a lunatic asylum'. Consider, then, Gideon's reaction to Julia Hazeltine's fit of laughter at his erratic behaviour in the houseboat:

'I speak as your sincere well-wisher, but this can only be called levity.'
Julia made great eyes at him.
'I cannot withdraw the word' he said.

After he has poured forth his miserable story she is obliged to apologize; and clearly no lasting damage has been done, since he proposes to her a few minutes later. Yet Gideon is not the only character to be seriously disturbed by levity. Earlier in the novel, Michael Finsbury tells William Dent Pitman (whose nerve is failing as he realizes the implications, both legal and logistical, of disposing of a corpse): 'I am not going to embark on such a business and have no fun for my money.' The artist is shocked by this callousness in the face of death; but the lawyer replies: 'Nothing like a little judicious levity.'

At first glance, Michael's 'judicious levity' may seem comforting, appearing not as an ideal, but instead as a reassuringly jaunty declaration which informs Pitman that the situation, while critical, is by no means grave. Yet the need to assert levity so expediently suggests that a body of evidence as considerable as a corpse may be disposed of neither easily nor decently. No doubt Stevenson and Osbourne meant the phrase to sound hollow, since 'levity''s terms cannot go without saying, but depend on a consensus—or even an aquiescence—wrought from other people. Throughout Stevenson's fiction, however, 'the ultimate decency of things' cannot be established with neutrality except in relation to the politics of established professions and institutions such as the law, banking, medicine, or even kingship; the claims of mere individuals are invalid. In this novel, it is such decency that Pitman cannot see in Michael; and later, on the houseboat, that Gideon is not prepared to grant even in Julia; but these deficiencies are irrelevant. The crux of this extraordinary book is that decency must speak, yet it cannot speak for itself; that it can receive, adapt to, comprehend, and aid action, but it cannot initiate it, for in the comedy of *The Wrong Box* only error carries any conviction of rightness, even though that conviction may, in fact, be criminal. In this absurd world, any other qualities must strive for compromised expression; and so Michael's 'levity' is imperilled by the larger practicalities implied by 'judicious'. The words are invoked in the novel's Preface: ' "Nothing like a piece of judicious levity," says Michael Finsbury in the text; nor can any better excuse be found for the volume in the reader's hand'; consequently, those who enjoy the novel must be prepared to accept the expediency of the narrative's frivolity. Stevenson once described *The Wrong Box* as 'a real lark' (*Letters*, iii. 95), and laughing at the right time, at the capriciousness of so many, one can come to appreciate the vital humour inherent in the disposal and disappearance of a body. But it is a lark whose sheer vitality precludes any thoughts that, within its darker depths, the dead are being mocked.

Stevenson's idea of responsible social comedy may derive from his reading of George Meredith's novels. The two first met in 1878 at Meredith's home, Box Hill, and, throughout his career, Stevenson championed the older man's work. His favourite book was *The Egoist* (1879), which he thought 'strange and admirable' (*Letters*, ii. 186), but singling out its ruthless satire—'the angry picture of human faults'—for particular praise: 'It is yourself that is hunted down; these are your own faults that are dragged into the day and numbered, with lingering relish, with cruel cunning and precision.'[8] Meredith's novel is introduced by a 'Prelude' in which he explains that 'the Comic Spirit', however dark or bizarre, is the ultimate civilizer in a dull, hard world; 'it deals with human nature in the drawing-room of civilized men and women, where we have no dust of the struggling outer world, no mire, no violent clashes'. It is on guard against sentimentalism and vanity, and strips us of our affectations, presenting 'the singular scene of charity issuing of disdain under the stroke of honorable laughter'; what Stevenson and Osbourne might call 'judicious levity'. This 'Prelude' needs to be supplemented with the less well-known lecture Meredith delivered to the London Institution in early 1877, which has become one of the most important accounts in English of the morality of comedy.

Men's future on earth does not attract it; their honesty and shapeliness in the present does; and whenever they wax out of proportion, overblown, affected, pretentious, bombastical, hypocritical, pedantic, fantastically delicate; whenever it sees them self-deceived or hoodwinked, given to run riot in idolatries, drifting into vanities, congregating in absurdities, planning short-sightedly, plotting dementedly; whenever they are at variance with their professions, and violate the unwritten but perceptible laws binding them in consideration one to another; whenever they offend sound reason, fair justice; are false in humility or mined with conceit, individually or in the bulk; the Spirit overhead will look humanely malign, and cast an oblique light on them followed by volleys of silvery laughter. That is the Comic Spirit.[9]

This could be a prescription for the characters in this novel: the bombast and pedantry of Joseph Finsbury's lectures; the fantastic delicacy of Pitman; the demented plotting of Morris Finsbury; the short-sighted planning of Gideon Forsyth; both he and Michael Finsbury at variance with their professions as lawyers. In the final analysis, as Michael takes over the Tontine, as John and Morris are left with the leather business, and as Gideon elects to do 'nothing in the world' with the 'criminals' assembled before him in Chancery Lane, that 'humanely malign' levity is a sure sign of the decency that can emerge out of the most absurd human error.

[8] RLS, 'Books Which Have Influenced Me' in *Essays and Criticisms* (1903), 230.
[9] George Meredith, 'An Essay On Comedy', repr. in Wylie Sypher, ed., *Comedy* (Baltimore, 1956).

J. B. Priestley thought that Stevenson 'was often most happily himself . . . when he was larking on paper with Lloyd Osbourne', and that in the case of the novel in question, 'the result was glorious'. Other critics, though, have treated Osbourne's literary aspirations with extraordinary hostility; Frank McLynn, for instance, submits that the young man 'suffered from a well-known syndrome, whereby frequent contact with a genuine writer induces the feeling that "anyone can do it" '.[10] Yet he cannot be treated as a spoilt child, for although *The Wrong Box* was the first of three novels on which Stevenson and his stepson collaborated, even before they actually wrote together, Lloyd helped bring about his stepfather's work. In a preface to *Treasure Island*, he recalls being summoned to hear the opening chapter of the novel: 'I was called up mysteriously to [RLS's] bedroom (he always spent his mornings writing in bed), and the first thing I saw was my beloved map lying on the coverlet.' The role that his little handpainted map played in the conception of a great adventure story is celebrated: 'Had it not been for me, and my childish box of paints, there would have been no such book as *Treasure Island*.'[11] This is arguable; but it is true that *The Wrong Box* would not have been launched on the tides of critical opinion were it not for the exertions of the young man Stevenson nicknamed 'the Port Admiral' (*Letters*, iii. 27).

According to Osbourne's own account, between October and November 1887, when he was 19, he wrote (entirely on his own) a work first entitled *The Finsbury Tontine*. His health had broken down in 1886, and he feared for his sight; a typewriter was procured so he could write even if blind. Writing to J. A. Symonds on 6 December 1887, Stevenson reports: 'Lloyd has learned to use the typewriter, and has gallantly completed upon that the draft of a tale, which seems to me not without merit and promise, it is so silly, so gay, so absurd, in spots (to my partial eyes) so genuinely humorous' (*Letters*, iii. 25). That parenthesis is a beautiful fatherly touch, even though some of the draft must have given him 'spots' before his 'eyes', for he told his wife Fanny: 'I quite chortle over some of it. Some of it, of course, is incredibly bad.'[12] The idea of collaboration occurred soon after, and

[10] J. B. Priestley, 'R.L.S.: The Real Romantic', *Observer*, 12 Nov. 1950; McLynn, 284.

[11] Lloyd Osbourne, 'Stevenson at Thirty-two', in RLS, *Treasure Island* (1924).

[12] Quoted in McLynn, 284.

by mid-March 1888, Stevenson had 'taken it in hand' (*Letters*, iii. 53) like some unruly child, revising it for publication, but leaving the essentials of the work unchanged. Osbourne recalls: 'Louis had to follow the text very closely, being unable to break without jeopardising the succeeding chapters. He breathed into it of course, his own incomparable power, humour and vivacity, and forced the thing to live as it had never lived before.'[13] At this point it was entitled *A Game of Bluff*; and not until January 1889 just before he offered it to Burlingame, editor of *Scribner's*, 'cash down' for $5,000, would it be rechristened *The Wrong Box*. During this long period of revision, Stevenson claimed to be 'toiling like a galley slave' on several other works, including *The Master of Ballantrae*; but things were not too bleak in Honolulu, since he also reported that 'this spasm of activity has been chequered with champagne parties' (*Letters*, iii. 102).

In a letter written during the composition of the next book he and Osbourne wrote together, *The Wrecker* (1892), Stevenson described their manner of collaboration: 'one person being responsible and giving the *coup de pouce* to every part of the work' (*Letters*, iv. 305). The finishing touches to *The Wrong Box* were generally provided by Stevenson, who tidied Osbourne's youthful excesses, clarified much of the characterization, and administered his distinctive treatment, though this was often done so slickly that it may be true—as Chesterton observed—that 'we remember the treatment more than the subject'. Yet just as this is remembered, what should not be forgotten along with the subject, is that the novel had two authors:

long after the details of the Tontine system have become blurred and all the far less interesting details of our own daily life along with them, when all lesser things have diminished and life itself is fading from my eyes— I shall still see before me the Form called up by that inspired paragraph: 'His costume was of a mercantile brilliancy best described as stylish; nor could anything be said against him, except that he was a little too like a wedding guest to be quite a gentleman.'[14]

This is wrong in two ways; first, the passage is misquoted, and secondly, the distinctively Stevensonian description is, in fact, Osbourne's. As Ernest Mehew points out in his magisterial edition, in the proof Stevenson struck out 'quite a gentleman' and replaced it

---

[13] Quoted in Graham Balfour, *The Life of Robert Louis Stevenson*, 2 vols. (1901), ii. 34.

[14] Chesterton, 161.

with 'perfectly genteel', but his corrections never reached his publishers, and so Osbourne's words have stood the test of time.[15] (See 'Note on the Text'.)

However, we do know that Stevenson added one or two of his favourite words. For instance, he inserted the paragraph in which Joseph Finsbury makes a 'sedulous review' of his pockets to find only one and ninepence halfpenny. The adjective recalls the essay, 'A College Magazine' (1887) in which Stevenson, looking back, claimed to have 'played the sedulous ape' to many other writers including Hazlitt, Defoe, and Baudelaire. Chesterton, commenting on this passage, observed: 'I do not think that Hazlitt would have added that word . . . some would say that the word is in the strict sense too *recherché*.'[16] It is a standard criticism of Stevenson: style impedes content. When George Moore first read 'Markheim' he found his enjoyment was compromised by the deployment of a single unexpected verb: 'my admiration waxed until I happened upon a man who stopped a clock with an "interjected finger".' At this point he realized the insupportability of Stevenson's style which, he claimed, was 'but a conjuror's trick.'

He spins one plate, two plates, three plates; he goes on throwing up plates until a dozen are whirling in the air. He throws up the thirteenth, and, lo! one comes down crashing.[17]

Reading Moore, Chesterton, ever ready to defend Stevenson, found it difficult to accept 'that because the word is unusual in that use, it showed that there was nothing but artificial verbalism in the whole tragedy of *Jekyll and Hyde* or the fun of *The Wrong Box*'.[18] This sounds like special pleading, for there is something in Moore's general charge which applies specifically to the farce of the latter. Rather than plates, its plot must be kept spinning, and consequently, in the midst of muddle, the novel lacks a significant reality. It is artificial, but that artifice is oddly knowing, a worldliness perhaps encapsulated in the exchange between Pitman and Michael over their newly assumed identities as Ezra Thomas and John Dickson:

[15] Robert Louis Stevenson and Lloyd Osbourne, *The Wrong Box*, ed. Ernest Mehew (1989), p. xviii.

[16] Chesterton, 141–2.

[17] George Moore, *The Daily Chronicle*, 22 May 1897.   [18] Chesterton, 143.

'But I can't invent,' protested Pitman. 'I never could invent in all my life.'

'You'll find you'll have to, my boy.'

From such desperation emerges the art of our necessities.

With a more characteristic brilliance, Chesterton also observed of Stevenson: 'He treated everything with an economy of detail and a suppression of irrelevance which had at last something about it stark and unnatural'; and such starkness could have its lighter consequences. For instance, it could engender that 'Comic Spirit' which Meredith defines in his 'Prelude' as conceiving 'a definite situation for a number of characters, and rejects all accessories in the exclusive pursuit of them'. Yet the plot of *The Wrong Box*, which seems as carefully constructed as the movement of a clock, is itself in error. In 'A Ramble in Barsetshire', Ronald Knox wrote: 'Consistency is, in romance, almost unattainable . . . there is even a mistake in *The Wrong Box*'. He did not elaborate, but the slip is both trivial and profound.[19] In Chapter XIV Gideon and Morris fail to recognize each other even though they have already met earlier, when Gideon rescues Julia from Morris's incandescent rage; and, what is more, there is no good reason for Gideon to be at the station on that Sunday, save the expediencies of fictional coincidence. Stevenson and Osbourne's ignorance of, or arrogance toward, detail saves the work from the charges of artificial verbalism, for its sheer wrongness is an imperfectly decent reaction towards the baggage of the late Victorian novel, in which boxes of irrelevant particulars had obstructed narrative drive. As Stevenson argued elsewhere: 'the great change of the past century has been effected by the admission of detail. . . . The introduction of these details developed a particular ability of hand; and that ability has led to the works that now amaze us on a railway journey.'[20]

To a great extent, *The Wrong Box* depends upon narratives associated with such journeys for its existence. Without the fortuitous rail disaster the plot would not get under way; the switching of luggage labels takes place on a train; and the denouement requires us to be at Waterloo station on a Sunday afternoon. Yet even as we are rushing

[19] Ronald Knox, *Essays in Satire* (1928), 197.
[20] RLS, 'A Note on Realism' in *Essays and Criticisms*, 214.

towards the novel's climax, Stevenson and Osbourne are keen to remind us of the sort of texts associated with mass travel: 'the backs of Mr Haggard's novels, with which (upon a week-day) the book-stall shines emblazoned, discreetly hidden behind dingy shutters.' These Railway Books—popular fantasies such as Rider Haggard's *King Solomon's Mines* (1885) and *She* (1887)—were a phenomenon which began in the 1840s, when publishers realized that there was a market for a cheap portable fiction, which, as Stevenson and Osbourne suggest in their novel's opening lines, could be used 'to while away an hour . . . in a railway train'. George Routledge's firm made the most of this new possibility, and, in 1848, created the Railway Library, which, in due course would have a thousand or so titles in print. Within twenty years a new line of instantly recognizable 'yellowbacks'— frequently translations of popular European novels—had been pioneered by Chapman and Hall to supply W. H. Smith's monopoly of station bookstalls; hence, Gideon Forsyth's chambers contain many 'yellow-backed French novels'. By the 1880s, two genres were coming to dominate the railway station: detective fictions and novels of sensation, both of which are parodied in Chapter xiii, where each of Morris's tribulations—as described by the brilliantly faked titles: *Where is the Body? or, The Mystery of Bent Pitman*; *The Fraud of the Tontine; or, Is my Uncle dead?*; *The Cottage at Browndean; or, The Underpaid Accomplice*; and *The Leather Business; or, The Shutters at Last: a Tale of the City*—'would have graced and commended the cover of a railway novel'.

Gideon Forsyth, of course, is the author of a novel entitled *Who Put Back the Clock?*, 'which appeared for several days upon the railway bookstalls and then vanished entirely from the face of the earth', and whose investigator bears the apposite name of Robert Skill: 'To readers of a critical turn, Robert appeared scarce upon a level with his surname, but it is a difficulty of the police romance that the reader is always a man of such vastly greater ingenuity than the writer'; and so it is that, when Gideon invokes his fictional creation, and imagines how Skill would have reacted had he found a corpse in a piano in his rooms, his course of action—to assume the guise of a composer and retire to a houseboat—is astoundingly stupid. Throughout *The Wrong Box*, characters make facetious reference to the popularity of *le roman policier*. Gideon's novel was 'inspired by the muse who presides over the police romance, a lady presumably of French extraction'; and

Michael invokes the name of 'Fortuné du Boisgobey', a prolific *roman-feuilletoniste* whose works dealt with the crimes committed by (and against) ordinary French people. His most famous novel, *Le Coup de Pouce* (1875) depicts a kindly old *curé* who sets out to discover the murderer of one of his parishioners, only to discover that the killing was committed by a newcomer whose false alibi had been contrived by tampering with the hands of the village clock. It's conceivable that the title of Gideon's novel may recall to the central mystery in du Boisgobey's novel, which was published in an English translation by Routledge's Railway Library in 1884.

Stevenson was not averse to such fiction; but it was to be read and written only as a last resort. In his essay, 'My First Book', he recalls how, during the writing of *Treasure Island*, when inspiration failed him, he buried himself 'in the novels of M. de Boisgobey', which rejuvenated him; and while there are detective elements in *New Arabian Nights*, *The Dynamiter* (1885), and *The Wrecker* (1892) ultimately these works remain 'novels of adventure', a genre to which *The Wrong Box*, avowedly, does not belong. In the Epilogue to *The Wrecker*, Stevenson and Osbourne discuss the police novel, and claim to have been 'attracted by its peculiar interest when done, and the peculiar difficulties that attend its execution; repelled by that appearance of insincerity and shallowness of tone, which seems its inevitable drawback'. Too often its form was 'an airless elaborate mechanism', and part of the distinction of *The Wrong Box* is that it interferes with the workings of the detective story.

Chesterton argued that 'the best sort of police novel' is one 'in which the police are never called in', and, in this novel, Stevenson and Osbourne wanted to suggest how easily the detective form could turn comic when there was a pressing need to keep the police out of the matter. Hence, Morris's bumbling attempts at cheque fraud are brought to a premature end when he is told that 'the whole affair must go at once into the hands of the police'; Michael thinks better of using the name 'Fortuné du Boisgobey', that writer so well-known in railway and police stations, since 'it would hang us both'; later, responding to Dent Pitman's suggestion to call in the police, Michael argues that it would only 'make a Scandal'; while for Gideon to do the same, though 'an easy course, a safe course', was 'not a pleasant one'. His Uncle Ned, with an eye on his political career, thinks similarly: 'not the police, Gid'; and, as the stolen carrier's cart, containing the unique Broadwood, is driven quickly away from the houseboat by the desperate Sergeant Brand, 'the word "detective" might have been heard to gurgle in the sergeant's throat'. Behind such comedy, Stevenson and Osbourne depict a society that is not only impossible, but unnecessary, to police.

Both the anarchy and the failure that the absence of authority might be assumed to invite, are thwarted by the improvised self-sufficiency of an urban world whose own free operation somehow remains in perfect accord with the policy it does not require. For so many, like Morris or John, existence only means 'keeping up the farce'. Michael sees himself 'condemned to be the instrument of Providence'; and something like providence is at work in what other characters believe to be the most ordinary psychological processes and social interactions, arranging things so that everyone goes his own way to arrive at a place tolerable, if not positively gratifying. And only one person, Sergeant Brand, goes astray. Despite all the plotting, the characters in the novel are not circumspect enough to feel themselves trapped between error and decency. They lack conscience, which in this novel is nothing more than the ability to put rightness into words. In its closing lines, Gideon makes an attempt to do just this when he admits to having 'qualms of conscience' about Brand, but Michael tells him that he can do 'nothing but sympathise'; this is the indecent thing to do, but according to the moral logic of this novel, there is really no alternative. *The Wrong Box*, then, presents a comedy of conduct without conscience; of disloyalty without guilt; of being in the wrong, but not boxed into the wrong course of action. Indecently buried by critics for so long, it deserves a decent exhumation now.

A NOTE ON THE TEXT

Apart from minor emendations to spelling and punctuation, the text is reproduced from the Swanston Edition (1912) of *The Wrong Box*: this has been checked with both the First and the Edinburgh editions of the novel. It was in this state that the book became so well-loved, or reviled, at the turn of the century; recently, however, this familiar text has become controversial.

In March 1889 Stevenson sent to his publisher, Burlingame, a final version of *The Wrong Box* for publication. Having been set from the typescript and his own manuscript of the closing chapters, the proofs of the novel were returned to Stevenson in May 1889. He corrected and sent back the first batch early in June, but retained a section to revise. In fact, he re-wrote about five pages of manuscript and introduced a new chapter heading, 'The Battle of Waterloo', in the midst of Chapter XV; but Scribner's seem not to have waited for the return of all the proofs and published the book uncorrected on 15 June. Clearly, the firm thought that he had made all the changes he wished to make, and neither Stevenson nor Osbourne seem to have been bothered by this textual confusion, for the corrections are not mentioned in any subsequent correspondence.

None of the changes appear in this edition of *The Wrong Box*, but interested readers can find them in Ernest Mehew's critical edition of the novel (1989), published on the centenary of its first appearance.

SELECT BIBLIOGRAPHY

The Wrong Box was first published simultaneously in the United States by Charles Scribner & Sons and in England by Longmans, Green and Co. on 15 June 1889. Ernest J. Mehew's critical edition (1989) restores the revisions, and contains some useful bibliographical information, and some excellent annotations; but many of the textual changes remain minor.

Collected Editions of the Works of R. L. Stevenson include: The Edinburgh Edition, ed. Sidney Colvin (1894–8); the Pentland Edition, with bibliographical notes by Edmund Gosse (1906–7); the Swanston Edition, with an introduction by Andrew Lang (1911–12); the Vailima Edition, ed. Lloyd Osbourne, with Prefatory Notes by Fanny van de Grift Stevenson (1922–3); and the Tusitala Edition (1923–4).

For a full bibliography of RLS see W. F. Prideaux, *Bibliography of Robert Louis Stevenson* (1903; rev. 1917), and Roger G. Swearingen, *The Prose Writings of Robert Louis Stevenson: A Guide* (1980). The Stevenson entry in the *New Cambridge History of English Literature* can be found in vol. iii, pp. 1004–14.

Letters have been edited variously by S. Colvin (4 vols., 1912); J. A. Smith, *Henry James and Robert Louis Stevenson: A Record of Friendship and Criticism* (1948); J. DeLancey Ferguson and Marshall Waingrow, *RLS: Stevenson's Letters to Charles Baxter* (1956). A definitive new edition of the complete correspondence is being prepared by Ernest Mehew (1994–). The official life by Graham Balfour (2 vols., 1901) has never been surpassed, but J. C. Furnas, *Voyage to Windward* (1951) is equally authoritative but also concise. More recently, the account by James Pope Hennessy, *Robert Louis Stevenson* (1974) is readable; Jenni Calder's *RLS: A Life Study* (1980) is thorough; and Frank McLynn's *Robert Louis Stevenson: A Life* (1993) is wayward but stimulating. Less formal accounts are common, and vary in relevance: J. A. Hammerton, *Stevensoniana: An Anecdotal Life and Appreciation of Robert Louis Stevenson* (1910) is diverting, while George L. McKay, *Some Notes on Robert Louis Stevenson, His Finances and His Agents and Publishers* (1958) contains a massive amount of useful information; and Lloyd Osbourne wrote some affectionate vignettes of his stepfather in *An Intimate Portrait of RLS* (1924), and gives a good account of the composition of *The Wrong Box*.

There is a fine anthology of Victorian criticism, *Robert Louis Stevenson: The Critical Heritage* (1981), edited by Paul Mainer, which includes commentary on *The Wrong Box*. Of the works written this century, G. K. Chesterton's *Robert Louis Stevenson* (1927) remains exciting, if impressionistic, and is particularly astute discussing the work as a response to the Puritanism of RLS's childhood; but some will be of the opinion of T. S. Eliot, who criticized Chesterton for being 'diffuse and dissipated', and observed: 'what we should have liked is a critical essay showing that Stevenson is a writer of permanent importance, and why.' One such essay is Leslie Fiedler's influential 'RLS Revisited', published in *No! In Thunder* (1960), which argues that Stevenson's fiction makes 'a series of variations on the theme of the beauty of evil—and conversely the unloveliness of good'. Other excellent introductions include Graham Good's 'Rereading Robert Louis Stevenson', *Dalhousie Review*, 62 (1982), 44–59; and Jeremy Treglown's 'Out of the Diving Suit: Robert Louis Stevenson', *Grand Street*, 6 (1986), 122–40. Worthwhile general accounts are David Daiches's two books, *Robert Louis Stevenson* (1947) and *Stevenson and the Art of Fiction* (1951); Robert Kiely's *Robert Louis Stevenson and the Fiction of Adventure* (1964); Edwin Eigner's *Robert Louis Stevenson and the Romantic Tradition* (1966).

Although it has long had its champions, few critics have written on *The Wrong Box*, and the best remain anonymous. Witness the three-part essay by V.R. and E.D., 'Stevenson: *The Wrong Box*: Notes and Comments' in *Notes and Queries*, 182 (4 Apr. 1942), 187; 183 (15 Aug. 1942), 101; and 183 (21 Nov. 1942), 302. On the novel's contribution to the conventions of late Victorian detective fiction, see A. E. Murch, *The Development of Detective Fiction* (1968).

A film version of *The Wrong Box*, directed by Bryan Forbes, was released in 1966. Based only loosely on Stevenson and Osbourne's novel, it starred Sir Ralph Richardson, John Mills, and Michael Caine. The role of Dr Pratt, a chaotic physician, was created for Peter Sellers; his best line, 'I was not always as you see me now', characterizes this dismal attempt at revising a singular novel for the screen.

The Wrong Box

WRITTEN IN
COLLABORATION WITH
LLOYD OSBOURNE

PREFACE

'Nothing like a little judicious levity,' says Michael Finsbury in the text: nor can any better excuse be found for the volume in the reader's hand. The authors can but add that one of them is old enough to be ashamed of himself, and the other young enough to learn better.

R. L. S.
L. O.

CHAPTER I

In Which Morris Suspects

How very little does the amateur, dwelling at home at ease, comprehend the labours and perils of the author, and, when he smilingly
skims the surface of a work of fiction, how little does he consider the
hours of toil, consultation of authorities, researches in the Bodleian,
correspondence with learned and illegible Germans—in one word,
the vast scaffolding that was first built up and then knocked down, to
while away an hour for him in a railway train! Thus I might begin this
tale with a biography of Tonti—birthplace, parentage, genius probably inherited from his mother, remarkable instance of precocity,
etc.—and a complete treatise on the system to which he bequeathed
his name. The material is all beside me in a pigeon-hole, but I scorn
to appear vainglorious. Tonti is dead, and I never saw anyone who
even pretended to regret him; and, as for the tontine system, a word
will suffice for all the purposes of this unvarnished narrative.

A number of sprightly youths (the more the merrier) put up a
certain sum of money, which is then funded in a pool under trustees;
coming on for a century later, the proceeds are fluttered for a moment
in the face of the last survivor, who is probably deaf, so that he cannot
even hear of his success—and who is certainly dying, so that he might
just as well have lost. The peculiar poetry and even humour of the
scheme is now apparent, since it is one by which nobody concerned
can possibly profit; but its fine, sportsmanlike character endeared it to
our grandparents.

When Joseph Finsbury and his brother Masterman were little lads
in white-frilled trousers, their father—a well-to-do merchant in
Cheapside—caused them to join a small but rich tontine of seven-
and-thirty lives. A thousand pounds was the entrance fee; and Joseph
Finsbury can remember to this day the visit to the lawyer's, where the
members of the tontine—all children like himself—were assembled
together, and sat in turn in the big office chair, and signed their names
with the assistance of a kind old gentleman in spectacles and Wellington boots. He remembers playing with the children afterwards on the

lawn at the back of the lawyer's house, and a battle-royal that he had
with a brother tontiner who had kicked his shins. The sound of war
called forth the lawyer from where he was dispensing cake and wine
to the assembled parents in the office, and the combatants were
separated, and Joseph's spirit (for he was the smaller of the two)
commended by the gentleman in the Wellington boots, who vowed
he had been just such another at the same age. Joseph wondered to
himself if he had worn at that time little Wellingtons and a little bald
head, and when, in bed at night, he grew tired of telling himself
stories of sea-fights, he used to dress himself up as the old gentleman,
and entertain other little boys and girls with cake and wine.

In the year 1840 the thirty-seven were all alive; in 1850 their
number had decreased by six; in 1856 and 1857 business was more
lively, for the Crimea and the Mutiny carried off no less than nine.
There remained in 1870 but five of the original members, and at the
date of my story, including the two Finsburys, but three.

By this time Masterman was in his seventy-third year; he had long
complained of the effects of age, had long since retired from business,
and now lived in absolute seclusion under the roof of his son Michael,
the well-known solicitor. Joseph, on the other hand, was still up and
about, and still presented but a semi-venerable figure on the streets
in which he loved to wander. This was the more to be deplored
because Masterman had led (even to the least particular) a model
British life. Industry, regularity, respectability, and a preference for
the four per cents are understood to be the very foundations of a
green old age. All these Masterman had eminently displayed, and
here he was, *ab agendo*, at seventy-three; while Joseph, barely two
years younger, and in the most excellent preservation, had disgraced
himself through life by idleness and eccentricity. Embarked in the
leather trade, he had early wearied of business, for which he was
supposed to have small parts. A taste for general information, not
promptly checked, had soon begun to sap his manhood. There is no
passion more debilitating to the mind, unless, perhaps, it be that itch
of public speaking which it not infrequently accompanies or begets.
The two were conjoined in the case of Joseph; the acute stage of this
double malady, that in which the patient delivers gratuitous lectures,
soon declared itself with severity, and not many years had passed over
his head before he would have travelled thirty miles to address an
infant school. He was no student; his reading was confined to elemen-

tary textbooks and the daily papers; he did not even fly as high as cyclopedias; life, he would say, was his volume. His lectures were not meant, he would declare, for college professors; they were addressed direct to 'the great heart of the people', and the heart of the people must certainly be sounder than its head, for his lucubrations were received with favour. That entitled 'How to Live Cheerfully on Forty Pounds a Year', created a sensation among the unemployed. 'Education: Its Aims, Objects, Purposes, and Desirability', gained him the respect of the shallow-minded. As for his celebrated essay on 'Life Insurance Regarded in its Relation to the Masses', read before the Working Men's Mutual Improvement Society, Isle of Dogs, it was received with a 'literal ovation' by an unintelligent audience of both sexes, and so marked was the effect that he was next year elected honorary president of the institution, an office of less than no emolument—since the holder was expected to come down with a donation—but one which highly satisfied his self-esteem.

While Joseph was thus building himself up a reputation among the more cultivated portion of the ignorant, his domestic life was suddenly overwhelmed by orphans. The death of his younger brother Jacob saddled him with the charge of two boys, Morris and John; and in the course of the same year his family was still further swelled by the addition of a little girl, the daughter of John Henry Hazeltine, Esq., a gentleman of small property and fewer friends. He had met Joseph only once, at a lecture-hall in Holloway; but from that formative experience he returned home to make a new will, and consign his daughter and her fortune to the lecturer. Joseph had a kindly disposition; and yet it was not without reluctance that he accepted this new responsibility, advertised for a nurse, and purchased a second-hand perambulator. Morris and John he made more readily welcome; not so much because of the tie of consanguinity as because the leather business (in which he hastened to invest their fortune of thirty thousand pounds) had recently exhibited inexplicable symptoms of decline. A young but capable Scot was chosen as manager to the enterprise, and the cares of business never again afflicted Joseph Finsbury. Leaving his charges in the hands of the capable Scot (who was married), he began his extensive travels on the Continent and in Asia Minor.

With a polyglot Testament in one hand and a phrase-book in the other, he groped his way among the speakers of eleven European languages. The first of these guides is hardly applicable to the purposes of the philosophic traveller, and even the second is designed more expressly for the tourist than for the expert in life. But he pressed interpreters into his service—whenever he could get their services for nothing—and by one means and another filled many notebooks with the results of his researches.

In these wanderings he spent several years, and only returned to England when the increasing age of his charges needed his attention. The two lads had been placed in a good but economical school, where they had received a sound commercial education; which was somewhat awkward, as the leather business was by no means in a state to court enquiry. In fact, when Joseph went over his accounts preparatory to surrendering his trust, he was dismayed to discover that his brother's fortune had not increased by his stewardship; even by making over to his two wards every penny he had in the world, there would still be a deficit of seven thousand eight hundred pounds. When these facts were communicated to the two brothers in the presence of a lawyer, Morris Finsbury threatened his uncle with all the terrors of the law, and was only prevented from taking extreme steps by the advice of the professional man.

'You cannot get blood from a stone,' observed the lawyer.

And Morris saw the point and came to terms with his uncle. On the one side, Joseph gave up all that he possessed, and assigned to his nephew his contingent interest in the tontine, already quite a hopeful speculation. On the other, Morris agreed to harbour his uncle and Miss Hazeltine (who had come to grief with the rest), and to pay to each of them one pound a month as pocket-money. The allowance was amply sufficient for the old man; it scarce appears how Miss Hazeltine contrived to dress upon it; but she did, and, what is more, she never complained. She was, indeed, sincerely attached to her incompetent guardian. He had never been unkind; his age spoke for him loudly; there was something appealing in his whole-souled quest of knowledge and innocent delight in the smallest mark of admiration; and, though the lawyer had warned her she was being sacrificed, Julia had refused to add to the perplexities of Uncle Joseph.

In a large, dreary house in John Street, Bloomsbury, these four dwelt together; a family in appearance, in reality a financial association. Julia and Uncle Joseph were, of course, slaves; John, a gentleman with a taste for the banjo, the music-hall, the Gaiety bar, and the sporting papers, must have been anywhere a secondary figure; and the cares and delights of empire devolved entirely upon Morris. That these are inextricably intermixed is one of the commonplaces with which the bland essayist consoles the incompetent and the obscure, but in the case of Morris the bitter must have largely outweighed the sweet. He grudged no trouble to himself, he spared none to others; he called the servants in the morning, he served out the stores with his own hand, he took soundings of the sherry, he numbered the remainder biscuits; painful scenes took place over the weekly bills, and the cook was frequently impeached, and the tradespeople came and hectored with him in the back parlour upon a question of three farthings. The superficial might have deemed him a miser; in his own eyes he was simply a man who had been defrauded; the world owed him seven thousand eight hundred pounds, and he intended that the world should pay.

But it was in his dealings with Joseph that Morris's character particularly shone. His uncle was a rather gambling stock in which he had invested heavily; and he spared no pains in nursing the security. The old man was seen monthly by a physician, whether he was well or ill. His diet, his raiment, his occasional outings, now to Brighton, now to Bournemouth, were doled out to him like pap to infants. In bad weather he must keep the house. In good weather, by half-past nine, he must be ready in the hall; Morris would see that he had gloves and that his shoes were sound; and the pair would start for the leather business arm in arm. The way there was probably dreary enough, for there was no pretence of friendly feeling; Morris had never ceased to upbraid his guardian with his defalcation and to lament the burthen of Miss Hazeltine; and Joseph, though he was a mild enough soul, regarded his nephew with something very near akin to hatred. But the way there was nothing to the journey back; for the mere sight of the place of business, as well as every detail of its transactions, was enough to poison life for any Finsbury.

Joseph's name was still over the door; it was he who still signed the cheques; but this was only policy on the part of Morris, and designed to discourage other members of the tontine. In reality the business was entirely his; and he found it an inheritance of sorrows. He tried to sell it, and the offers he received were quite derisory. He tried to extend it, and it was only the liabilities he succeeded in extending; to restrict it, and it was only the profits he managed to restrict. Nobody had ever made money out of that concern except the capable Scot, who retired (after his discharge) to the neighbourhood of Banff and built a castle with his profits. The memory of this fallacious Caledonian Morris would revile daily, as he sat in the private office opening his mail, with old Joseph at another table, sullenly awaiting orders, or savagely affixing signatures to he knew not what. And when the man of the heather pushed cynicism so far as to send him the announcement of his second marriage (to Davida, eldest daughter of the Revd. Alexander McCraw), it was really supposed that Morris would have had a fit.

Business hours, in the Finsbury leather trade, had been cut to the quick; even Morris's strong sense of duty to himself was not strong enough to dally within those walls and under the shadow of that bankruptcy; and presently the manager and the clerks would draw a long breath, and compose themselves for another day of procrastination. Raw Haste, on the authority of my Lord Tennyson, is half-sister to Delay; but the Business Habits are certainly her uncles. Meanwhile, the leather merchant would lead his living investment back to John Street like a puppy dog; and, having there immured him in the hall, would depart for the day on the quest of seal rings, the only passion of his life. Joseph had more than the vanity of man, he had that of lecturers. He owned he was in fault, although more sinned against (by the capable Scot) than sinning; but had he steeped his hands in gore, he would still not deserve to be thus dragged at the chariot-wheels of a young man, to sit a captive in the halls of his own leather business, to be entertained with mortifying comments on his whole career—to have his costume examined, his collar pulled up, the presence of his mittens verified, and to be taken out and brought home in custody, like an infant with a nurse. At the thought of it his soul would swell with venom, and he would make haste to hang up his hat and coat and the detested mittens, and slink upstairs to Julia and his notebooks. The drawing-room at least was sacred from Morris; it belonged to the old man and the young girl; it was there that she made her dresses; it was there that he inked his spectacles over the registration of disconnected facts and the calculation of insignificant statistics.

Here he would sometimes lament his connection with the tontine. 'If it were not for that,' he cried one afternoon, 'he would not care to keep me. I might be a free man, Julia. And I could so easily support myself by giving lectures.'

'To be sure you could,' said she; 'and I think it one of the meanest things he ever did to deprive you of that amusement. There were those nice people at the Isle of Cats (wasn't it?) who wrote and asked you so very kindly to give them an address. I did think he might have let you go to the Isle of Cats.'

'He is a man of no intelligence,' cried Joseph. 'He lives here literally surrounded by the absorbing spectacle of life, and for all the good it does him, he might just as well be in his coffin. Think of his opportunities! The heart of any other young man would burn within him at the chance. The amount of information that I have it in my power to convey, if he would only listen, is a thing that beggars language, Julia.'

'Whatever you do, my dear, you mustn't excite yourself,' said Julia; 'for you know, if you look at all ill, the doctor will be sent for.'

'That is very true,' returned the old man humbly, 'I will compose myself with a little study.' He thumbed his gallery of notebooks. 'I wonder,' he said, 'I wonder (since I see your hands are occupied) whether it might not interest you——'

'Why, of course it would,' cried Julia. 'Read me one of your nice stories, there's a dear!'

He had the volume down and his spectacles upon his nose instanter, as though to forestall some possible retractation. 'What I propose to read to you,' said he, skimming through the pages, 'is the notes of a highly important conversation with a Dutch courier of the name of David Abbas, which is the Latin for abbot. Its results are well worth the money it cost me, for, as Abbas at first appeared somewhat impatient, I was induced to (what is, I believe, singularly called) stand him drink. It runs only to about five-and-twenty pages. Yes, here it is.' He cleared his throat, and began to read.

Mr Finsbury (according to his own report) contributed about four hundred and ninety-nine five-hundredths of the interview, and elicited from Abbas literally nothing. It was dull for Julia, who did not require to listen; for the Dutch courier, who had to answer, it must have been a perfect nightmare. It would seem as if he had consoled himself by frequent appliances to the bottle; it would even seem that (toward the end) he had ceased to depend on Joseph's frugal generosity and called for the flagon on his own account. The effect, at least, of some mellowing influence was visible in the record: Abbas became suddenly a willing witness; he began to volunteer disclosures; and Julia had just looked up from her seam with something like a smile, when Morris burst into the house, eagerly calling for his uncle, and the next instant plunged into the room, waving in the air the evening paper.

It was indeed with great news that he came charged. The demise was announced of Lieutenant-General Sir Glasgow Biggar, KCSI, KCMG, etc., and the prize of the tontine now lay between the Finsbury brothers. Here was Morris's opportunity at last. The brothers had never, it is true, been cordial. When word came that Joseph was in Asia Minor, Masterman had expressed himself with irritation. 'I call it simply indecent,' he had said. 'Mark my words—we shall hear of him next at the North Pole.' And these bitter expressions had been reported to the traveller on his return. What was worse, Masterman had refused to attend the lecture on 'Education: Its Aims, Objects, Purposes, and Desirability', although invited to the platform. Since then the brothers had not met. On the other hand, they never had openly quarrelled; Joseph (by Morris's orders) was prepared to waive the advantage of his juniority; Masterman had enjoyed all through life the reputation of a man neither greedy nor unfair. Here, then, were all the elements of compromise assembled; and Morris, suddenly beholding his seven thousand eight hundred pounds restored to him, and himself dismissed from the vicissitudes of the leather trade, hastened the next morning to the office of his cousin Michael.

Michael was something of a public character. Launched upon the law at a very early age, and quite without protectors, he had become a trafficker in shady affairs. He was known to be the man for a lost cause; it was known he could extract testimony from a stone, and interest from a gold-mine; and his office was besieged in consequence by all that numerous class of persons who have still some reputation to lose, and find themselves upon the point of losing it; by those who have made undesirable acquaintances, who have mislaid a compromising correspondence, or who are blackmailed by their own butlers. In private life Michael was a man of pleasure; but it was thought his dire experience at the office had gone far to sober him, and it was known that (in the matter of investments) he preferred the solid to the brilliant. What was yet more to the purpose, he had been all his life a consistent scoffer at the Finsbury tontine.

It was therefore with little fear for the result that Morris presented himself before his cousin, and proceeded feverishly to set forth his scheme. For near upon a quarter of an hour the lawyer suffered him to dwell upon its manifest advantages uninterrupted. Then Michael rose from his seat, and, ringing for his clerk, uttered a single clause:

'It won't do, Morris.'

It was in vain that the leather merchant pleaded and reasoned, and returned day after day to plead and reason. It was in vain that he offered a bonus of one thousand, of two thousand, of three thousand pounds; in vain that he offered, in Joseph's name, to be content with only one-third of the pool. Still there came the same answer: 'It won't do.'

'I can't see the bottom of this,' he said at last. 'You answer none of my arguments; you haven't a word to say. For my part, I believe it's malice.'

The lawyer smiled at him benignly. 'You may believe one thing,' said he. 'Whatever else I do, I am not going to gratify any of your curiosity. You see I am a trifle more communicative today, because this is our last interview upon the subject.'

'Our last interview!' cried Morris.

'The stirrup-cup, dear boy,' returned Michael. 'I can't have my business hours encroached upon. And, by the by, have you no business of your own? Are there no convulsions in the leather trade?'

'I believe it to be malice,' repeated Morris doggedly. 'You always hated and despised me from a boy.'

'No, no—not hated,' returned Michael soothingly. 'I rather like you than otherwise; there's such a permanent surprise about you, you look so dark and attractive from a distance. Do you know that to the naked eye you look romantic?—like what they call a man with a history? And indeed, from all that I can hear, the history of the leather trade is full of incident.'

'Yes,' said Morris, disregarding these remarks, 'it's no use coming here. I shall see your father.'

'O no, you won't,' said Michael. 'Nobody shall see my father.'

'I should like to know why,' cried his cousin.

'I never make any secret of that,' replied the lawyer. 'He is too ill.'

'If he is as ill as you say,' cried the other, 'the more reason for accepting my proposal. I *will* see him.'

'Will you?' said Michael, and he rose and rang for his clerk.

It was now time, according to Sir Faraday Bond, the medical baronet whose name is so familiar at the foot of bulletins, that Joseph (the poor Golden Goose) should be removed into the purer air of Bournemouth; and for that uncharted wilderness of villas the family now shook off the dust of Bloomsbury; Julia delighted, because at Bournemouth she sometimes made acquaintances; John in despair, for he was a man of city tastes; Joseph indifferent where he was, so long as there was pen and ink and daily papers, and he could avoid martyrdom at the office; Morris himself, perhaps, not displeased to pretermit these visits to the city, and have a quiet time for thought. He was prepared for any sacrifice; all he desired was to get his money again and clear his feet of leather; and it would be strange, since he was so modest in his desires, and the pool amounted to upward of a hundred and sixteen thousand pounds—it would be strange indeed if he could find no way of influencing Michael. 'If I could only guess his reason,' he repeated to himself; and by day, as he walked in Branksome Woods, and by night, as he turned upon his bed, and at meal-times, when he forgot to eat, and in the bathing machine, when he forgot to dress himself, that problem was constantly before him: Why had Michael refused?

At last, one night, he burst into his brother's room and woke him.

'What's all this?' asked John.

'Julia leaves this place tomorrow,' replied Morris. 'She must go up to town and get the house ready, and find servants. We shall all follow in three days.'

'Oh, brayvo!' cried John. 'But why?'

'I've found it out, John,' returned his brother gently.

'It? What?' enquired John.

'Why Michael won't compromise,' said Morris. 'It's because he can't. It's because Masterman's dead, and he's keeping it dark.'

'Golly!' cried the impressionable John. 'But what's the use? Why does he do it, anyway?'

'To defraud us of the tontine,' said his brother.

'He couldn't; you have to have a doctor's certificate,' objected John.

'Did you never hear of venal doctors?' enquired Morris. 'They're as common as blackberries: you can pick 'em up for three-pound-ten a head.'

'I wouldn't do it under fifty if I were a sawbones,' ejaculated John.

'And then Michael,' continued Morris, 'is in the very thick of it. All his clients have come to grief; his whole business is rotten eggs. If any man could arrange it, he could; and depend upon it, he has his plan all straight; and depend upon it, it's a good one, for he's clever, and be damned to him! But I'm clever too; and I'm desperate. I lost seven thousand eight hundred pounds when I was an orphan at school.'

'O, don't be tedious,' interrupted John. 'You've lost far more already trying to get it back.'

CHAPTER II

In Which Morris takes Action

Some days later, accordingly, the three males of this depressing family might have been observed (by a reader of G. P. R. James) taking their departure from the East Station of Bournemouth. The weather was raw and changeable, and Joseph was arrayed in consequence according to the principles of Sir Faraday Bond, a man no less strict (as is well known) on costume than on diet. There are few polite invalids who have not lived, or tried to live, by that punctilious physician's orders. 'Avoid tea, madam,' the reader has doubtless heard him say, 'avoid tea, fried liver, antimonial wine, and bakers' bread. Retire nightly at 10.45; and clothe yourself (if you please) throughout in hygienic flannel. Externally, the fur of the marten is indicated. Do not forget to procure a pair of health boots at Messrs Dall and Crumbie's.' And he has probably called you back, even after you have paid your fee, to add with stentorian emphasis: 'I had forgotten one caution: avoid kippered sturgeon as you would the very devil!' The unfortunate Joseph was cut to the pattern of Sir Faraday in every button; he was shod with the health boot; his suit was of genuine ventilating cloth; his shirt of hygienic flannel, a somewhat dingy fabric; and he was draped to the knees in the inevitable greatcoat of marten's fur. The very railway porters at Bournemouth (which was a favourite station of the doctor's) marked the old gentleman for a creature of Sir Faraday. There was but one evidence of personal taste, a vizarded forage cap; from this form of headpiece, since he had fled from a dying jackal on the plains of Ephesus, and weathered a bora in the Adriatic, nothing could divorce our traveller.

The three Finsburys mounted into their compartment, and fell immediately to quarrelling, a step unseemly in itself and (in this case) highly unfortunate for Morris. Had he lingered a moment longer by the window, this tale need never have been written. For he might then have observed (as the porters did not fail to do) the arrival of a second passenger in the uniform of Sir Faraday Bond. But he had other matters on hand, which he judged (God knows how erroneously) to be more important.

'I never heard of such a thing,' he cried, resuming a discussion which had scarcely ceased all morning. 'The bill is not yours; it is mine.'

'It is payable to me,' returned the old gentleman, with an air of bitter obstinacy. 'I will do what I please with my own property.'

The bill was one for eight hundred pounds, which had been given him at breakfast to endorse, and which he had simply pocketed.

'Hear him, Johnny!' cried Morris. 'His property! the very clothes upon his back belong to me.'

'Let him alone,' said John. 'I am sick of both of you.'

'That is no way to speak of your uncle, sir,' cried Joseph. 'I will not endure this disrespect. You are a pair of exceedingly forward, impudent, and ignorant young men, and I have quite made up my mind to put an end to the whole business.'

'O skittles!' said the graceful John.

But Morris was not so easy in his mind. This unusual act of insubordination had already troubled him; and these mutinous words now sounded ominously in his ears. He looked at the old gentleman uneasily. Upon one occasion, many years before, when Joseph was delivering a lecture, the audience had revolted in a body; finding their entertainer somewhat dry, they had taken the question of amusement into their own hands; and the lecturer (along with the board schoolmaster, the Baptist clergyman, and a working-man's candidate, who made up his bodyguard) was ultimately driven from the scene. Morris had not been present on that fatal day; if he had, he would have recognized a certain fighting glitter in his uncle's eye, and a certain chewing movement of his lips, as old acquaintances. But even to the inexpert these symptoms breathed of something dangerous.

'Well, well,' said Morris. 'I have no wish to bother you further till we get to London.'

Joseph did not so much as look at him in answer; with tremulous hands he produced a copy of the *British Mechanic*, and ostentatiously buried himself in its perusal.

'I wonder what can make him so cantankerous?' reflected the nephew. 'I don't like the look of it at all.' And he dubiously scratched his nose.

The train travelled forth into the world, bearing along with it the customary freight of obliterated voyagers, and along with these old Joseph, affecting immersion in his paper, and John slumbering over the columns of the *Pink Un*, and Morris revolving in his mind a dozen grudges, and suspicions, and alarms. It passed Christchurch by the sea, Herne with its pinewoods, Ringwood on its mazy river. A little behind time, but not much for the South-Western, it drew up at the platform of a station, in the midst of the New Forest, the real name of which (in case the railway company 'might have the law of me') I shall veil under the alias of Browndean.

Many passengers put their heads to the window, and among the rest an old gentleman on whom I willingly dwell, for I am nearly done with him now, and (in the whole course of the present narrative) I am not in the least likely to meet another character so decent. His name is immaterial, not so his habits. He had passed his life wandering in a tweed suit on the continent of Europe; and years of *Galignani's Messenger* having at length undermined his eyesight, he suddenly remembered the rivers of Assyria and came to London to consult an oculist. From the oculist to the dentist, and from both to the physician, the step appears inevitable; presently he was in the hands of Sir Faraday, robed in ventilating cloth and sent to Bournemouth; and to that domineering baronet (who was his only friend upon his native soil) he was now returning to report. The case of these tweed-suited wanderers is unique. We have all seen them entering the table d'hôte (at Spezzia, or Grätz, or Venice) with a genteel melancholy and a faint appearance of having been to India and not succeeded. In the offices of many hundred hotels they are known by name; and yet, if the whole of this wandering cohort were to disappear tomorrow, their absence would be wholly unremarked. How much more, if only one—say this one in the ventilating cloth—should vanish! He had paid his bills at Bournemouth; his worldly effects were all in the van in two portmanteaux, and these after the proper interval would be sold as unclaimed baggage to a Jew; Sir Faraday's butler would be a half-crown poorer at the year's end, and the hotel-keepers of Europe about the same date would be mourning a small but quite observable decline in profits. And that would be literally all. Perhaps the old gentleman thought something of the sort, for he looked melancholy enough as he pulled his bare, grey head back into the carriage, and the train smoked under the bridge, and forth, with ever quickening speed, across the mingled heaths and woods of the New Forest.

Not many hundred yards beyond Browndean, however, a sudden jarring of brakes set everybody's teeth on edge, and there was a brutal stoppage. Morris Finsbury was aware of a confused uproar of voices, and sprang to the window. Women were screaming, men were tumbling from the windows on the track, the guard was crying to them to stay where they were; at the same time the train began to gather way and move very slowly backward toward Browndean; and the next moment, all these various sounds were blotted out in the apocalyptic whistle and the thundering onslaught of the down express.

The actual collision Morris did not hear. Perhaps he fainted. He had a wild dream of having seen the carriage double up and fall to pieces like a pantomime trick; and sure enough, when he came to himself, he was lying on the bare earth and under the open sky. His head ached savagely; he carried his hand to his brow, and was not surprised to see it red with blood. The air was filled with an intolerable, throbbing roar, which he expected to find die away with the return of consciousness; and instead of that it seemed but to swell the louder and to pierce the more cruelly through his ears. It was a raging, bellowing thunder, like a boiler-riveting factory.

And now curiosity began to stir, and he sat up and looked about him. The track at this point ran in a sharp curve about a wooded hillock; all of the near side was heaped with the wreckage of the Bournemouth train; that of the express was mostly hidden by the trees; and just at the turn, under clouds of vomiting steam and piled about with cairns of living coal, lay what remained of the two engines, one upon the other. On the heathy margin of the line were many people running to and fro, and crying aloud as they ran, and many others lying motionless like sleeping tramps.

Morris suddenly drew an inference. 'There has been an accident!' thought he, and was elated at his perspicacity. Almost at the same time his eye lighted on John, who lay close by as white as paper. 'Poor old John! poor old cove!' he thought, the schoolboy expression popping forth from some forgotten treasury, and he took his brother's hand in his with childish tenderness. It was perhaps the touch that recalled him; at least John opened his eyes, sat suddenly up, and after several ineffectual movements of his lips, 'What's the row?' said he, in a phantom voice.

The din of that devil's smithy still thundered in their ears. 'Let us get away from that,' Morris cried, and pointed to the vomit of steam that still spouted from the broken engines. And the pair helped each other up, and stood and quaked and wavered and stared about them at the scene of death.

Just then they were approached by a party of men who had already organized themselves for the purposes of rescue.

'Are you hurt?' cried one of these, a young fellow with the sweat streaming down his pallid face, and who, by the way he was treated, was evidently the doctor.

Morris shook his head, and the young man, nodding grimly, handed him a bottle of some spirit.

'Take a drink of that,' he said; 'your friend looks as if he needed it badly. We want every man we can get,' he added; 'there's terrible work before us, and nobody should shirk. If you can do no more, you can carry a stretcher.'

The doctor was hardly gone before Morris, under the spur of the dram, awoke to the full possession of his wits.

'My God!' he cried. 'Uncle Joseph!'

'Yes,' said John, 'where can he be? He can't be far off. I hope the old party isn't damaged.'

'Come and help me to look,' said Morris, with a snap of savage determination strangely foreign to his ordinary bearing; and then, for one moment, he broke forth. 'If he's dead!' he cried, and shook his fist at heaven.

To and fro the brothers hurried, staring in the faces of the wounded, or turning the dead upon their backs. They must have thus examined forty people, and still there was no word of Uncle Joseph. But now the course of their search brought them near the centre of the collision, where the boilers were still blowing off steam with a deafening clamour. It was a part of the field not yet gleaned by the rescuing party. The ground, especially on the margin of the wood, was full of inequalities—here a pit, there a hillock surmounted with a bush of furze. It was a place where many bodies might lie concealed, and they beat it like pointers after game. Suddenly Morris, who was leading, paused and reached forth his index with a tragic gesture. John followed the direction of his brother's hand.

In the bottom of a sandy hole lay something that had once been human. The face had suffered severely, and it was unrecognizable;

but that was not required. The snowy hair, the coat of marten, the ventilating cloth, the hygienic flannel—everything down to the health boots from Messrs Dall and Crumbie's, identified the body as that of Uncle Joseph. Only the forage cap must have been lost in the convulsion, for the dead man was bareheaded.

'The poor old beggar!' said John, with a touch of natural feeling; 'I would give ten pounds if we hadn't chivied him in the train!'

But there was no sentiment in the face of Morris as he gazed upon the dead. Gnawing his nails, with introverted eyes, his brow marked with the stamp of tragic indignation and tragic intellectual effort, he stood there silent. Here was a last injustice; he had been robbed while he was an orphan at school, he had been lashed to a decadent leather business, he had been saddled with Miss Hazeltine, his cousin had been defrauding him of the tontine, and he had borne all this, we might almost say, with dignity, and now they had gone and killed his uncle!

'Here!' he said suddenly, 'take his heels, we must get him into the woods. I'm not going to have anybody find this.'

'O, fudge!' said John, 'where's the use?'

'Do what I tell you,' spirted Morris, as he took the corpse by the shoulders. 'Am I to carry him myself?'

They were close upon the borders of the wood; in ten or twelve paces they were under cover; and a little further back, in a sandy clearing of the trees, they laid their burthen down, and stood and looked at it with loathing.

'What do you mean to do?' whispered John.

'Bury him, to be sure!' responded Morris, and he opened his pocket-knife and began feverishly to dig.

'You'll never make a hand of it with that,' objected the other.

'If you won't help me, you cowardly shirk,' screamed Morris, 'you can go to the devil!'

'It's the childishest folly,' said John; 'but no man shall call me a coward,' and he began to help his brother grudgingly.

The soil was sandy and light, but matted with the roots of the surrounding firs. Gorse tore their hands; and as they baled the sand from the grave, it was often discoloured with their blood. An hour passed of unremitting energy upon the part of Morris, of lukewarm help on that of John; and still the trench was barely nine inches in depth. Into this the body was rudely flung: sand was piled upon it, and then more sand must be dug, and gorse had to be cut to pile on that; and still from one end of the sordid mound a pair of feet projected and caught the light upon their patent-leather toes. But by this time the nerves of both were shaken; even Morris had enough of his grisly task; and they skulked off like animals into the thickest of the neighbouring covert.

'It's the best that we can do,' said Morris, sitting down.

'And now,' said John, 'perhaps you'll have the politeness to tell me what it's all about.'

'Upon my word,' cried Morris, 'if you do not understand for yourself, I almost despair of telling you.'

'O, of course it's some rot about the tontine,' returned the other. 'But it's the merest nonsense. We've lost it, and there's an end.'

'I tell you,' said Morris, 'Uncle Masterman is dead. I know it, there's a voice that tells me so.'

'Well, and so is Uncle Joseph,' said John.

'He's not dead, unless I choose,' returned Morris.

'And come to that,' cried John, 'if you're right, and Uncle Masterman's been dead ever so long, all we have to do is to tell the truth and expose Michael.'

'You seem to think Michael is a fool,' sneered Morris. 'Can't you understand he's been preparing this fraud for years? He has the whole thing ready: the nurse, the doctor, the undertaker, all bought, the certificate all ready but the date! Let him get wind of this business, and you mark my words, Uncle Masterman will die in two days and be buried in a week. But see here, Johnny; what Michael can do, I can do. If he plays a game of bluff, so can I. If his father is to live for ever, by God, so shall my uncle!'

'It's illegal, ain't it?' said John.

'A man must have *some* moral courage,' replied Morris with dignity.

'And then suppose you're wrong? Suppose Uncle Masterman's alive and kicking?'

'Well, even then,' responded the plotter, 'we are no worse off than we were before; in fact, we're better. Uncle Masterman must die some day; as long as Uncle Joseph was alive, he might have died any day; but we're out of all that trouble now: there's no sort of limit to the game that I propose—it can be kept up till Kingdom Come.'

'If I could only see how you meant to set about it!' sighed John. 'But you know, Morris, you always were such a bungler.'

'I'd like to know what I ever bungled,' cried Morris; 'I have the best collection of signet rings in London.'

'Well, you know, there's the leather business,' suggested the other. 'That's considered rather a hash.'

It was a mark of singular self-control in Morris that he suffered this to pass unchallenged, and even unresented.

'About the business in hand,' said he, 'once we can get him up to Bloomsbury, there's no sort of trouble. We bury him in the cellar, which seems made for it; and then all I have to do is to start out and find a venal doctor.'

'Why can't we leave him where he is?' asked John.

'Because we know nothing about the country,' retorted Morris. 'This wood may be a regular lovers' walk. Turn your mind to the real difficulty. How are we to get him up to Bloomsbury?'

Various schemes were mooted and rejected. The railway station at Browndean was, of course, out of the question, for it would now be a centre of curiosity and gossip, and (of all things) they would be least able to dispatch a dead body without remark. John feebly proposed getting an ale-cask and sending it as beer, but the objections to this course were so overwhelming that Morris scorned to answer. The purchase of a packing-case seemed equally hopeless, for why should two gentlemen without baggage of any kind require a packing-case? They would be more likely to require clean linen.

'We are working on wrong lines,' cried Morris at last. 'The thing must be gone about more carefully. Suppose now,' he added excitedly, speaking by fits and starts, as if he were thinking aloud, 'suppose we rent a cottage by the month. A householder can buy a packing-case without remark. Then suppose we clear the people out today, get the packing-case tonight, and tomorrow I hire a carriage—or a cart that we could drive ourselves—and take the box, or whatever we get, to Ringwood or Lyndhurst or somewhere; we could label it "specimens", don't you see? Johnny, I believe I've hit the nail at last.'

'Well, it sounds more feasible,' admitted John.

'Of course we must take assumed names,' continued Morris. 'It would never do to keep our own. What do you say to "Masterman" itself? It sounds quiet and dignified.'

'I will *not* take the name of Masterman,' returned his brother; 'you may, if you like. I shall call myself Vance—the Great Vance; positively the last six nights. There's some go in a name like that.'

'Vance!' cried Morris. 'Do you think we are playing a pantomime for our amusement? There was never anybody named Vance who wasn't a music-hall singer.'

'That's the beauty of it,' returned John; 'it gives you some standing at once. You may call yourself Fortescue till all's blue, and nobody cares; but to be Vance gives a man a natural nobility.'

'But there's lots of other theatrical names,' cried Morris. 'Leybourne, Irving, Brough, Toole——'

'Devil a one will I take!' returned his brother. 'I am going to have my little lark out of this as well as you.'

'Very well,' said Morris, who perceived that John was determined to carry his point, 'I shall be Robert Vance.'

'And I shall be George Vance,' cried John, 'the only original George Vance! Rally round the only original!'

Repairing as well as they were able the disorder of their clothes, the Finsbury brothers returned to Browndean by a circuitous route in quest of luncheon and a suitable cottage. It is not always easy to drop at a moment's notice on a furnished residence in a retired locality; but fortune presently introduced our adventurers to a deaf carpenter, a man rich in cottages of the required description, and unaffectedly eager to supply their wants. The second place they visited, standing, as it did, about a mile and a half from any neighbours, caused them to exchange a glance of hope. On a nearer view, the place was not without depressing features. It stood in a marshy-looking hollow of a heath; tall trees obscured its windows; the thatch visibly rotted on the rafters; and the walls were stained with splashes of unwholesome green. The rooms were small, the ceilings low, the furniture merely nominal; a strange chill and a haunting smell of damp pervaded the kitchen; and the bedroom boasted only of one bed.

Morris, with a view to cheapening the place, remarked on this defect.

'Well,' returned the man; 'if you can't sleep two abed, you'd better take a villa residence.'

'And then,' pursued Morris, 'there's no water. How do you get your water?'

'We fill *that* from the spring,' replied the carpenter, pointing to a big barrel that stood beside the door. 'The spring ain't so *very* far off, after all, and it's easy brought in buckets. There's a bucket there.'

Morris nudged his brother as they examined the water-butt. It was new, and very solidly constructed for its office. If anything had been wanting to decide them, this eminently practical barrel would have turned the scale. A bargain was promptly struck, the month's rent was paid upon the nail, and about an hour later the Finsbury brothers might have been observed returning to the blighted cottage, having along with them the key, which was the symbol of their tenancy, a spirit-lamp, with which they fondly told themselves they would be able to cook, a pork pie of suitable dimensions, and a quart of the worst whisky in Hampshire. Nor was this all they had effected; already (under the plea that they were landscape-painters) they had hired for dawn on the morrow a light but solid two-wheeled cart; so that when they entered in their new character, they were able to tell themselves that the back of the business was already broken.

John proceeded to get tea; while Morris, foraging about the house, was presently delighted by discovering the lid of the water-butt upon the kitchen shelf. Here, then, was the packing-case complete; in the absence of straw, the blankets (which he himself, at least, had not the smallest intention of using for their present purpose) would exactly take the place of packing; and Morris, as the difficulties began to vanish from his path, rose almost to the brink of exultation. There was, however, one difficulty not yet faced, one upon which his whole scheme depended. Would John consent to remain alone in the cottage? He had not yet dared to put the question.

It was with high good-humour that the pair sat down to the deal table, and proceeded to fall-to on the pork pie. Morris retailed the discovery of the lid, and the Great Vance was pleased to applaud by beating on the table with his fork in true music-hall style.

'That's the dodge,' he cried. 'I always said a water-butt was what you wanted for this business.'

'Of course,' said Morris, thinking this a favourable opportunity to prepare his brother, 'of course you must stay on in this place till I give the word; I'll give out that uncle is resting in the New Forest. It would not do for both of us to appear in London; we could never conceal the absence of the old man.'

John's jaw dropped.

'O, come!' he cried. 'You can stay in this hole yourself. I won't.'

The colour came into Morris's cheeks. He saw that he must win his brother at any cost.

'You must please remember, Johnny,' he said, 'the amount of the tontine. If I succeed, we shall have each fifty thousand to place to our bank account; ay, and nearer sixty.'

'But if you fail,' returned John, 'what then? What'll be the colour of our bank account in that case?'

'I will pay all expenses,' said Morris, with an inward struggle; 'you shall lose nothing.'

'Well,' said John, with a laugh, 'if the ex-s are yours, and half-profits mine, I don't mind remaining here for a couple of days.'

'A couple of days!' cried Morris, who was beginning to get angry and controlled himself with difficulty; 'why, you would do more to win five pounds on a horse-race!'

'Perhaps I would,' returned the Great Vance; 'it's the artistic temperament.'

'This is monstrous!' burst out Morris. 'I take all risks; I pay all expenses; I divide profits; and you won't take the slightest pains to help me. It's not decent; it's not honest; it's not even kind.'

'But suppose,' objected John, who was considerably impressed by his brother's vehemence, 'suppose that Uncle Masterman is alive after all, and lives ten years longer; must I rot here all that time?'

'Of course not,' responded Morris, in a more conciliatory tone; 'I only ask a month at the outside; and if Uncle Masterman is not dead by that time you can go abroad.'

'Go abroad?' repeated John eagerly. 'Why shouldn't I go at once? Tell 'em that Joseph and I are seeing life in Paris.'

'Nonsense,' said Morris.

'Well, but look here,' said John; 'it's this house, it's such a pig-sty, it's so dreary and damp. You said yourself that it was damp.'

'Only to the carpenter,' Morris distinguished, 'and that was to reduce the rent. But really, you know, now we're in it, I've seen worse.'

'And what am I to do?' complained the victim. 'How can I entertain a friend?'

'My dear Johnny, if you don't think the tontine worth a little trouble, say so, and I'll give the business up.'

'You're dead certain of the figures, I suppose?' asked John. 'Well'— with a deep sigh—'send me the *Pink Un* and all the comic papers regularly. I'll face the music.'

As afternoon drew on, the cottage breathed more thrillingly of its native marsh; a creeping chill inhabited its chambers; the fire smoked, and a shower of rain, coming up from the channel on a slant of wind, tingled on the window-panes. At intervals, when the gloom deepened toward despair, Morris would produce the whisky-bottle, and at first John welcomed the diversion—not for long. It has been said this spirit was the worst in Hampshire; only those acquainted with the county can appreciate the force of that superlative; and at length even the Great Vance (who was no connoisseur) waved the decoction from his lips. The approach of dusk, feebly combated with a single tallow candle, added a touch of tragedy; and John suddenly stopped whistling through his fingers—an art to the practice of which he had been reduced—and bitterly lamented his concessions.

'I can't stay here a month,' he cried. 'No one could. The thing's nonsense, Morris. The parties that lived in the Bastille would rise against a place like this.'

With an admirable affectation of indifference, Morris proposed a game of pitch-and-toss. To what will not the diplomatist condescend! It was John's favourite game; indeed his only game—he had found all the rest too intellectual—and he played it with equal skill and good fortune. To Morris himself, on the other hand, the whole business was detestable; he was a bad pitcher, he had no luck in tossing, and he was one who suffered torments when he lost. But John was in a dangerous humour, and his brother was prepared for any sacrifice.

By seven o'clock, Morris, with incredible agony, had lost a couple of half-crowns. Even with the tontine before his eyes, this was as much as he could bear; and, remarking that he would take his revenge some other time, he proposed a bit of supper and a grog.

Before they had made an end of this refreshment it was time to be at work. A bucket of water for present necessities was withdrawn from the water-butt, which was then emptied and rolled before the kitchen fire to dry; and the two brothers set forth on their adventure under a starless heaven.

CHAPTER III

The Lecturer at Large

Whether mankind is really partial to happiness is an open question. Not a month passes by but some cherished son runs off into the merchant service, or some valued husband decamps to Texas with a lady help; clergymen have fled from their parishioners; and even judges have been known to retire. To an open mind, it will appear (upon the whole) less strange that Joseph Finsbury should have been led to entertain ideas of escape. His lot (I think we may say) was not a happy one. My friend, Mr Morris, with whom I travel up twice or thrice a week from Snaresbrook Park, is certainly a gentleman whom I esteem; but he was scarce a model nephew. As for John, he is of course an excellent fellow; but if he was the only link that bound one to a home, I think the most of us would vote for foreign travel. In the case of Joseph, John (if he were a link at all) was not the only one; endearing bonds had long enchained the old gentleman to Bloomsbury; and by these expressions I do not in the least refer to Julia Hazeltine (of whom, however, he was fond enough), but to that collection of manuscript notebooks in which his life lay buried. That he should ever have made up his mind to separate himself from these collections, and go forth upon the world with no other resources than his memory supplied, is a circumstance highly pathetic in itself, and but little creditable to the wisdom of his nephews.

The design, or at least the temptation, was already some months old; and when a bill for eight hundred pounds, payable to himself, was suddenly placed in Joseph's hand, it brought matters to an issue. He retained that bill, which, to one of his frugality, meant wealth; and he promised himself to disappear among the crowds at Waterloo, or (if that should prove impossible) to slink out of the house in the course of the evening and melt like a dream into the millions of London. By a peculiar interposition of Providence and railway mismanagement he had not so long to wait.

He was one of the first to come to himself and scramble to his feet after the Browndean catastrophe, and he had no sooner remarked his prostrate nephews than he understood his opportunity and fled. A man of upwards of seventy, who has just met with a railway accident, and who is cumbered besides with the full uniform of Sir Faraday Bond, is not very likely to flee far, but the wood was close at hand and offered the fugitive at least a temporary covert. Hither, then, the old gentleman skipped with extraordinary expedition, and, being somewhat winded and a good deal shaken, here he lay down in a convenient grove and was presently overwhelmed by slumber. The way of fate is often highly entertaining to the looker-on, and it is certainly a pleasant circumstance, that while Morris and John were delving in the sand to conceal the body of a total stranger, their uncle lay in dreamless sleep a few hundred yards deeper in the wood.

He was awakened by the jolly note of a bugle from the neighbouring high road, where a *char-à-banc* was bowling by with some belated tourists. The sound cheered his old heart, it directed his steps into the bargain, and soon he was on the highway, looking east and west from under his vizor, and doubtfully revolving what he ought to do. A deliberate sound of wheels arose in the distance, and then a cart was seen approaching, well filled with parcels, driven by a good-natured looking man on a double bench, and displaying on a board the legend, 'I. Chandler, carrier'. In the infamously prosaic mind of Mr Finsbury, certain streaks of poetry survived and were still efficient; they had carried him to Asia Minor as a giddy youth of forty, and now, in the first hours of his recovered freedom, they suggested to him the idea of continuing his flight in Mr Chandler's cart. It would be cheap; properly broached, it might even cost nothing, and, after years of mittens and hygienic flannel, his heart leaped out to meet the notion of exposure.

Mr Chandler was perhaps a little puzzled to find so old a gentleman, so strangely clothed, and begging for a lift on so retired a roadside. But he was a good-natured man, glad to do a service, and so he took the stranger up; and he had his own idea of civility, and so he asked no questions. Silence, in fact, was quite good enough for Mr Chandler; but the cart had scarcely begun to move forward ere he found himself involved in a one-sided conversation.

'I can see,' began Mr Finsbury, 'by the mixture of parcels and boxes that are contained in your cart, each marked with its individual label, and by the good Flemish mare you drive, that you occupy the post of carrier in that great English system of transport which, with all its defects, is the pride of our country.'

'Yes, sir,' returned Mr Chandler vaguely, for he hardly knew what to reply; 'them parcels posts has done us carriers a world of harm.'

'I am not a prejudiced man,' continued Joseph Finsbury. 'As a young man I travelled much. Nothing was too small or too obscure for me to acquire. At sea I studied seamanship, learned the complicated knots employed by mariners, and acquired the technical terms. At Naples, I would learn the art of making macaroni; at Nice, the principles of making candied fruit. I never went to the opera without first buying the book of the piece, and making myself acquainted with the principal airs by picking them out on the piano with one finger.'

'You must have seen a deal, sir,' remarked the carrier, touching up his horse; 'I wish I could have had your advantages.'

'Do you know how often the word whip occurs in the Old Testament?' continued the old gentleman. 'One hundred and (if I remember exactly) forty-seven times.'

'Do it indeed, sir?' said Mr Chandler. 'I never should have thought it.'

'The Bible contains three million five hundred and one thousand two hundred and forty-nine letters. Of verses I believe there are upward of eighteen thousand. There have been many editions of the Bible; Wycliff was the first to introduce it into England about the year 1300. The "Paragraph Bible", as it is called, is a well-known edition, and is so called because it is divided into paragraphs. The "Breeches Bible" is another well-known instance, and gets its name either because it was printed by one Breeches, or because the place of publication bore that name.'

The carrier remarked drily that he thought that was only natural, and turned his attention to the more congenial task of passing a cart of hay; it was a matter of some difficulty, for the road was narrow, and there was a ditch on either hand.

'I perceive,' began Mr Finsbury, when they had successfully passed the cart, 'that you hold your reins with one hand; you should employ two.'

'Well, I like that!' cried the carrier contemptuously. 'Why?'

'You do not understand,' continued Mr Finsbury. 'What I tell you is a scientific fact, and reposes on the theory of the lever, a branch of

mechanics. There are some very interesting little shilling books upon
the field of study, which I should think a man in your station would
take a pleasure to read. But I am afraid you have not cultivated the art
of observation; at least we have now driven together for some time,
and I cannot remember that you have contributed a single fact. This
is a very false principle, my good man. For instance, I do not know if
you observed that (as you passed the hay-cart man) you took your
left?'

'Of course I did,' cried the carrier, who was now getting belligerent;
'he'd have the law on me if I hadn't.'

'In France, now,' resumed the old man, 'and also, I believe, in the
United States of America, you would have taken the right.'

'I would not,' cried Mr Chandler indignantly. 'I would have taken
the left.'

'I observe again,' continued Mr Finsbury, scorning to reply, 'that
you mend the dilapidated parts of your harness with string. I have
always protested against this carelessness and slovenliness of the
English poor. In an essay that I once read before an appreciative
audience——'

'It ain't string,' said the carrier sullenly, 'it's pack-thread.'

'I have always protested,' resumed the old man, 'that in their
private and domestic life, as well as in their labouring career, the
lower classes of this country are improvident, thriftless, and extravagant. A stitch in time——'

'Who the devil *are* the lower classes?' cried the carrier. 'You are the
lower classes yourself! If I thought you were a blooming aristocrat, I
shouldn't have given you a lift.'

The words were uttered with undisguised ill-feeling; it was
plain the pair were not congenial, and further conversation, even to
one of Mr Finsbury's pathetic loquacity, was out of the question.
With an angry gesture, he pulled down the brim of the forage-
cap over his eyes, and, producing a notebook and a blue pencil
from one of his innermost pockets, soon became absorbed in
calculations.

On his part the carrier fell to whistling with fresh zest; and if (now
and again) he glanced at the companion of his drive, it was with
mingled feelings of triumph and alarm—triumph because he had
succeeded in arresting that prodigy of speech, and alarm lest (by any
accident) it should begin again. Even the shower, which presently

overtook and passed them, was endured by both in silence; and it was still in silence that they drove at length into Southampton.

Dusk had fallen; the shop windows glimmered forth into the streets of the old seaport; in private houses lights were kindled for the evening meal; and Mr Finsbury began to think complacently of his night's lodging. He put his papers by, cleared his throat, and looked doubtfully at Mr Chandler.

'Will you be civil enough,' said he, 'to recommend me to an inn?'

Mr Chandler pondered for a moment.

'Well,' he said at last, 'I wonder how about the "Tregonwell Arms".'

'The "Tregonwell Arms" will do very well,' returned the old man, 'if it's clean and cheap, and the people civil.'

'I wasn't thinking so much of you,' returned Mr Chandler thoughtfully. 'I was thinking of my friend Watts as keeps the 'ouse; he's a friend of mine, you see, and he helped me through my trouble last year. And I was thinking, would it be fair-like on Watts to saddle him with an old party like you, who might be the death of him with general information. Would it be fair to the 'ouse?' enquired Mr Chandler, with an air of candid appeal.

'Mark me,' cried the old gentleman with spirit. 'It was kind in you to bring me here for nothing, but it gives you no right to address me in such terms. Here's a shilling for your trouble; and, if you do not choose to set me down at the "Tregonwell Arms", I can find it for myself.'

Chandler was surprised and a little startled; muttering something apologetic, he returned the shilling, drove in silence through several intricate lanes and small streets, drew up at length before the bright windows of an inn, and called loudly for Mr Watts.

'Is that you, Jem?' cried a hearty voice from the stableyard. 'Come in and warm yourself.'

'I only stopped here,' Mr Chandler explained, 'to let down an old gent that wants food and lodging. Mind, I warn you agin him; he's worse nor a temperance lecturer.'

Mr Finsbury dismounted with difficulty, for he was cramped with his long drive, and the shaking he had received in the accident. The friendly Mr Watts, in spite of the carter's scarcely agreeable introduction, treated the old gentleman with the utmost courtesy, and led him into the back parlour, where there was a big fire burning in the grate.

Presently a table was spread in the same room, and he was invited to seat himself before a stewed fowl—somewhat the worse for having seen service before—and a big pewter mug of ale from the tap.

He rose from supper a giant refreshed; and, changing his seat to one nearer the fire, began to examine the other guests with an eye to the delights of oratory. There were near a dozen present, all men, and (as Joseph exulted to perceive) all working men. Often already had he seen cause to bless that appetite for disconnected fact and rotatory argument which is so marked a character of the mechanic. But even an audience of working men has to be courted, and there was no man more deeply versed in the necessary arts than Joseph Finsbury. He placed his glasses on his nose, drew from his pocket a bundle of papers, and spread them before him on a table. He crumpled them, he smoothed them out; now he skimmed them over, apparently well pleased with their contents; now, with tapping pencil and contracted brows, he seemed maturely to consider some particular statement. A stealthy glance about the room assured him of the success of his manœuvres; all eyes were turned on the performer, mouths were open, pipes hung suspended; the birds were charmed. At the same moment the entrance of Mr Watts afforded him an opportunity.

'I observe,' said he, addressing the landlord, but taking at the same time the whole room into his confidence with an encouraging look, 'I observe that some of these gentlemen are looking with curiosity in my direction; and certainly it is unusual to see anyone immersed in literary and scientific labours in the public apartment of an inn. I have here some calculations I made this morning upon the cost of living in this and other countries—a subject, I need scarcely say, highly interesting to the working classes. I have calculated a scale of living for incomes of eighty, one hundred and sixty, two hundred, and two hundred and forty pounds a year. I must confess that the income of eighty pounds has somewhat baffled me, and the others are not so exact as I could wish; for the price of washing varies largely in foreign countries, and the different cokes, coals and firewoods fluctuate surprisingly. I will read my researches, and I hope you won't scruple to point out to me any little errors that I may have committed either from oversight or ignorance. I will begin, gentlemen, with the income of eighty pounds a year.'

Whereupon the old gentleman, with less compassion than he would have had for brute beasts, delivered himself of all his tedious calculations. As he occasionally gave nine versions of a single income, placing the imaginary person in London, Paris, Bagdad, Spitzbergen, Bassorah, Heligoland, the Scilly Islands, Brighton, Cincinnati, and Nijni-Novgorod, with an appropriate outfit for each locality, it is no wonder that his hearers look back on that evening as the most tiresome they ever spent.

Long before Mr Finsbury had reached Nijni-Novgorod with the income of one hundred and sixty pounds, the company had dwindled and faded away to a few old topers and the bored but affable Watts. There was a constant stream of customers from the outer world, but so soon as they were served they drank their liquor quickly and departed with the utmost celerity for the next public-house.

By the time the young man with two hundred a year was vegetating in the Scilly Islands, Mr Watts was left alone with the economist; and that imaginary person had scarce commenced life at Brighton before the last of his pursuers desisted from the chase.

Mr Finsbury slept soundly after the manifold fatigues of the day. He rose late, and, after a good breakfast, ordered the bill. Then it was that he made a discovery which has been made by many others, both before and since: that it is one thing to order your bill, and another to discharge it. The items were moderate and (what does not always follow) the total small; but, after the most sedulous review of all his pockets, one and nine pence halfpenny appeared to be the total of the old gentleman's available assets. He asked to see Mr Watts.

'Here is a bill on London for eight hundred pounds,' said Mr Finsbury, as that worthy appeared. 'I am afraid, unless you choose to discount it yourself, it may detain me a day or two till I can get it cashed.'

Mr Watts looked at the bill, turned it over, and dogs-eared it with his fingers. 'It will keep you a day or two?' he said, repeating the old man's words. 'You have no other money with you?'

'Some trifling change,' responded Joseph. 'Nothing to speak of.'

'Then you can send it me; I should be pleased to trust you.'

'To tell the truth,' answered the old gentleman, 'I am more than half inclined to stay; I am in need of funds.'

'If a loan of ten shillings would help you, it is at your service,' responded Watts, with eagerness.

'No, I think I would rather stay,' said the old man, 'and get my bill discounted.'

'You shall not stay in my house,' cried Mr Watts. 'This is the last time you shall have a bed at the "Tregonwell Arms".'

'I insist upon remaining,' replied Mr Finsbury, with spirit; 'I remain by Act of Parliament; turn me out if you dare.'

'Then pay your bill,' said Mr Watts.

'Take that,' cried the old man, tossing him the negotiable bill.

'It is not legal tender,' replied Mr Watts. 'You must leave my house at once.'

'You cannot appreciate the contempt I feel for you, Mr Watts,' said the old gentleman, resigning himself to circumstances. 'But you shall feel it in one way: I refuse to pay my bill.'

'I don't care for your bill,' responded Mr Watts. 'What I want is your absence.'

'That you shall have!' said the old gentleman, and, taking up his forage cap as he spoke, he crammed it on his head. 'Perhaps you are too insolent,' he added, 'to inform me of the time of the next London train?'

'It leaves in three-quarters of an hour,' returned the innkeeper with alacrity. 'You can easily catch it.'

Joseph's position was one of considerable weakness. On the one hand, it would have been well to avoid the direct line of railway, since it was there he might expect his nephews to lie in wait for his recapture; on the other, it was highly desirable, it was even strictly needful, to get the bill discounted ere it should be stopped. To London, therefore, he decided to proceed on the first train; and there remained but one point to be considered, how to pay his fare.

Joseph's nails were never clean; he ate almost entirely with his knife. I doubt if you could say he had the manners of a gentleman; but he had better than that, a touch of genuine dignity. Was it from his stay in Asia Minor? Was it from a strain in the Finsbury blood sometimes alluded to by customers? At least, when he presented himself before the station-master, his salaam was truly Oriental, palm-trees appeared to crowd about the little office, and the simoom or the bulbul—but I leave this image to persons better acquainted with the East. His appearance, besides, was highly in his favour; the uniform of Sir Faraday, however inconvenient and conspicuous, was, at least, a costume in which no swindler could have hoped to prosper; and the exhibition of a valuable watch and a bill for eight hundred pounds completed what deportment had begun. A quarter of an hour later, when the train came up, Mr Finsbury was introduced to the guard and installed in a first-class compartment, the station-master smilingly assuming all responsibility.

As the old gentleman sat waiting the moment of departure, he was the witness of an incident strangely connected with the fortunes of his house. A packing-case of cyclopean bulk was borne along the platform by some dozen of tottering porters, and ultimately, to the delight of a considerable crowd, hoisted on board the van. It is often the cheering task of the historian to direct attention to the designs and (if it may be reverently said) the artifices of Providence. In the luggage van, as Joseph was borne out of the station of Southampton East upon his way to London, the egg of his romance lay (so to speak) unhatched. The huge packing-case was directed to lie at Waterloo till called for, and addressed to one 'William Dent Pitman'; and the very next article, a goodly barrel jammed into the corner of the van, bore the superscription, 'M. Finsbury, 16 John Street, Bloomsbury. Carriage paid.'

In this juxtaposition, the train of powder was prepared; and there was now wanting only an idle hand to fire it off.

CHAPTER IV

The Magistrate in the Luggage Van

The city of Winchester is famed for a cathedral, a bishop—but he was unfortunately killed some years ago while riding—a public school, a considerable assortment of the military, and the deliberate passage of the trains of the London and South-Western line. These and many similar associations would have doubtless crowded on the mind of Joseph Finsbury; but his spirit had at that time flitted from the railway compartment to a heaven of populous lecture-halls and endless oratory. His body, in the meanwhile, lay doubled on the cushions, the forage-cap rakishly tilted back after the fashion of those that lie in wait for nursery-maids, the poor old face quiescent, one arm clutching to his heart *Lloyd's Weekly Newspaper*.

To him, thus unconscious, enter and exeunt again a pair of voyagers. These two had saved the train and no more. A tandem urged to its last speed, an act of something closely bordering on brigandage at the ticket office, and a spasm of running, had brought them on the platform just as the engine uttered its departing snort. There was but one carriage easily within their reach; and they had sprung into it, and the leader and elder already had his feet upon the floor, when he observed Mr Finsbury.

'Good God!' he cried. 'Uncle Joseph! This'll never do.'

And he backed out, almost upsetting his companion, and once more closed the door upon the sleeping patriarch.

The next moment the pair had jumped into the baggage van.

'What's the row about your Uncle Joseph?' enquired the younger traveller, mopping his brow. 'Does he object to smoking?'

'I don't know that there's anything the row with him,' returned the other. 'He's by no means the first comer, my Uncle Joseph, I can tell you! Very respectable old gentleman; interested in leather; been to Asia Minor; no family, no assets—and a tongue, my dear Wickham, sharper than a serpent's tooth.'

'Cantankerous old party, eh?' suggested Wickham.

'Not in the least,' cried the other; 'only a man with a solid talent for being a bore; rather cheery I dare say, on a desert island, but on a railway journey insupportable. You should hear him on Tonti, the ass that started tontines. He's incredible on Tonti.'

'By Jove!' cried Wickham, 'then you're one of these Finsbury tontine fellows. I hadn't a guess of that.'

'Ah!' said the other, 'do you know that old boy in the carriage is worth a hundred thousand pounds to me? There he was asleep, and nobody there but you! But I spared him, because I'm a Conservative in politics.'

Mr Wickham, pleased to be in a luggage van, was flitting to and fro like a gentlemanly butterfly.

'By Jingo!' he cried, 'here's something for you! "M. Finsbury, 16 John Street, Bloomsbury, London." M. stands for Michael, you sly dog; you keep two establishments, do you?'

'O, that's Morris,' responded Michael from the other end of the van, where he had found a comfortable seat upon some sacks. 'He's a little cousin of mine. I like him myself, because he's afraid of me. He's one of the ornaments of Bloomsbury, and has a collection of some kind—birds' eggs or something that's supposed to be curious. I bet it's nothing to my clients!'

'What a lark it would be to play billy with the labels!' chuckled Mr Wickham. 'By George, here's a tack-hammer! We might send all these things skipping about the premises like what's-his-name!'

At this moment, the guard, surprised by the sound of voices, opened the door of his little cabin.

'You had best step in here, gentlemen,' said he, when he had heard their story.

'Won't you come, Wickham?' asked Michael.

'Catch me—I want to travel in a van,' replied the youth.

And so the door of communication was closed; and for the rest of the run Mr Wickham was left alone over his diversions on the one side, and on the other Michael and the guard were closeted together in familiar talk.

'I can get you a compartment here, sir,' observed the official, as the train began to slacken speed before Bishopstoke station. 'You had best get out at my door, and I can bring your friend.'

Mr Wickham, whom we left (as the reader has shrewdly suspected) beginning to 'play billy' with the labels in the van, was a young gentleman of much wealth, a pleasing but sandy exterior, and a highly vacant mind. Not many months before, he had contrived to get himself blackmailed by the family of a Wallachian Hospodar, resident for political reasons in the gay city of Paris. A common friend (to whom he had confided his distress) recommended him to Michael; and the lawyer was no sooner in possession of the facts than he instantly assumed the offensive, fell on the flank of the Wallachian forces, and, in the inside of three days, had the satisfaction to behold them routed and fleeing for the Danube. It is no business of ours to follow them on this retreat, over which the police were so obliging as to preside paternally. Thus relieved from what he loved to refer to as the Bulgarian Atrocity, Mr Wickham returned to London with the most unbounded and embarrassing gratitude and admiration for his saviour. These sentiments were not repaid either in kind or degree; indeed, Michael was a trifle ashamed of his new client's friendship; it had taken many invitations to get him to Winchester and Wickham Manor; but he had gone at last, and was now returning. It has been remarked by some judicious thinker (possibly J. F. Smith) that Providence despises to employ no instrument, however humble; and it is now plain to the dullest that both Mr Wickham and the Wallachian Hospodar were liquid lead and wedges in the hand of Destiny.

Smitten with the desire to shine in Michael's eyes and show himself a person of original humour and resources, the young gentleman (who was a magistrate, more by token, in his native county) was no sooner alone in the van than he fell upon the labels with all the zeal of a reformer; and, when he rejoined the lawyer at Bishopstoke, his face was flushed with his exertions, and his cigar, which he had suffered to go out was almost bitten in two.

'By George, but this has been a lark!' he cried. 'I've sent the wrong thing to everybody in England. These cousins of yours have a packing-case as big as a house. I've muddled the whole business up to that extent, Finsbury, that if it were to get out it's my belief we should get lynched.'

It was useless to be serious with Mr Wickham. 'Take care,' said Michael. 'I am getting tired of your perpetual scrapes; my reputation is beginning to suffer.'

'Your reputation will be all gone before you finish with me,' replied his companion with a grin. 'Clap it in the bill, my boy. "For total loss of reputation, six and eightpence." But,' continued Mr Wickham with more seriousness, 'could I be bowled out of the Commission for this little jest? I know it's small, but I like to be a JP. Speaking as a professional man, do you think there's any risk?'

'What does it matter?' responded Michael, 'they'll chuck you out sooner or later. Somehow you don't give the effect of being a good magistrate.'

'I only wish I was a solicitor,' retorted his companion, 'instead of a poor devil of a country gentleman. Suppose we start one of those tontine affairs ourselves; I to pay five hundred a year, and you to guarantee me against every misfortune except illness or marriage.'

'It strikes me,' remarked the lawyer with a meditative laugh, as he lighted a cigar, 'it strikes me that you must be a cursed nuisance in this world of ours.'

'Do you really think so, Finsbury?' responded the magistrate, leaning back in his cushions, delighted with the compliment. 'Yes, I suppose I am a nuisance. But, mind you, I have a stake in the country: don't forget that, dear boy.'

CHAPTER V

Mr Gideon Forsyth and the Gigantic Box

It has been mentioned that at Bournemouth Julia sometimes made acquaintances; it is true she had but a glimpse of them before the doors of John Street closed again upon its captives, but the glimpse was sometimes exhilarating, and the consequent regret was tempered with hope. Among those whom she had thus met a year before was a young barrister of the name of Gideon Forsyth.

About three o'clock of the eventful day when the magistrate tampered with the labels, a somewhat moody and distempered ramble had carried Mr Forsyth to the corner of John Street; and about the same moment Miss Hazeltine was called to the door of No. 16 by a thundering double knock.

Mr Gideon Forsyth was a happy enough young man; he would have been happier if he had had more money and less uncle. One hundred and twenty pounds a year was all his store; but his uncle, Mr Edward Hugh Bloomfield, supplemented this with a handsome allowance and a great deal of advice, couched in language that would probably have been judged intemperate on board a pirate ship. Mr Bloomfield was indeed a figure quite peculiar to the days of Mr Gladstone; what we may call (for the lack of an accepted expression) a Squirradical. Having acquired years without experience, he carried into the Radical side of politics those noisy, after-dinner-table passions, which we are more accustomed to connect with Toryism in its severe and senile aspects. To the opinions of Mr Bradlaugh, in fact, he added the temper and the sympathies of that extinct animal, the Squire; he admired pugilism, he carried a formidable oaken staff, he was a reverent churchman, and it was hard to know which would have more volcanically stirred his choler—a person who should have defended the established church, or one who should have neglected to attend its celebrations. He had besides some levelling catchwords, justly dreaded in the family circle; and when he could not go so far as to declare a step un-English, he might still (and with hardly less effect) denounce it as unpractical. It was under the ban of this lesser excommunication that Gideon had fallen. His views on the study of law had been pronounced unpractical; and it had been intimated to him, in a vociferous interview punctuated with the oaken staff, that he must either take a new start and get a brief or two, or prepare to live on his own money.

No wonder if Gideon was moody. He had not the slightest wish to modify his present habits; but he would not stand on that, since the recall of Mr Bloomfield's allowance would revolutionize them still more radically. He had not the least desire to acquaint himself with law; he had looked into it already, and it seemed not to repay attention; but upon this also he was ready to give way. In fact, he would go as far as he could to meet the views of his uncle, the Squirradical. But there was one part of the programme that appeared independent of his will. How to get a brief? there was the question. And there was another and a worse. Suppose he got one, should he prove the better man?

Suddenly he found his way barred by a crowd. A garishly illuminated van was backed against the kerb; from its open stern, half resting on the street, half supported by some glistening athletes, the end of the largest packing-case in the county of Middlesex might have been seen protruding; while, on the steps of the house, the burly person of the driver and the slim figure of a young girl stood as upon a stage, disputing.

'It is not for us,' the girl was saying. 'I beg you to take it away; it couldn't get into the house, even if you managed to get it out of the van.'

'I shall leave it on the pavement, then, and M. Finsbury can arrange with the Vestry as he likes,' said the vanman.

'But I am not M. Finsbury,' expostulated the girl.

'It doesn't matter who you are,' said the vanman.

'You must allow me to help you, Miss Hazeltine,' said Gideon, putting out his hand.

Julia gave a little cry of pleasure. 'O, Mr Forsyth,' she cried, 'I am so glad to see you; we must get this horrid thing, which can only have come here by mistake, into the house. The man says we'll have to take off the door, or knock two of our windows into one, or be fined by the Vestry or Custom House or something for leaving our parcels on the pavement.'

The men by this time had successfully removed the box from the van, had plumped it down on the pavement, and now stood leaning against it, or gazing at the door of No. 16, in visible physical distress and mental embarrassment. The windows of the whole street had filled, as if by magic, with interested and entertained spectators.

With as thoughtful and scientific an expression as he could assume, Gideon measured the doorway with his cane, while Julia entered his observations in a drawing-book. He then measured the box, and, upon comparing his data, found that there was just enough space for it to enter. Next, throwing off his coat and waistcoat, he assisted the men to take the door from its hinges. And lastly, all bystanders being pressed into the service, the packing-case mounted the steps upon some fifteen pairs of wavering legs—scraped, loudly grinding, through the doorway—and was deposited at length, with a formidable convulsion, in the far end of the lobby, which it almost blocked. The artisans of this victory smiled upon each other as the dust subsided. It was true they had smashed a bust of Apollo and ploughed the wall into deep ruts; but, at least, they were no longer one of the public spectacles of London.

'Well, sir,' said the vanman, 'I never see such a job.'

Gideon eloquently expressed his concurrence in this sentiment by pressing a couple of sovereigns in the man's hand.

'Make it three, sir, and I'll stand Sam to everybody here!' cried the latter, and, this having been done, the whole body of volunteer porters swarmed into the van, which drove off in the direction of the nearest reliable public-house. Gideon closed the door on their departure, and turned to Julia; their eyes met; the most uncontrollable mirth seized upon them both, and they made the house ring with their laughter. Then curiosity awoke in Julia's mind, and she went and examined the box, and more especially the label.

'This is the strangest thing that ever happened,' she said, with another burst of laughter. 'It is certainly Morris's handwriting, and I had a letter from him only this morning, telling me to expect a barrel. Is there a barrel coming too, do you think, Mr Forsyth?'

' "Statuary with Care, Fragile," ' read Gideon aloud from the painted warning on the box. 'Then you were told nothing about this?'

'No,' responded Julia. 'O, Mr Forsyth, don't you think we might take a peep at it?'

'Yes, indeed,' cried Gideon. 'Just let me have a hammer.'

'Come down, and I'll show you where it is,' cried Julia. 'The shelf is too high for me to reach'; and, opening the door of the kitchen stair, she bade Gideon follow her. They found both the hammer and a chisel; but Gideon was surprised to see no sign of a servant. He also discovered that Miss Hazeltine had a very pretty little foot and ankle; and the discovery embarrassed him so much that he was glad to fall at once upon the packing-case.

He worked hard and earnestly, and dealt his blows with the precision of a blacksmith; Julia the while standing silently by his side, and regarding rather the workman than the work. He was a handsome fellow; she told herself she had never seen such beautiful arms. And suddenly, as though he had overheard these thoughts, Gideon turned and smiled to her. She, too, smiled and coloured; and the double change became her so prettily that Gideon forgot to turn away his eyes, and, swinging the hammer with a will, discharged a smashing blow on his own knuckles. With admirable presence of mind he crushed down an oath and substituted the harmless comment, 'Butter fingers!' But the pain was sharp, his nerve was shaken, and after an abortive trial he found he must desist from further operations.

In a moment Julia was off to the pantry; in a moment she was back again with a basin of water and a sponge, and had begun to bathe his wounded hand.

'I am dreadfully sorry!' said Gideon apologetically. 'If I had had any manners I should have opened the box first and smashed my hand afterward. It feels much better,' he added. 'I assure you it does.'

'And now I think you are well enough to direct operations,' said she. 'Tell me what to do, and I'll be your workman.'

'A very pretty workman,' said Gideon, rather forgetting himself. She turned and looked at him, with a suspicion of a frown; and the indiscreet young man was glad to direct her attention to the packing-case. The bulk of the work had been accomplished; and presently Julia had burst through the last barrier and disclosed a zone of straw. In a moment they were kneeling side by side, engaged like hay-makers; the next they were rewarded with a glimpse of something white and polished; and the next again laid bare an unmistakable marble leg.

'He is surely a very athletic person,' said Julia.

'I never saw anything like it,' responded Gideon. 'His muscles stand out like penny rolls.'

Another leg was soon disclosed, and then what seemed to be a third. This resolved itself, however, into a knotted club resting upon a pedestal.

'It is a Hercules,' cried Gideon; 'I might have guessed that from his calf. I'm supposed to be rather partial to statuary, but when it comes to Hercules, the police should interfere. I should say,' he added, glancing with disaffection at the swollen leg, 'that this was about the biggest and the worst in Europe. What in heaven's name can have induced him to come here?'

'I suppose nobody else would have a gift of him,' said Julia. 'And for that matter, I think we could have done without the monster very well.'

'O, don't say that,' returned Gideon. 'This has been one of the most amusing experiences of my life.'

'I don't think you'll forget it very soon,' said Julia. 'Your hand will remind you.'

'Well, I suppose I must be going,' said Gideon reluctantly.

'No,' pleaded Julia. 'Why should you? Stay and have tea with me.'

'If I thought you really wished me to stay,' said Gideon, looking at his hat, 'of course I should only be too delighted.'

'What a silly person you must take me for!' returned the girl. 'Why, of course I do; and, besides, I want some cakes for tea, and I've nobody to send. Here is the latchkey.'

Gideon put on his hat with alacrity, and casting one look at Miss Hazeltine, and another at the legs of Hercules, threw open the door and departed on his errand.

He returned with a large bag of the choicest and most tempting of cakes and tartlets, and found Julia in the act of spreading a small tea-table in the lobby.

'The rooms are all in such a state,' she cried, 'that I thought we should be more cosy and comfortable in our own lobby, and under our own vine and statuary.'

'Ever so much better,' cried Gideon delightedly.

'O what adorable cream tarts!' said Julia, opening the bag, 'and the dearest little cherry tartlets, with all the cherries spilled out into the cream!'

'Yes,' said Gideon, concealing his dismay, 'I knew they would mix beautifully; the woman behind the counter told me so.'

'Now,' said Julia, as they began their little festival, 'I am going to show you Morris's letter; read it aloud, please; perhaps there's something I have missed.'

Gideon took the letter, and spreading it out on his knee, read as follows:

DEAR JULIA, I write you from Browndean, where we are stopping over for a few days. Uncle was much shaken in that dreadful accident, of which, I dare say, you have seen the account. Tomorrow I leave him here with John, and come up alone; but before that, you will have received a barrel *containing specimens for a friend*. Do not open it on any account, but leave it in the lobby till I come.

Yours in haste,
M. FINSBURY.

P.S.—Be sure and leave the barrel in the lobby.

'No,' said Gideon, 'there seems to be nothing about the monument,' and he nodded, as he spoke, at the marble legs. 'Miss Hazeltine,' he continued, 'would you mind me asking a few questions?'

'Certainly not,' replied Julia; 'and if you can make me understand why Morris has sent a statue of Hercules instead of a barrel containing specimens for a friend, I shall be grateful till my dying day. And what are specimens for a friend?'

'I haven't a guess,' said Gideon. 'Specimens are usually bits of stone, but rather smaller than our friend the monument. Still, that is not the point. Are you quite alone in this big house?'

'Yes, I am at present,' returned Julia. 'I came up before them to prepare the house, and get another servant. But I couldn't get one I liked.'

'Then you are utterly alone,' said Gideon in amazement. 'Are you not afraid?'

'No,' responded Julia stoutly. 'I don't see why I should be more afraid than you would be; I am weaker, of course, but when I found I must sleep alone in the house I bought a revolver wonderfully cheap, and made the man show me how to use it.'

'And how do you use it?' demanded Gideon, much amused at her courage.

'Why,' said she, with a smile, 'you pull the little trigger thing on top, and then pointing it very low, for it springs up as you fire, you pull the underneath little trigger thing, and it goes off as well as if a man had done it.'

'And how often have you used it?' asked Gideon.

'O, I have not used it yet,' said the determined young lady; 'but I know how, and that makes me wonderfully courageous, especially when I barricade my door with a chest of drawers.'

'I'm awfully glad they are coming back soon,' said Gideon. 'This business strikes me as excessively unsafe; if it goes on much longer, I could provide you with a maiden aunt of mine, or my landlady if you preferred.'

'Lend me an aunt!' cried Julia. 'O, what generosity! I begin to think it must have been you that sent the Hercules.'

'Believe me,' cried the young man, 'I admire you too much to send you such an infamous work of art.'

Julia was beginning to reply, when they were both startled by a knocking at the door.

'O, Mr Forsyth!'

'Don't be afraid, my dear girl,' said Gideon, laying his hand tenderly on her arm.

'I know it's the police,' she whispered. 'They are coming to complain about the statue.'

The knock was repeated. It was louder than before, and more impatient.

'It's Morris,' cried Julia, in a startled voice, and she ran to the door and opened it.

It was indeed Morris that stood before them; not the Morris of ordinary days, but a wild-looking fellow, pale and haggard, with bloodshot eyes, and a two-days' beard upon his chin.

'The barrel!' he cried. 'Where's the barrel that came this morning?' And he stared about the lobby, his eyes, as they fell upon the legs of Hercules, literally goggling in his head. 'What is that?' he screamed. 'What is that waxwork? Speak, you fool! What is that? And where's the barrel—the water-butt?'

'No barrel came, Morris,' responded Julia coldly. 'This is the only thing that has arrived.'

'This!' shrieked the miserable man. 'I never heard of it!'

'It came addressed in your hand,' replied Julia; 'we had nearly to pull the house down to get it in, that is all that I can tell you.'

Morris gazed at her in utter bewilderment. He passed his hand over his forehead; he leaned against the wall like a man about to faint. Then his tongue was loosed, and he overwhelmed the girl with torrents of abuse. Such fire, such directness, such a choice of ungentlemanly language, none had ever before suspected Morris to possess; and the girl trembled and shrank before his fury.

'You shall not speak to Miss Hazeltine in that way,' said Gideon sternly. 'It is what I will not suffer.'

'I shall speak to the girl as I like,' returned Morris, with a fresh outburst of anger. 'I'll speak to the hussy as she deserves.'

'Not a word more, sir, not one word,' cried Gideon. 'Miss Hazeltine,' he continued, addressing the young girl, 'you cannot stay a moment longer in the same house with this unmanly fellow. Here is my arm; let me take you where you will be secure from insult.'

'Mr Forsyth,' returned Julia, 'you are right; I cannot stay here longer, and I am sure I trust myself to an honourable gentleman.'

Pale and resolute, Gideon offered her his arm, and the pair descended the steps, followed by Morris clamouring for the latchkey.

Julia had scarcely handed the key to Morris before an empty hansom drove smartly into John Street. It was hailed by both men, and as the cabman drew up his restive horse, Morris made a dash into the vehicle.

'Sixpence above fare,' he cried recklessly. 'Waterloo Station for your life. Sixpence for yourself!'

'Make it a shilling, guv'ner,' said the man, with a grin; 'the other parties were first.'

'A shilling then,' cried Morris, with the inward reflection that he would reconsider it at Waterloo. The man whipped up his horse, and the hansom vanished from John Street.

CHAPTER VI

The Tribulations of Morris: Part the First

As the hansom span through the streets of London, Morris sought to rally the forces of his mind. The water-butt with the dead body had miscarried, and it was essential to recover it. So much was clear; and if, by some blest good fortune, it was still at the station, all might be well. If it had been sent out, however, if it were already in the hands of some wrong person, matters looked more ominous. People who receive unexplained packages are usually keen to have them open; the example of Miss Hazeltine (whom he cursed again) was there to remind him of the circumstance; and if anyone had opened the water-butt—'O Lord!' cried Morris at the thought, and carried his hand to his damp forehead. The private conception of any breach of law is apt to be inspiriting, for the scheme (while yet inchoate) wears dashing and attractive colours. Not so in the least that part of the criminal's later reflections which deal with the police. That useful corps (as Morris now began to think) had scarce been kept sufficiently in view when he embarked upon his enterprise. 'I must play devilish close,' he reflected, and he was aware of an exquisite thrill of fear in the region of the spine.

'Main line or loop?' enquired the cabman, through the scuttle.

'Main line,' replied Morris, and mentally decided that the man should have his shilling after all. 'It would be madness to attract attention,' thought he. 'But what this thing will cost me, first and last, begins to be a nightmare!'

He passed through the booking-office and wandered disconsolately on the platform. It was a breathing-space in the day's traffic. There were few people there, and these for the most part quiescent on the benches. Morris seemed to attract no remark, which was a good thing; but, on the other hand, he was making no progress in his quest. Something must be done, something must be risked. Every passing instant only added to his dangers. Summoning all his courage, he stopped a porter, and asked him if he remembered receiving a barrel by the morning train. He was anxious to get information, for the barrel belonged to a friend. 'It is a matter of some moment,' he added, 'for it contains specimens.'

'I was not here this morning, sir,' responded the porter, somewhat reluctantly, 'but I'll ask Bill. Do you recollect, Bill, to have got a barrel from Bournemouth this morning containing specimens?'

'I don't know about specimens,' replied Bill; 'but the party as received the barrel I mean raised a sight of trouble.'

'What's that?' cried Morris, in the agitation of the moment pressing a penny into the man's hand.

'You see, sir, the barrel arrived at one-thirty. No one claimed it till about three, when a small, sickly-looking gentleman (probably a curate) came up, and sez he, "Have you got anything for Pitman?" or "Will'm Bent Pitman," if I recollect right. "I don't exactly know," sez I, "but I rather fancy that there barrel bears that name." The little man went up to the barrel, and seemed regularly all took aback when he saw the address, and then he pitched into us for not having brought what he wanted. "I don't care a damn what you want," sez I to him, "but if you are Will'm Bent Pitman, there's your barrel."'

'Well, and did he take it?' cried the breathless Morris.

'Well, sir,' returned Bill, 'it appears it was a packing-case he was after. The packing-case came; that's sure enough, because it was about the biggest packing-case ever I clapped eyes on. And this Pitman he seemed a good deal cut up, and he had the superintendent out, and they got hold of the vanman—him as took the packing-case. Well, sir,' continued Bill, with a smile, 'I never see a man in such a state. Everybody about that van was mortal, bar the horses. Some gen'leman (as well as I could make out) had given the vanman a sov.; and so that was where the trouble come in, you see.'

'But what did he say?' gasped Morris.

'I don't know as he *said* much, sir,' said Bill. 'But he offered to fight this Pitman for a pot of beer. He had lost his book, too, and the receipts, and his men were all as mortal as himself. O, they were all like'—and Bill paused for a simile—'like lords! The superintendent sacked them on the spot.'

'O, come, but that's not so bad,' said Morris, with a bursting sigh. 'He couldn't tell where he took the packing-case, then?'

'Not he,' said Bill, 'nor yet nothink else.'

'And what—what did Pitman do?' asked Morris.

'O, he went off with the barrel in a four-wheeler, very trembling like,' replied Bill. 'I don't believe he's a gentleman as has good health.'

'Well, so the barrel's gone,' said Morris, half to himself.

'You may depend on that, sir,' returned the porter. 'But you had better see the superintendent.'

'Not in the least; it's of no account,' said Morris. 'It only contained specimens.' And he walked hastily away.

Ensconced once more in a hansom, he proceeded to reconsider his position. Suppose (he thought), suppose he should accept defeat and declare his uncle's death at once? He should lose the tontine, and with that the last hope of his seven thousand eight hundred pounds. But on the other hand, since the shilling to the hansom cabman, he had begun to see that crime was expensive in its course, and, since the loss of the water-butt, that it was uncertain in its consequences. Quietly at first, and then with growing heat, he reviewed the advantages of backing out. It involved a loss; but (come to think of it) no such great loss after all; only that of the tontine, which had been always a toss-up, which at bottom he had never really expected. He reminded himself of that eagerly; he congratulated himself upon his constant moderation. He had never really expected the tontine; he had never even very definitely hoped to recover his seven thousand eight hundred pounds; he had been hurried into the whole thing by Michael's obvious dishonesty. Yes, it would probably be better to draw back from this high-flying venture, settle back on the leather business——

'Great God!' cried Morris, bounding in the hansom like a Jack-in-a-box. 'I have not only not gained the tontine—I have lost the leather business!'

Such was the monstrous fact. He had no power to sign; he could not draw a cheque for thirty shillings. Until he could produce legal evidence of his uncle's death, he was a penniless outcast—and as soon as he produced it he had lost the tontine! There was no hesitation on the part of Morris; to drop the tontine like a hot chestnut, to concentrate all his forces on the leather business and the rest of his small but legitimate inheritance, was the decision of a single instant. And the next, the full extent of his calamity was suddenly disclosed to him. Declare his uncle's death? He couldn't! Since the body was lost Joseph had (in a legal sense) become immortal.

There was no created vehicle big enough to contain Morris and his woes. He paid the hansom off and walked on he knew not whither.

'I seem to have gone into this business with too much precipitation,' he reflected, with a deadly sigh. 'I fear it seems too ramified for a person of my powers of mind.'

And then a remark of his uncle's flashed into his memory: If you want to think clearly, put it all down on paper. 'Well, the old boy knew a thing or two,' said Morris. 'I will try; but I don't believe the paper was ever made that will clear my mind.'

He entered a place of public entertainment, ordered bread and cheese, and writing materials, and sat down before them heavily. He tried the pen. It was an excellent pen, but what was he to write? 'I have it,' cried Morris. 'Robinson Crusoe and the double columns!' He prepared his paper after that classic model, and began as follows:

Bad.	*Good.*
1. I have lost my uncle's body.	1. But then Pitman has found it.

'Stop a bit,' said Morris. 'I am letting the spirit of antithesis run away with me. Let's start again.'

Bad.	*Good.*
1. I have lost my uncle's body.	1. But then I no longer require to bury it.
2. I have lost the tontine.	2. But I may still save that if Pitman disposes of the body, and if I can find a physician who will stick at nothing.
3. I have lost the leather business and the rest of my uncle's succession.	3. But not if Pitman gives the body up to the police.

'O, but in that case I go to gaol; I had forgot that,' thought Morris. 'Indeed, I don't know that I had better dwell on that hypothesis at all; it's all very well to talk of facing the worst; but in a case of this kind a man's first duty is to his own nerve. Is there any answer to No. 3? Is there any possible good side to such a beastly bungle? There must be, of course, or where would be the use of this double-entry business?

And—by George, I have it!' he exclaimed; 'it's exactly the same as the last!' And he hastily re-wrote the passage:

Bad.	*Good.*
3. I have lost the leather business and the rest of my uncle's succession.	3. But not if I can find a physician who will stick at nothing.

'This venal doctor seems quite a desideratum,' he reflected. 'I want him first to give me a certificate that my uncle is dead, so that I may get the leather business; and then that he's alive—but here we are again at the incompatible interests!' And he returned to his tabulation:

Bad.	*Good.*
4. I have almost no money.	4. But there is plenty in the bank.
5. Yes, but I can't get the money in the bank.	5. But—well, that seems unhappily to be the case.
6. I have left the bill for eight hundred pounds in Uncle Joseph's pocket.	6. But if Pitman is only a dishonest man, the presence of this bill may lead him to keep the whole thing dark and throw the body into the New Cut.
7. Yes, but if Pitman is dishonest and finds the bill, he will know who Joseph is, and he may blackmail me.	7. Yes, but if I am right about Uncle Masterman, I can blackmail Michael.
8. But I can't blackmail Michael (which is, besides, a very dangerous thing to do) until I find out.	8. Worse luck!
9. The leather business will soon want money for current expenses, and I have none to give.	9. But the leather business is a sinking ship.
10. Yes, but it's all the ship I have.	10. A fact.
11. John will soon want money, and I have none to give.	11.
12. And the venal doctor will want money down.	12.
13. And if Pitman is dishonest and don't send me to gaol, he will want a fortune.	13.

'O, this seems to be a very one-sided business,' exclaimed Morris. 'There's not so much in this method as I was led to think.' He crumpled the paper up and threw it down; and then, the next moment, picked it up again and ran it over. 'It seems it's on the financial point that my position is weakest,' he reflected. 'Is there positively no way of raising the wind? In a vast city like this, and surrounded by all the resources of civilization, it seems not to be conceived! Let us have no more precipitation. Is there nothing I can sell? My collection of signet——' But at the thought of scattering these loved treasures the blood leaped into Morris's cheek. 'I would rather die!' he exclaimed, and, cramming his hat upon his head, strode forth into the streets.

'I *must* raise funds,' he thought. 'My uncle being dead, the money in the bank is mine, or would be mine but for the cursed injustice that has pursued me ever since I was an orphan in a commercial academy. I know what any other man would do; any other man in Christendom would forge; although I don't know why I call it forging, either, when Joseph's dead, and the funds are my own. When I think of that, when I think that my uncle is really as dead as mutton, and that I can't prove it, my gorge rises at the injustice of the whole affair. I used to feel bitterly about that seven thousand eight hundred pounds; it seems a trifle now! Dear me, why, the day before yesterday I was comparatively happy.'

And Morris stood on the sidewalk and heaved another sobbing sigh.

'Then there's another thing,' he resumed; 'can I? Am I able? Why didn't I practise different handwritings while I was young? How a fellow regrets those lost opportunities when he grows up! But there's one comfort: it's not morally wrong; I can try it on with a clear conscience, and even if I was found out, I wouldn't greatly care—morally, I mean. And then, if I succeed, and if Pitman is staunch—there's nothing to do but find a venal doctor; and that ought to be simple enough in a place like London. By all accounts the town's alive with them. It wouldn't do, of course, to advertise for a corrupt physician; that would be impolitic. No, I suppose a fellow has simply to spot along the streets for a red lamp and herbs in the window, and then you go in and—and—and put it to him plainly; though it seems a delicate step.'

He was near home now, after many devious wanderings, and turned up John Street. As he thrust his latchkey in the lock, another mortifying reflection struck him to the heart.

'Not even this house is mine till I can prove him dead,' he snarled, and slammed the door behind him so that the windows in the attic rattled.

Night had long fallen; long ago the lamps and the shop-fronts had begun to glitter down the endless streets; the lobby was pitch-dark; and, as the devil would have it, Morris barked his shins and sprawled all his length over the pedestal of Hercules. The pain was sharp; his temper was already thoroughly undermined; by a last misfortune his hand closed on the hammer as he fell; and, in a spasm of childish irritation, he turned and struck at the offending statue. There was a splintering crash.

'O Lord, what have I done next?' wailed Morris; and he groped his way to find a candle. 'Yes,' he reflected, as he stood with the light in his hand and looked upon the mutilated leg, from which about a pound of muscle was detached. 'Yes, I have destroyed a genuine antique; I may be in for thousands!' And then there sprung up in his bosom a sort of angry hope. 'Let me see,' he thought. 'Julia's got rid of; there's nothing to connect me with that beast Forsyth; the men were all drunk, and (what's better) they've been all discharged. O, come, I think this is another case of moral courage! I'll deny all knowledge of the thing.'

A moment more, and he stood again before the Hercules, his lips sternly compressed, the coal-axe and the meat-cleaver under his arm. The next, he had fallen upon the packing-case. This had been already seriously undermined by the operations of Gideon; a few well-directed blows, and it already quaked and gaped; yet a few more, and it fell about Morris in a shower of boards followed by an avalanche of straw.

And now the leather-merchant could behold the nature of his task: and at the first sight his spirit quailed. It was, indeed, no more ambitious a task for De Lesseps, with all his men and horses, to attack the hills of Panama, than for a single, slim young gentleman, with no previous experience of labour in a quarry, to measure himself against that bloated monster on his pedestal. And yet the pair were well encountered: on the one side, bulk—on the other, genuine heroic fire.

'Down you shall come, you great big ugly brute!' cried Morris aloud, with something of that passion which swept the Parisian mob against the walls of the Bastille. 'Down you shall come, this night. I'll have none of you in my lobby.'

The face, from its indecent expression, had particularly animated the zeal of our iconoclast; and it was against the face that he began his operations. The great height of the demigod—for he stood a fathom and half in his stocking-feet—offered a preliminary obstacle to this attack. But here, in the first skirmish of the battle, intellect already began to triumph over matter. By means of a pair of library steps, the injured householder gained a posture of advantage; and, with great swipes of the coal-axe, proceeded to decapitate the brute.

Two hours later, what had been the erect image of a gigantic coal-porter turned miraculously white, was now no more than a medley of disjected members; the quadragenarian torso prone against the pedestal; the lascivious countenance leering down the kitchen stair; the legs, the arms, the hands, and even the fingers, scattered broadcast on the lobby floor. Half an hour more, and all the debris had been laboriously carted to the kitchen; and Morris, with a gentle sentiment of triumph, looked round upon the scene of his achievements. Yes, he could deny all knowledge of it now: the lobby, beyond the fact that it was partly ruinous, betrayed no trace of the passage of Hercules. But it was a weary Morris that crept up to bed; his arms and shoulders ached, the palms of his hands burned from the rough kisses of the coal-axe, and there was one smarting finger that stole continually to his mouth. Sleep long delayed to visit the dilapidated hero, and with the first peep of day it had again deserted him.

The morning, as though to accord with his disastrous fortunes, dawned inclemently. An easterly gale was shouting in the streets; flaws of rain angrily assailed the windows; and as Morris dressed, the draught from the fireplace vividly played about his legs.

'I think,' he could not help observing bitterly, 'that with all I have to bear, they might have given me decent weather.'

There was no bread in the house, for Miss Hazeltine (like all women left to themselves) had subsisted entirely upon cake. But some of this was found, and (along with what the poets call a glass of fair, cold water) made up a semblance of a morning meal, and then down he sat undauntedly to his delicate task.

Nothing can be more interesting than the study of signatures, written (as they are) before meals and after, during indigestion and intoxication; written when the signer is trembling for the life of his child or has come from winning the Derby, in his lawyer's office, or under the bright eyes of his sweetheart. To the vulgar, these seem never the same; but to the expert, the bank clerk, or the lithographer, they are constant quantities, and as recognizable as the North Star to the night-watch on deck.

To all this Morris was alive. In the theory of that graceful art in which he was now embarking, our spirited leather-merchant was beyond all reproach. But, happily for the investor, forgery is an affair of practice. And as Morris sat surrounded by examples of his uncle's signature and of his own incompetence, insidious depression stole upon his spirits. From time to time the wind wuthered in the chimney at his back; from time to time there swept over Bloomsbury a squall so dark that he must rise and light the gas; about him was the chill and the mean disorder of a house out of commission—the floor bare, the sofa heaped with books and accounts enveloped in a dirty table-cloth, the pens rusted, the paper glazed with a thick film of dust; and yet these were but adminicles of misery, and the true root of his depression lay round him on the table in the shape of misbegotten forgeries.

'It's one of the strangest things I ever heard of,' he complained. 'It almost seems as if it was a talent that I didn't possess.' He went once more minutely through his proofs. 'A clerk would simply gibe at them,' said he. 'Well, there's nothing else but tracing possible.'

He waited till a squall had passed and there came a blink of scowling daylight. Then he went to the window, and in the face of all John Street traced his uncle's signature. It was a poor thing at the best. 'But it must do,' said he, as he stood gazing woefully on his handiwork. 'He's dead, anyway.' And he filled up the cheque for a couple of hundred and sallied forth for the Anglo-Patagonian Bank.

There, at the desk at which he was accustomed to transact business, and with as much indifference as he could assume, Morris presented the forged cheque to the big, red-bearded Scots teller. The teller seemed to view it with surprise; and as he turned it this way and that, and even scrutinized the signature with a magnifying-glass, his surprise appeared to warm into disfavour. Begging to be excused for a moment, he passed away into the rearmost quarters of the bank; whence, after an appreciable interval, he returned again in earnest talk with a superior, an oldish and a baldish, but a very gentlemanly man.

'Mr Morris Finsbury, I believe,' said the gentlemanly man, fixing Morris with a pair of double eye-glasses.

'That is my name,' said Morris, quavering. 'Is there anything wrong?'

'Well, the fact is, Mr Finsbury, you see we are rather surprised at receiving this,' said the other, flicking at the cheque. 'There are no effects.'

'No effects?' cried Morris. 'Why, I know myself there must be eight-and-twenty hundred pounds, if there's a penny.'

'Two seven six four, I think,' replied the gentlemanly man; 'but it was drawn yesterday.'

'Drawn!' cried Morris.

'By your uncle himself, sir,' continued the other. 'Not only that, but we discounted a bill for him for—let me see—how much was it for, Mr Bell?'

'Eight hundred, Mr Judkin,' replied the teller.

'Bent Pitman!' cried Morris, staggering back.

'I beg your pardon,' said Mr Judkin.

'It's—it's only an expletive,' said Morris.

'I hope there's nothing wrong, Mr Finsbury,' said Mr Bell.

'All I can tell you,' said Morris, with a harsh laugh, 'is that the whole thing's impossible. My uncle is at Bournemouth, unable to move.'

'Really!' cried Mr Bell, and he recovered the cheque from Mr Judkin. 'But this cheque is dated in London, and today,' he observed. 'How d'ye account for that, sir?'

'O, that was a mistake,' said Morris, and a deep tide of colour dyed his face and neck.

'No doubt, no doubt,' said Mr Judkin, but he looked at his customer enquiringly.

'And—and—' resumed Morris, 'even if there were no effects—this is a very trifling sum to overdraw—our firm—the name of Finsbury, is surely good enough for such a wretched sum as this.'

'No doubt, Mr Finsbury,' returned Mr Judkin; 'and if you insist I will take it into consideration; but I hardly think—in short, Mr Finsbury, if there had been nothing else, the signature seems hardly all that we could wish.'

'That's of no consequence,' replied Morris nervously. 'I'll get my uncle to sign another. The fact is,' he went on, with a bold stroke, 'my uncle is so far from well at present that he was unable to sign this cheque without assistance, and I fear that my holding the pen for him may have made the difference in the signature.'

Mr Judkin shot a keen glance into Morris's face; and then turned and looked at Mr Bell.

'Well,' he said, 'it seems as if we had been victimized by a swindler. Pray tell Mr Finsbury we shall put detectives on at once. As for this cheque of yours, I regret that, owing to the way it was signed, the bank can hardly consider it—what shall I say?—businesslike,' and he returned the cheque across the counter.

Morris took it up mechanically; he was thinking of something very different.

'In a case of this kind,' he began, 'I believe the loss falls on us; I mean upon my uncle and myself.'

'It does not, sir,' replied Mr Bell; 'the bank is responsible, and the bank will either recover the money or refund it, you may depend on that.'

Morris's face fell; then it was visited by another gleam of hope.

'I'll tell you what,' he said, 'you leave this entirely in my hands. I'll sift the matter. I've an idea, at any rate; and detectives,' he added appealingly, 'are so expensive.'

'The bank would not hear of it,' returned Mr Judkin. 'The bank stands to lose between three and four thousand pounds; it will spend as much more if necessary. An undiscovered forger is a permanent danger. We shall clear it up to the bottom, Mr Finsbury; set your mind at rest on that.'

'Then I'll stand the loss,' said Morris boldly. 'I order you to abandon the search.' He was determined that no enquiry should be made.

'I beg your pardon,' returned Mr Judkin, 'but we have nothing to do with you in this matter, which is one between your uncle and ourselves. If he should take this opinion, and will either come here himself or let me see him in his sick-room——'

'Quite impossible,' cried Morris.

'Well, then, you see,' said Mr Judkin, 'how my hands are tied. The whole affair must go at once into the hands of the police.'

Morris mechanically folded the cheque and restored it to his pocket-book.

'Good-morning,' said he, and scrambled somehow out of the bank.

'I don't know what they suspect,' he reflected; 'I can't make them out, their whole behaviour is thoroughly unbusinesslike. But it doesn't matter; all's up with everything. The money has been paid;

the police are on the scent; in two hours that idiot Pitman will be nabbed—and the whole story of the dead body in the evening papers.'

If he could have heard what passed in the bank after his departure he would have been less alarmed, perhaps more mortified.

'That was a curious affair, Mr Bell,' said Mr Judkin.

'Yes, sir,' said Mr Bell, 'but I think we have given him a fright.'

'O, we shall hear no more of Mr Morris Finsbury,' returned the other; it was a first attempt, and the house have dealt with us so long that I was anxious to deal gently. But I suppose, Mr Bell, there can be no mistake about yesterday? It was old Mr Finsbury himself?'

'There could be no possible doubt of that,' said Mr Bell with a chuckle. 'He explained to me the principles of banking.'

'Well, well,' said Mr Judkin. 'The next time he calls ask him to step into my room. It is only proper he should be warned.'

CHAPTER VII

In Which William Dent Pitman takes Legal Advice

Norfolk Street, King's Road—jocularly known among Mr Pitman's lodgers as 'Norfolk Island'—is neither a long, a handsome, nor a pleasing thoroughfare. Dirty, undersized maids-of-all-work issue from it in pursuit of beer, or linger on its sidewalk listening to the voice of love. The cat's-meat man passes twice a day. An occasional organ-grinder wanders in and wanders out again, disgusted. In holiday-time the street is the arena of the young bloods of the neighbourhood, and the householders have an opportunity of studying the manly art of self-defence. And yet Norfolk Street has one claim to be respectable, for it contains not a single shop—unless you count the public-house at the corner, which is really in the King's Road.

The door of No. 7 bore a brass plate inscribed with the legend 'W. D. Pitman, Artist'. It was not a particularly clean brass plate, nor was No. 7 itself a particularly inviting place of residence. And yet it had a character of its own, such as may well quicken the pulse of the reader's curiosity. For here was the home of an artist—and a distinguished artist too, highly distinguished by his ill-success—which had never been made the subject of an article in the illustrated magazines. No wood-engraver had ever reproduced 'a corner in the back drawing-room' or 'the studio mantelpiece' of No. 7; no young lady author had ever commented on 'the unaffected simplicity' with which Mr Pitman received her in the midst of his 'treasures'. It is an omission I would gladly supply, but our business is only with the backward parts and 'abject rear' of this aesthetic dwelling.

Here was a garden, boasting a dwarf fountain (that never played) in the centre, a few grimy-looking flowers in pots, two or three newly planted trees which the spring of Chelsea visited without noticeable consequence, and two or three statues after the antique, representing satyrs and nymphs in the worst possible style of sculptured art. On one side the garden was overshadowed by a pair of crazy studios, usually hired out to the more obscure and youthful practitioners of British art. Opposite these another lofty out-building, somewhat more carefully finished, and boasting of a communication with the house and a private door on the back lane, enshrined the multifarious industry of Mr Pitman. All day, it is true, he was engaged in the work of education at a seminary for young ladies; but the evenings at least were his own, and these he would prolong far into the night, now dashing off 'A landscape with waterfall' in oil, now a volunteer bust ('in marble', as he would gently but proudly observe) of some public character, now stooping his chisel to a mere 'nymph' ('for a gas-bracket on a stair, sir'), or a life-size 'Infant Samuel' for a religious nursery. Mr Pitman had studied in Paris, and he had studied in Rome, supplied with funds by a fond parent who went subsequently bank-rupt in consequence of a fall in corsets; and though he was never thought to have the smallest modicum of talent, it was at one time supposed that he had learned his business. Eighteen years of what is called 'tuition' had relieved him of the dangerous knowledge. His artist lodgers would sometimes reason with him; they would point out to him how impossible it was to paint by gaslight, or to sculpture life-sized nymphs without a model.

'I know that,' he would reply. 'No one in Norfolk Street knows it better; and if I were rich I should certainly employ the best models in London; but, being poor, I have taught myself to do without them. An occasional model would only disturb my ideal conception of the figure, and be a positive impediment in my career. As for painting by an artificial light,' he would continue, 'that is simply a knack I have found it necessary to acquire, my days being engrossed in the work of tuition.'

At the moment when we must present him to our readers, Pitman was in his studio alone, by the dying light of the October day. He sat (sure enough with 'unaffected simplicity') in a Windsor chair, his low-crowned black felt hat by his side; a dark, weak, harmless, pathetic little man, clad in the hue of mourning, his coat longer than is usual with the laity, his neck enclosed in a collar without a parting, his neckcloth pale in hue and simply tied; the whole outward man, except for a pointed beard, tentatively clerical. There was a thinning on the top of Pitman's head, there were silver hairs at Pitman's temple. Poor gentleman, he was no longer young; and years, and poverty, and humble ambition thwarted, make a cheerless lot.

In front of him, in the corner by the door, there stood a portly barrel; and let him turn them where he might, it was always to the barrel that his eyes and his thoughts returned.

'Should I open it? Should I return it? Should I communicate with Mr Semitopolis at once?' he wondered. 'No,' he concluded finally, 'nothing without Mr Finsbury's advice.' And he arose and produced a shabby leathern desk. It opened without the formality of unlocking, and displayed the thick cream-coloured notepaper on which Mr Pitman was in the habit of communicating with the proprietors of schools and the parents of his pupils. He placed the desk on the table by the window, and taking a saucer of Indian ink from the chimney-piece, laboriously composed the following letter:

'My dear Mr Finsbury,' it ran, 'would it be presuming on your kindness if I asked you to pay me a visit here this evening? It is in no trifling matter that I invoke your valuable assistance, for need I say more than it concerns the welfare of Mr Semitopolis's statue of Hercules? I write you in great agitation of mind; for I have made all enquiries, and greatly fear that this work of ancient art has been mislaid. I labour besides under another perplexity, not unconnected with the first. Pray excuse the inelegance of this scrawl, and believe me yours in haste, William D. Pitman.'

Armed with this he set forth and rang the bell of No. 233 King's Road, the private residence of Michael Finsbury. He had met the lawyer at a time of great public excitement in Chelsea; Michael, who had a sense of humour and a great deal of careless kindness in his nature, followed the acquaintance up, and, having come to laugh, remained to drop into a contemptuous kind of friendship. By this time, which was four years after the first meeting, Pitman was the lawyer's dog.

'No,' said the elderly housekeeper, who opened the door in person, 'Mr Michael's not in yet. But ye're looking terribly poorly, Mr Pitman. Take a glass of sherry, sir, to cheer ye up.'

'No, I thank you, ma'am,' replied the artist. 'It is very good in you, but I scarcely feel in sufficient spirits for sherry. Just give Mr Finsbury this note, and ask him to look round—to the door in the lane, you will please tell him; I shall be in the studio all evening.'

And he turned again into the street and walked slowly homeward. A hairdresser's window caught his attention, and he stared long and earnestly at the proud, high-born, waxen lady in evening dress, who circulated in the centre of the show. The artist woke in him, in spite of his troubles.

'It is all very well to run down the men who make these things,' he cried, 'but there's a something—there's a haughty, indefinable something about that figure. It's what I tried for in my "Empress Eugénie",' he added, with a sigh.

And he went home reflecting on the quality. 'They don't teach you that direct appeal in Paris,' he thought. 'It's British. Come, I am going to sleep, I must wake up, I must aim higher—aim higher,' cried the little artist to himself. All through his tea and afterward, as he was giving his eldest boy a lesson on the fiddle, his mind dwelt no longer on his troubles, but he was rapt into the better land; and no sooner was he at liberty than he hastened with positive exhilaration to his studio.

Not even the sight of the barrel could entirely cast him down. He flung himself with rising zest into his work—a bust of Mr Gladstone from a photograph; turned (with extraordinary success) the difficulty of the back of the head, for which he had no documents beyond a hazy recollection of a public meeting; delighted himself by his treatment of the collar; and was only recalled to the cares of life by Michael Finsbury's rattle at the door.

'Well, what's wrong?' said Michael, advancing to the grate, where, knowing his friend's delight in a bright fire, Mr Pitman had not spared the fuel. 'I suppose you have come to grief somehow.'

'There is no expression strong enough,' said the artist. 'Mr Semitopolis's statue has not turned up, and I am afraid I shall be answerable for the money; but I think nothing of that—what I fear, my dear Mr Finsbury, what I fear—alas that I should have to say it!— is exposure. The Hercules was to be smuggled out of Italy; a thing positively wrong, a thing of which a man of my principles and in my responsible position should have taken (as I now see too late) no part whatever.'

'This sounds like very serious work,' said the lawyer. 'It will require a great deal of drink, Pitman.'

'I took the liberty of—in short, of being prepared for you,' replied the artist, pointing to a kettle, a bottle of gin, a lemon, and glasses.

Michael mixed himself a grog, and offered the artist a cigar.

'No, thank you,' said Pitman. 'I used occasionally to be rather partial to it, but the smell is so disagreeable about the clothes.'

'All right,' said the lawyer. 'I am comfortable now. Unfold your tale.'

At some length Pitman set forth his sorrows. He had gone today to Waterloo, expecting to receive the colossal Hercules, and he had received instead a barrel not big enough to hold Discobolus; yet the barrel was addressed in the hand (with which he was perfectly acquainted) of his Roman correspondent. What was stranger still, a case had arrived by the same train, large enough and heavy enough to contain the Hercules; and this case had been taken to an address now undiscoverable. 'The vanman (I regret to say it) had been drinking, and his language was such as I could never bring myself to repeat. He was at once discharged by the superintendent of the line, who behaved most properly throughout, and is to make enquiries at Southampton. In the meanwhile, what was I to do? I left my address and brought the barrel home; but, remembering an old adage, I determined not to open it except in the presence of my lawyer.'

'Is that all?' asked Michael. 'I don't see any cause to worry. The Hercules has stuck upon the road. It will drop in tomorrow or the day after; and as for the barrel, depend upon it, it's a testimonial from one of your young ladies, and probably contains oysters.'

'O, don't speak so loud!' cried the little artist. 'It would cost me my place if I were heard to speak lightly of the young ladies; and besides, why oysters from Italy? and why should they come to me addressed in Signor Ricardi's hand?'

'Well, let's have a look at it,' said Michael. 'Let's roll it forward to the light.'

The two men rolled the barrel from the corner, and stood it on end before the fire.

'It's heavy enough to be oysters,' remarked Michael judiciously.

'Shall we open it at once?' enquired the artist, who had grown decidedly cheerful under the combined effects of company and gin; and without waiting for a reply, he began to strip as if for a prize-fight, tossed his clerical collar in the wastepaper basket, hung his clerical coat upon a nail, and with a chisel in one hand and a hammer in the other, struck the first blow of the evening.

'That's the style, William Dent!' cried Michael. 'There's fire for your money! It may be a romantic visit from one of the young ladies—a sort of Cleopatra business. Have a care and don't stave in Cleopatra's head.'

But the sight of Pitman's alacrity was infectious. The lawyer could sit still no longer. Tossing his cigar into the fire, he snatched the instrument from the unwilling hands of the artist, and fell to himself. Soon the sweat stood in beads upon his large, fair brow; his stylish trousers were defaced with iron rust, and the state of his chisel testified to misdirected energies.

A cask is not an easy thing to open, even when you set about it in the right way; when you set about it wrongly, the whole structure must be resolved into its elements. Such was the course pursued alike by the artist and the lawyer. Presently the last hoop had been removed—a couple of smart blows tumbled the staves upon the ground—and what had once been a barrel was no more than a confused heap of broken and distorted boards.

In the midst of these, a certain dismal something, swathed in blankets, remained for an instant upright, and then toppled to one side and heavily collapsed before the fire. Even as the thing subsided, an eye-glass tingled to the floor and rolled toward the screaming Pitman.

'Hold your tongue!' said Michael. He dashed to the house door and locked it; then, with a pale face and bitten lip, he drew near, pulled aside a corner of the swathing blanket, and recoiled, shuddering.

There was a long silence in the studio.

'Now tell me,' said Michael, in a low voice: 'Had you any hand in it?' and he pointed to the body.

The little artist could only utter broken and disjointed sounds.

Michael poured some gin into a glass. 'Drink that,' he said. 'Don't be afraid of me. I'm your friend through thick and thin.'

Pitman put the liquor down untasted.

'I swear before God,' he said, 'this is another mystery to me. In my worst fears I never dreamed of such a thing. I would not lay a finger on a sucking infant.'

'That's all square,' said Michael, with a sigh of huge relief. 'I believe you, old boy.' And he shook the artist warmly by the hand. 'I thought for a moment,' he added with rather a ghastly smile, 'I thought for a moment you might have made away with Mr Semitopolis.'

'It would make no difference if I had,' groaned Pitman. 'All is at an end for me. There's the writing on the wall.'

'To begin with,' said Michael, 'let's get him out of sight; for to be quite plain with you, Pitman, I don't like your friend's appearance.' And with that the lawyer shuddered. 'Where can we put it?'

'You might put it in the closet there—if you could bear to touch it,' answered the artist.

'Somebody has to do it, Pitman,' returned the lawyer; 'and it seems as if it had to be me. You go over to the table, turn your back, and mix me a grog; that's a fair division of labour.'

About ninety seconds later the closet-door was heard to shut.

'There,' observed Michael, 'that's more homelike. You can turn now, my pallid Pitman. Is this the grog?' he ran on. 'Heaven forgive you, it's a lemonade.'

'But, O, Finsbury, what are we to do with it?' wailed the artist, laying a clutching hand upon the lawyer's arm.

'Do with it?' repeated Michael. 'Bury it in one of your flower-beds, and erect one of your own statues for a monument. I tell you we should look devilish romantic shovelling out the sod by the moon's pale ray. Here, put some gin in this.'

'I beg of you, Mr Finsbury, do not trifle with my misery,' cried Pitman. 'You see before you a man who has been all his life—I do not hesitate to say it—eminently respectable. Even in this solemn hour I can lay my hand upon my heart without a blush. Except on the really trifling point of the smuggling of the Hercules (and even of that I now humbly repent), my life has been entirely fit for publication. I never feared the light,' cried the little man; 'and now—now——!'

'Cheer up, old boy,' said Michael. 'I assure you we should count this little contretemps a trifle at the office; it's the sort of thing that may occur to any one; and if you're perfectly sure you had no hand in it——'

'What language am I to find——' began Pitman.

'O, I'll do that part of it,' interrupted Michael, 'you have no experience. But the point is this: If—or rather since—you know nothing of the crime, since the—the party in the closet—is neither your father, nor your brother, nor your creditor, nor your mother-in-law, nor what they call an injured husband——'

'O, my dear sir!' interjected Pitman, horrified.

'Since, in short,' continued the lawyer, 'you had no possible interest in the crime, we have a perfectly free field before us and a safe game to play. Indeed, the problem is really entertaining; it is one I have long contemplated in the light of an A. B. case; here it is at last under my hand in specie; and I mean to pull you through. Do you hear that?—I mean to pull you through. Let me see: it's a long time since I have had what I call a genuine holiday; I'll send an excuse tomorrow to the office. We had best be lively,' he added significantly; 'for we must not spoil the market for the other man.'

'What do you mean?' enquired Pitman. 'What other man? The inspector of police?'

'Damn the inspector of police!' remarked his companion. 'If you won't take the short cut and bury this in your back garden, we must find some one who will bury it in his. We must place the affair, in short, in the hands of some one with fewer scruples and more resources.'

'A private detective, perhaps?' suggested Pitman.

'There are times when you fill me with pity,' observed the lawyer. 'By the way, Pitman,' he added in another key, 'I have always regretted that you have no piano in this den of yours. Even if you don't play yourself, your friends might like to entertain themselves with a little music while you were mudding.'

'I shall get one at once if you like,' said Pitman nervously, anxious to please. 'I play the fiddle a little as it is.'

'I know you do,' said Michael; 'but what's the fiddle—above all as you play it? What you want is polyphonic music. And I'll tell you what it is—since it's too late for you to buy a piano I'll give you mine.'

'Thank you,' said the artist blankly. 'You will give me yours? I am sure it's very good in you.'

'Yes, I'll give you mine,' continued Michael, 'for the inspector of police to play on while his men are digging up your back garden.'

Pitman stared at him in pained amazement.

'No, I'm not insane,' Michael went on. 'I'm playful, but quite coherent. See here, Pitman: follow me one half minute. I mean to profit by the refreshing fact that we are really and truly innocent; nothing but the presence of the—you know what—connects us with the crime; once let us get rid of it, no matter how, and there is no possible clue to trace us by. Well, I give you my piano; we'll bring it round this very night. Tomorrow we rip the fittings out, deposit the—our friend—inside, plump the whole on a cart, and carry it to the chambers of a young gentleman whom I know by sight.'

'Whom do you know by sight?' repeated Pitman.

'And what is more to the purpose,' continued Michael, 'whose chambers I know better than he does himself. A friend of mine—I call him my friend for brevity; he is now, I understand, in Demerara and (most likely) in gaol—was the previous occupant. I defended him, and I got him off too—all saved but honour; his assets were nil, but he gave me what he had, poor gentleman, and along with the rest—the key of his chambers. It's there that I propose to leave the piano and, shall we say, Cleopatra?'

'It seems very wild,' said Pitman. 'And what will become of the poor young gentleman whom you know by sight?'

'It will do him good,' said Michael cheerily. 'Just what he wants to steady him.'

'But, my dear sir, he might be involved in a charge of—a charge of murder,' gulped the artist.

'Well, he'll be just where we are,' returned the lawyer. 'He's innocent, you see. What hangs people, my dear Pitman, is the unfortunate circumstance of guilt.'

'But indeed, indeed,' pleaded Pitman, 'the whole scheme appears to me so wild. Would it not be safer, after all, just to send for the police?'

'And make a scandal?' enquired Michael. ' "The Chelsea Mystery; alleged innocence of Pitman"? How would that do at the Seminary?'

'It would imply my discharge,' admitted the drawing-master. 'I cannot deny that.'

'And besides,' said Michael, 'I am not going to embark in such a business and have no fun for my money.'

'O my dear sir, is that a proper spirit?' cried Pitman.

'O, I only said that to cheer you up,' said the unabashed Michael. 'Nothing like a little judicious levity. But it's quite needless to discuss. If you mean to follow my advice, come on, and let us get the piano at once. If you don't, just drop me the word, and I'll leave you to deal with the whole thing according to your better judgement.'

'You know perfectly well that I depend on you entirely,' returned Pitman. 'But O, what a night is before me with that—horror in my studio! How am I to think of it on my pillow?'

'Well, you know, my piano will be there too,' said Michael. 'That'll raise the average.'

An hour later a cart came up the lane, and the lawyer's piano—a momentous Broadwood grand—was deposited in Mr Pitman's studio.

CHAPTER VIII

In Which Michael Finsbury Enjoys a Holiday

Punctually at eight o'clock next morning the lawyer rattled (according to previous appointment) on the studio door. He found the artist sadly altered for the worse—bleached, bloodshot, and chalky—a man upon wires, the tail of his haggard eye still wandering to the closet. Nor was the professor of drawing less inclined to wonder at his friend. Michael was usually attired in the height of fashion, with a certain mercantile brilliancy best described perhaps as stylish; nor could anything be said against him, as a rule, but that he looked a trifle too like a wedding guest to be quite a gentleman. Today he had fallen altogether from these heights. He wore a flannel shirt of washed-out shepherd's tartan, and a suit of reddish tweeds, of the colour known to tailors as 'heather mixture'; his neckcloth was black, and tied loosely in a sailor's knot; a rusty ulster partly concealed these advantages; and his feet were shod with rough walking boots. His hat was an old soft felt, which he removed with a flourish as he entered.

'Here I am, William Dent!' he cried, and drawing from his pocket two little wisps of reddish hair, he held them to his cheeks like side-whiskers and danced about the studio with the filmy graces of a ballet-girl.

Pitman laughed sadly. 'I should never have known you,' said he.

'Nor were you intended to,' returned Michael, replacing his false whiskers in his pocket. 'Now we must overhaul you and your wardrobe, and disguise you up to the nines.'

'Disguise!' cried the artist. 'Must I indeed disguise myself? Has it come to that?'

'My dear creature,' returned his companion, 'disguise is the spice of life. What is life, passionately exclaimed a French philosopher, without the pleasures of disguise? I don't say it's always good taste, and I know it's unprofessional; but what's the odds, downhearted drawing-master? It has to be. We have to leave a false impression on the minds of many persons, and in particular on the mind of Mr

Gideon Forsyth—the young gentleman I know by sight—if he should have the bad taste to be at home.'

'If he be at home?' faltered the artist. 'That would be the end of all.'

'Won't matter a d——,' returned Michael airily. 'Let me see your clothes, and I'll make a new man of you in a jiffy.'

In the bedroom, to which he was at once conducted, Michael examined Pitman's poor and scanty wardrobe with a humorous eye, picked out a short jacket of black alpaca, and presently added to that a pair of summer trousers which somehow took his fancy as incongruous. Then, with the garments in his hand, he scrutinized the artist closely.

'I don't like that clerical collar,' he remarked. 'Have you nothing else?'

The professor of drawing pondered for a moment, and then brightened; 'I have a pair of low-necked shirts,' he said, 'that I used to wear in Paris as a student. They are rather loud.'

'The very thing!' ejaculated Michael. 'You'll look perfectly beastly. Here are spats, too,' he continued, drawing forth a pair of those offensive little gaiters. 'Must have spats! And now you jump into these, and whistle a tune at the window for (say) three-quarters of an hour. After that you can rejoin me on the field of glory.'

So saying, Michael returned to the studio. It was the morning of the easterly gale; the wind blew shrilly among the statues in the garden, and drove the rain upon the skylight in the studio ceiling; and at about the same moment of the time when Morris attacked the hundredth version of his uncle's signature in Bloomsbury, Michael, in Chelsea, began to rip the wires out of the Broadwood grand.

Three-quarters of an hour later Pitman was admitted, to find the closet-door standing open, the closet untenanted, and the piano discreetly shut.

'It's a remarkably heavy instrument,' observed Michael, and turned to consider his friend's disguise. 'You must shave off that beard of yours,' he said.

'My beard!' cried Pitman. 'I cannot shave my beard. I cannot tamper with my appearance—my principals would object. They hold very strong views as to the appearance of the professors—young ladies are considered so romantic. My beard was regarded as quite a feature when I went about the place. It was regarded,' said the artist, with rising colour, 'it was regarded as unbecoming.'

'You can let it grow again,' returned Michael, 'and then you'll be so precious ugly that they'll raise your salary.'

'But I don't want to be ugly,' cried the artist.

'Don't be an ass,' said Michael, who hated beards and was delighted to destroy one. 'Off with it like a man!'

'Of course, if you insist,' said Pitman; and then he sighed, fetched some hot water from the kitchen, and setting a glass upon his easel, first clipped his beard with scissors and then shaved his chin. He could not conceal from himself, as he regarded the result, that his last claims to manhood had been sacrificed, but Michael seemed delighted.

'A new man, I declare!' he cried. 'When I give you the window-glass spectacles I have in my pocket, you'll be the beau-idéal of a French commercial traveller.'

Pitman did not reply, but continued to gaze disconsolately on his image in the glass.

'Do you know,' asked Michael, 'what the Governor of South Carolina said to the Governor of North Carolina? "It's a long time between drinks," observed that powerful thinker; and if you will put your hand into the top left-hand pocket of my ulster, I have an impression you will find a flask of brandy. Thank you, Pitman,' he added, as he filled out a glass for each. 'Now you will give me news of this.'

The artist reached out his hand for the water-jug, but Michael arrested the movement.

'Not if you went upon your knees!' he cried. 'This is the finest liqueur brandy in Great Britain.'

Pitman put his lips to it, set it down again, and sighed.

'Well, I must say you're the poorest companion for a holiday!' cried Michael. 'If that's all you know of brandy, you shall have no more of it; and while I finish the flask, you may as well begin business. Come to think of it,' he broke off, 'I have made an abominable error: you should have ordered the cart before you were disguised. Why, Pitman, what the devil's the use of you? why couldn't you have reminded me of that?'

'I never even knew there was a cart to be ordered,' said the artist. 'But I can take off the disguise again,' he suggested eagerly.

'You would find it rather a bother to put on your beard,' observed the lawyer. 'No, it's a false step; the sort of thing that hangs people,' he continued, with eminent cheerfulness, as he sipped his brandy; 'and it can't be retraced now. Off to the mews with you, make all the arrangements; they're to take the piano from here, cart it to Victoria, and dispatch it thence by rail to Cannon Street, to lie till called for in the name of Fortuné du Boisgobey.'

'Isn't that rather an awkward name?' pleaded Pitman.

'Awkward?' cried Michael scornfully. 'It would hang us both! Brown is both safer and easier to pronounce. Call it Brown.'

'I wish,' said Pitman, 'for my sake, I wish you wouldn't talk so much of hanging.'

'Talking about it's nothing, my boy!' returned Michael. 'But take your hat and be off, and mind and pay everything beforehand.'

Left to himself, the lawyer turned his attention for some time exclusively to the liqueur brandy, and his spirits, which had been pretty fair all morning, now prodigiously rose. He proceeded to adjust his whiskers finally before the glass. 'Devilish rich,' he remarked, as he contemplated his reflection. 'I look like a purser's mate.' And at that moment the window-glass spectacles (which he had hitherto destined for Pitman) flashed into his mind; he put them on, and fell in love with the effect. 'Just what I required,' he said. 'I wonder what I look like now? A humorous novelist, I should think,' and he began to practise divers characters of walk, naming them to himself as he proceeded. 'Walk of a humorous novelist—but that would require an umbrella. Walk of a purser's mate. Walk of an Australian colonist revisiting the scenes of childhood. Walk of Sepoy colonel, ditto, ditto.' And in the midst of the Sepoy colonel (which was an excellent assumption, although inconsistent with the style of his make-up), his eye lighted on the piano. This instrument was made to lock both at the top and at the keyboard, but the key of the latter had been mislaid. Michael opened it and ran his fingers over the dumb keys. 'Fine instrument—full, rich tone,' he observed, and he drew in a seat.

When Mr Pitman returned to the studio, he was appalled to observe his guide, philosopher, and friend performing miracles of execution on the silent grand.

'Heaven help me!' thought the little man, 'I fear he has been drinking! Mr Finsbury,' he said aloud; and Michael, without rising, turned upon him a countenance somewhat flushed, encircled with the bush of the red whiskers, and bestridden by the spectacles. 'Capriccio in B-flat on the departure of a friend,' said he, continuing his noiseless evolutions.

Indignation awoke in the mind of Pitman. 'Those spectacles were to be mine,' he cried. 'They are an essential part of my disguise.'

'I am going to wear them myself,' replied Michael; and he added, with some show of truth, 'There would be a devil of a lot of suspicion aroused if we both wore spectacles.'

'O, well,' said the assenting Pitman, 'I rather counted on them; but of course, if you insist. And at any rate, here is the cart at the door.'

While the men were at work, Michael concealed himself in the closet among the debris of the barrel and the wires of the piano; and as soon as the coast was clear the pair sallied forth by the lane, jumped into a hansom in the King's Road, and were driven rapidly toward town. It was still cold and raw and boisterous; the rain beat strongly in their faces, but Michael refused to have the glass let down; he had now suddenly donned the character of cicerone, and pointed out and lucidly commented on the sights of London, as they drove. 'My dear fellow,' he said, 'you don't seem to know anything of your native city. Suppose we visited the Tower? No? Well, perhaps it's a trifle out of our way. But, anyway—Here, cabby, drive round by Trafalgar Square!' And on that historic battlefield he insisted on drawing up, while he criticized the statues and gave the artist many curious details (quite new to history) of the lives of the celebrated men they represented.

It would be difficult to express what Pitman suffered in the cab: cold, wet, terror in the capital degree, a grounded distrust of the commander under whom he served, a sense of imprudency in the matter of the low-necked shirt, a bitter sense of the decline and fall involved in the deprivation of his beard, all these were among the ingredients of the bowl. To reach the restaurant, for which they were deviously steering, was the first relief. To hear Michael bespeak a private room was a second and a still greater. Nor, as they mounted the stair under the guidance of an unintelligible alien, did he fail to note with gratitude the fewness of the persons present, or the still more cheering fact that the greater part of these were exiles from the land of France. It was thus a blessed thought that none of them would be connected with the Seminary; for even the French professor, though admittedly a Papist, he could scarce imagine frequenting so rakish an establishment.

The alien introduced them into a small bare room with a single table, a sofa, and a dwarfish fire; and Michael called promptly for more coals and a couple of brandies and sodas.

'O, no,' said Pitman, 'surely not—no more to drink.'

'I don't know what you would be at,' said Michael plaintively. 'It's positively necessary to do something; and one shouldn't smoke before meals—I thought that was understood. You seem to have no idea of hygiene.' And he compared his watch with the clock upon the chimney-piece.

Pitman fell into bitter musing; here he was, ridiculously shorn, absurdly disguised, in the company of a drunken man in spectacles, and waiting for a champagne luncheon in a restaurant painfully foreign. What would his principals think, if they could see him? What if they knew his tragic and deceitful errand?

From these reflections he was aroused by the entrance of the alien with the brandies and sodas. Michael took one and bade the waiter pass the other to his friend.

Pitman waved it from him with his hand. 'Don't let me lose all self-respect,' he said.

'Anything to oblige a friend,' returned Michael. 'But I'm not going to drink alone. Here,' he added to the waiter, 'you take it.' And, then, touching glasses, 'The health of Mr Gideon Forsyth,' said he.

'Meestare Gidden Borsye,' replied the waiter, and he tossed off the liquor in four gulps.

'Have another?' said Michael, with undisguised interest. 'I never saw a man drink faster. It restores one's confidence in the human race.'

But the waiter excused himself politely, and, assisted by some one from without, began to bring in lunch.

Michael made an excellent meal, which he washed down with a bottle of Heidsieck's dry monopole. As for the artist, he was far too uneasy to eat, and his companion flatly refused to let him share in the champagne unless he did.

'One of us must stay sober,' remarked the lawyer, 'and I won't give you champagne on the strength of a leg of grouse. I have to be cautious,' he added confidentially. 'One drunken man, excellent business—two drunken men, all my eye.'

On the production of coffee and departure of the waiter, Michael might have been observed to make portentous efforts after gravity of mien. He looked his friend in the face (one eye perhaps a trifle off), and addressed him thickly but severely.

'Enough of this fooling,' was his not inappropriate exordium. 'To business. Mark me closely. I am an Australian. My name is John Dickson, though you mightn't think it from my unassuming appearance. You will be relieved to hear that I am rich, sir, very rich. You can't go into this sort of thing too thoroughly, Pitman; the whole secret is preparation, and I can get up my biography from the beginning, and I could tell it you now, only I have forgotten it.'

'Perhaps I'm stupid——' began Pitman.

'That's it!' cried Michael. 'Very stupid; but rich too—richer than I am. I thought you would enjoy it, Pitman, so I've arranged that you were to be literally wallowing in wealth. But then, on the other hand, you're only an American, and a maker of india-rubber overshoes at that. And the worst of it is—why should I conceal it from you?—the worst of it is that you're called Ezra Thomas. Now,' said Michael, with a really appalling seriousness of manner, 'tell me who we are.'

The unfortunate little man was cross-examined till he knew these facts by heart.

'There!' cried the lawyer. 'Our plans are laid. Thoroughly consistent—that's the great thing.'

'But I don't understand,' objected Pitman.

'O, you'll understand right enough when it comes to the point,' said Michael, rising.

'There doesn't seem any story to it,' said the artist.

'We can invent one as we go along,' returned the lawyer.

'But I can't invent,' protested Pitman. 'I never could invent in all my life.'

'You'll find you'll have to, my boy,' was Michael's easy comment, and he began calling for the waiter, with whom he at once resumed a sparkling conversation.

It was a downcast little man that followed him. 'Of course he is very clever, but can I trust him in such a state?' he asked himself. And when they were once more in a hansom, he took heart of grace.

'Don't you think,' he faltered, 'it would be wiser, considering all things, to put this business off?'

'Put off till tomorrow what can be done today?' cried Michael, with indignation. 'Never heard of such a thing! Cheer up, it's all right, go in and win—there's a lion-hearted Pitman!'

At Cannon Street they enquired for Mr Brown's piano, which had duly arrived, drove thence to a neighbouring mews, where they contracted for a cart, and while that was being got ready, took shelter in the harness-room beside the stove. Here the lawyer presently toppled against the wall and fell into a gentle slumber; so that Pitman found himself launched on his own resources in the midst of several staring loafers, such as love to spend unprofitable days about a stable.

'Rough day, sir,' observed one. 'Do you go far?'

'Yes, it's a—rather a rough day,' said the artist; and then, feeling that he must change the conversation, 'My friend is an Australian; he is very impulsive,' he added.

'An Australian?' said another. 'I've a brother myself in Melbourne. Does your friend come from that way at all?'

'No, not exactly,' replied the artist, whose ideas of the geography of New Holland were a little scattered. 'He lives immensely far inland, and is very rich.'

The loafers gazed with great respect upon the slumbering colonist.

'Well,' remarked the second speaker, 'it's a mighty big place, is Australia. Do you come from thereaway too?'

'No, I do not,' said Pitman. 'I do not, and I don't want to,' he added irritably. And then, feeling some diversion needful, he fell upon Michael and shook him up.

'Hullo,' said the lawyer, 'what's wrong?'

'The cart is nearly ready,' said Pitman sternly. 'I will not allow you to sleep.'

'All right—no offence, old man,' replied Michael, yawning. 'A little sleep never did anybody any harm; I feel comparatively sober now. But what's all the hurry?' he added, looking round him glassily. 'I don't see the cart, and I've forgotten where we left the piano.'

What more the lawyer might have said, in the confidence of the moment, is with Pitman a matter of tremulous conjecture to this day; but by the most blessed circumstance the cart was then announced, and Michael must bend the forces of his mind to the more difficult task of rising.

'Of course you'll drive,' he remarked to his companion, as he clambered on the vehicle.

'I drive!' cried Pitman. 'I never did such a thing in my life. I cannot drive.'

'Very well,' responded Michael with entire composure, 'neither can I see. But just as you like. Anything to oblige a friend.'

A glimpse of the ostler's darkening countenance decided Pitman. 'All right,' he said desperately, 'you drive. I'll tell you where to go.'

On Michael in the character of charioteer (since this is not intended to be a novel of adventure) it would be superfluous to dwell at length. Pitman, as he sat holding on and gasping counsels, sole witness of this singular feat, knew not whether most to admire the driver's valour or his undeserved good fortune. But the latter at least prevailed, the cart reached Cannon Street without disaster; and Mr Brown's piano was speedily and cleverly got on board.

'Well, sir,' said the leading porter, smiling as he mentally reckoned up a handful of loose silver, 'that's a mortal heavy piano.'

'It's the richness of the tone,' returned Michael, as he drove away.

It was but a little distance in the rain, which now fell thick and quiet, to the neighbourhood of Mr Gideon Forsyth's chambers in the Temple. There, in a deserted by-street, Michael drew up the horses and gave them in charge to a blighted shoe-black; and the pair descending from the cart, whereon they had figured so incongruously, set forth on foot for the decisive scene of their adventure. For the first time Michael displayed a shadow of uneasiness.

'Are my whiskers right?' he asked. 'It would be the devil and all if I was spotted.'

'They are perfectly in their place,' returned Pitman, with scant attention. 'But is my disguise equally effective? There is nothing more likely than that I should meet some of my patrons.'

'O, nobody could tell you without your beard,' said Michael. 'All you have to do is to remember to speak slow; you speak through your nose already.'

'I only hope the young man won't be at home,' sighed Pitman.

'And I only hope he'll be alone,' returned the lawyer. 'It will save a precious sight of manœuvring.'

And sure enough, when they had knocked at the door, Gideon admitted them in person to a room, warmed by a moderate fire, framed nearly to the roof in works connected with the bench of British Themis, and offering, except in one particular, eloquent testimony to the legal zeal of the proprietor. The one particular was the chimney-piece, which displayed a varied assortment of pipes, tobacco, cigar-boxes, and yellow-backed French novels.

'Mr Forsyth, I believe?' It was Michael who thus opened the engagement. 'We have come to trouble you with a piece of business. I fear it's scarcely professional——'

'I am afraid I ought to be instructed through a solicitor,' replied Gideon.

'Well, well, you shall name your own, and the whole affair can be put on a more regular footing tomorrow,' replied Michael, taking a chair and motioning Pitman to do the same. 'But you see we didn't know any solicitors; we did happen to know of you, and time presses.'

'May I enquire, gentlemen,' asked Gideon, 'to whom it was I am indebted for a recommendation?'

'You may enquire,' returned the lawyer, with a foolish laugh; 'but I was invited not to tell you—till the thing was done.'

'My uncle, no doubt,' was the barrister's conclusion.

'My name is John Dickson,' continued Michael; 'a pretty well-known name in Ballarat; and my friend here is Mr Ezra Thomas, of the United States of America, a wealthy manufacturer of india-rubber overshoes.'

'Stop one moment till I make a note of that,' said Gideon; any one might have supposed he was an old practitioner.

'Perhaps you wouldn't mind my smoking a cigar?' asked Michael. He had pulled himself together for the entrance; now again there began to settle on his mind clouds of irresponsible humour and incipient slumber; and he hoped (as so many have hoped in the like case) that a cigar would clear him.

'Oh, certainly,' cried Gideon blandly. 'Try one of mine; I can confidently recommend them.' And he handed the box to his client.

'In case I don't make myself perfectly clear,' observed the Australian, 'it's perhaps best to tell you candidly that I've been lunching. It's a thing that may happen to any one.'

'O, certainly,' replied the affable barrister. 'But please be under no sense of hurry. I can give you,' he added, thoughtfully consulting his watch—'yes, I can give you the whole afternoon.'

'The business that brings me here,' resumed the Australian with gusto, 'is devilish delicate, I can tell you. My friend Mr Thomas, being an American of Portuguese extraction, unacquainted with our habits, and a wealthy manufacturer of Broadwood pianos——'

'Broadwood pianos?' cried Gideon, with some surprise. 'Dear me, do I understand Mr Thomas to be a member of the firm?'

'O, pirated Broadwoods,' returned Michael. 'My friend's the American Broadwood.'

'But I understood you to say,' objected Gideon, 'I certainly have it so in my notes—that your friend was a manufacturer of india-rubber overshoes.'

'I know it's confusing at first,' said the Australian, with a beaming smile. 'But he—in short, he combines the two professions. And many others besides—many, many, many others,' repeated Mr Dickson, with drunken solemnity. 'Mr Thomas's cotton-mills are one of the sights of Tallahassee; Mr Thomas's tobacco-mills are the pride of Richmond, Va.; in short, he's one of my oldest friends, Mr Forsyth, and I lay his case before you with emotion.'

The barrister looked at Mr Thomas and was agreeably prepossessed by his open although nervous countenance, and the simplicity and timidity of his manner. 'What a people are these Americans!' he thought. 'Look at this nervous, weedy, simple little bird in a low-necked shirt, and think of him wielding and directing interests so extended and seemingly incongruous! But had we not better,' he observed aloud, 'had we not perhaps better approach the facts?'

'Man of business, I perceive, sir!' said the Australian. 'Let's approach the facts. It's a breach of promise case.'

The unhappy artist was so unprepared for this view of his position that he could scarce suppress a cry.

'Dear me,' said Gideon, 'they are apt to be very troublesome. Tell me everything about it,' he added kindly; 'if you require my assistance, conceal nothing.'

'*You* tell him,' said Michael, feeling, apparently, that he had done his share. 'My friend will tell you all about it,' he added to Gideon, with a yawn. 'Excuse my closing my eyes a moment; I've been sitting up with a sick friend.'

Pitman gazed blankly about the room; rage and despair seethed in his innocent spirit; thoughts of flight, thoughts even of suicide, came and went before him; and still the barrister patiently waited, and still the artist groped in vain for any form of words, however insignificant.

'It's a breach of promise case,' he said at last, in a low voice. 'I—I am threatened with a breach of promise case.' Here, in desperate quest of inspiration, he made a clutch at his beard; his fingers closed upon the unfamiliar smoothness of a shaven chin; and with that, hope and courage (if such expressions could ever have been appropriate in the case of Pitman) conjointly fled. He shook Michael roughly. 'Wake up!' he cried, with genuine irritation in his tones. 'I cannot do it, and you know I can't.'

'You must excuse my friend,' said Michael; 'he's no hand as a narrator of stirring incident. The case is simple,' he went on. 'My friend is a man of very strong passions, and accustomed to a simple, patriarchal style of life. You see the thing from here: unfortunate visit to Europe, followed by unfortunate acquaintance with sham foreign count, who has a lovely daughter. Mr Thomas was quite carried away; he proposed, he was accepted, and he wrote—wrote in a style which I am sure he must regret today. If these letters are produced in court, sir, Mr Thomas's character is gone.'

'Am I to understand——' began Gideon.

'My dear sir,' said the Australian emphatically, 'it isn't possible to understand unless you saw them.'

'That is a painful circumstance,' said Gideon; he glanced pityingly in the direction of the culprit, and, observing on his countenance every mark of confusion, pityingly withdrew his eyes.

'And that would be nothing,' continued Mr Dickson sternly, 'but I wish—I wish from my heart, sir, I could say that Mr Thomas's hands were clean. He has no excuse; for he was engaged at the time—and is still engaged—to the belle of Constantinople, Ga. My friend's conduct was unworthy of the brutes that perish.'

'Ga.?' repeated Gideon enquiringly.

'A contraction in current use,' said Michael. 'Ga. for Georgia, in the same way as Co. for Company.'

'I was aware it was sometimes so written,' returned the barrister, 'but not that it was so pronounced.'

'Fact, I assure you,' said Michael. 'You now see for yourself, sir, that if this unhappy person is to be saved, some devilish sharp practice will be needed. There's money, and no desire to spare it. Mr Thomas could write a cheque tomorrow for a hundred thousand. And, Mr Forsyth, there's better than money. The foreign count—Count Tarnow, he calls himself—was formerly a tobacconist in Bayswater, and passed under the humble but expressive name of Schmidt; his daughter—if she is his daughter—there's another point—make a note of that, Mr Forsyth—his daughter at that time actually served in the shop—and she now proposes to marry a man of the eminence of Mr Thomas! Now do you see our game? We know they contemplate a move; and we wish to forestall 'em. Down you go to Hampton Court, where they live, and threaten, or bribe, or both, until you get the letters; if you can't, God help us, we must go to court and Thomas must be exposed. I'll be done with him for one,' added the unchivalrous friend.

'There seem some elements of success,' said Gideon. 'Was Schmidt at all known to the police?'

'We hope so,' said Michael. 'We have every ground to think so. Mark the neighbourhood—Bayswater! Doesn't Bayswater occur to you as very suggestive?'

For perhaps the sixth time during this remarkable interview, Gideon wondered if he were not becoming light-headed. 'I suppose it's just because he has been lunching,' he thought; and then added aloud, 'To what figure may I go?'

'Perhaps five thousand would be enough for today,' said Michael. 'And now, sir, do not let me detain you any longer; the afternoon wears on; there are plenty of trains to Hampton Court; and I needn't try to describe to you the impatience of my friend. Here is a five-pound note for current expenses; and here is the address.' And Michael began to write, paused, tore up the paper, and put the pieces in his pocket. 'I will dictate,' he said, 'my writing is so uncertain.'

Gideon took down the address, 'Count Tarnow, Kurnaul Villa, Hampton Court.' Then he wrote something else on a sheet of paper. 'You said you had not chosen a solicitor,' he said. 'For a case of this sort, here is the best man in London.' And he handed the paper to Michael.

'God bless me!' ejaculated Michael, as he read his own address.

'O, I daresay you have seen his name connected with some rather painful cases,' said Gideon. 'But he is himself a perfectly honest man, and his capacity is recognized. And now, gentlemen, it only remains for me to ask where I shall communicate with you.'

'The Langham, of course,' returned Michael. 'Till tonight.'

'Till tonight,' replied Gideon, smiling. 'I suppose I may knock you up at a late hour?'

'Any hour, any hour,' cried the vanishing solicitor.

'Now there's a young fellow with a head upon his shoulders,' he said to Pitman, as soon as they were in the street.

Pitman was indistinctly heard to murmur, 'Perfect fool.'

'Not a bit of him,' returned Michael. 'He knows who's the best solicitor in London, and it's not every man can say the same. But, I say, didn't I pitch it in hot?'

Pitman returned no answer.

'Hullo!' said the lawyer, pausing, 'what's wrong with the long-suffering Pitman?'

'You had no right to speak of me as you did,' the artist broke out; 'your language was perfectly unjustifiable; you have wounded me deeply.'

'I never said a word about you,' replied Michael. 'I spoke of Ezra Thomas; and do please remember that there's no such party.'

'It's just as hard to bear,' said the artist.

But by this time they had reached the corner of the by-street; and there was the faithful shoeblack, standing by the horses' heads with a splendid assumption of dignity; and there was the piano, figuring forlorn upon the cart, while the rain beat upon its unprotected sides and trickled down its elegantly varnished legs.

The shoeblack was again put in requisition to bring five or six strong fellows from the neighbouring public-house; and the last battle of the campaign opened. It is probable that Mr Gideon Forsyth had not yet taken his seat in the train for Hampton Court, before Michael opened the door of the chambers, and the grunting porters deposited the Broadwood grand in the middle of the floor.

'And now,' said the lawyer, after he had sent the men about their business, 'one more precaution. We must leave him the key of the piano, and we must contrive that he shall find it. Let me see.' And he built a square tower of cigars upon the top of the instrument, and dropped the key into the middle.

'Poor young man,' said the artist, as they descended the stairs.

'He is in a devil of a position,' assented Michael drily. 'It'll brace him up.'

'And that reminds me,' observed the excellent Pitman, 'that I fear I displayed a most ungrateful temper. I had no right, I see, to resent expressions, wounding as they were, which were in no sense directed.'

'That's all right,' cried Michael, getting on the cart. 'Not a word more, Pitman. Very proper feeling on your part; no man of self-respect can stand by and hear his alias insulted.'

The rain had now ceased, Michael was fairly sober, the body had been disposed of, and the friends were reconciled. The return to the mews was therefore (in comparison with previous stages of the day's adventures) quite a holiday outing; and when they had returned the cart and walked forth again from the stable-yard, unchallenged, and even unsuspected, Pitman drew a deep breath of joy.

'And now,' he said, 'we can go home.'

'Pitman,' said the lawyer, stopping short, 'your recklessness fills me with concern. What! we have been wet through the greater part of the day, and you propose, in cold blood, to go home! No, sir—hot Scotch.'

And taking his friend's arm he led him sternly towards the nearest public-house. Nor was Pitman (I regret to say) wholly unwilling. Now that peace was restored and the body gone, a certain innocent skittishness began to appear in the manners of the artist; and when he touched his steaming glass to Michael's, he giggled aloud like a venturesome schoolgirl at a picnic.

CHAPTER IX

Glorious Conclusion of Michael Finsbury's Holiday

I know Michael Finsbury personally; my business—I know the awkwardness of having such a man for a lawyer— still it's an old story now, and there is such a thing as gratitude, and, in short, my legal business, although now (I am thankful to say) of quite a placid character, remains entirely in Michael's hands. But the trouble is I have no natural talent for addresses; I learn one for every man—that is friendship's offering; and the friend who subsequently changes his residence is dead to me, memory refusing to pursue him. Thus it comes about that, as I always write to Michael at his office, I cannot swear to his number in the King's Road. Of course (like my neighbours), I have been to dinner there. Of late years, since his accession to wealth, neglect of business, and election to the club, these little festivals have become common. He picks up a few fellows in the smoking-room—all men of Attic wit—myself, for instance, if he has the luck to find me disengaged; a string of hansoms may be observed (by Her Majesty) bowling gaily through St James's Park; and in a quarter of an hour the party surrounds one of the best appointed boards in London.

But at the time of which we write the house in the King's Road (let us still continue to call it No. 233) was kept very quiet; when Michael entertained guests it was at the halls of Nichol or Verrey that he would convene them, and the door of his private residence remained closed against his friends. The upper storey, which was sunny, was set apart for his father; the drawing-room was never opened; the dining-room was the scene of Michael's life. It is in this pleasant apartment, sheltered from the curiosity of King's Road by wire blinds, and entirely surrounded by the lawyer's unrivalled library of poetry and criminal trials, that we find him sitting down to his dinner after his holiday with Pitman. A spare old lady, with very bright eyes and a mouth humorously compressed, waited upon the lawyer's needs; in every line of her countenance she betrayed the fact that she was an old retainer; in every word that fell from her lips she flaunted the glorious circumstance of a Scottish origin; and the fear with which this powerful combination fills the boldest was obviously no stranger to the bosom of our friend. The hot Scotch having somewhat warmed up the embers of the Heidsieck, it was touching to observe the master's eagerness to pull himself together under the servant's eye; and when he remarked, 'I think, Teena, I'll take a brandy and soda,' he spoke like a man doubtful of his elocution, and not half certain of obedience.

'No such a thing, Mr Michael,' was the prompt return. 'Clar't and water.'

'Well, well, Teena, I daresay you know best,' said the master. 'Very fatiguing day at the office, though.'

'What?' said the retainer, 'ye never were near the office!'

'O yes, I was though; I was repeatedly along Fleet Street,' returned Michael.

'Pretty pliskies ye've been at this day!' cried the old lady, with humorous alacrity; and then, 'Take care—don't break my crystal!' she cried, as the lawyer came within an ace of knocking the glasses off the table.

'And how is he keeping?' asked Michael.

'O, just the same, Mr Michael, just the way he'll be till the end, worthy man!' was the reply. 'But ye'll not be the first that's asked me that the day.'

'No?' said the lawyer. 'Who else?'

'Ay, that's a joke, too,' said Teena grimly. 'A friend of yours: Mr Morris.'

'Morris! What was the little beggar wanting here?' enquired Michael.

'Wantin'? To see him,' replied the housekeeper, completing her meaning by a movement of the thumb toward the upper storey. 'That's by his way of it; but I've an idee of my own. He tried to bribe me, Mr Michael. Bribe—me!' she repeated, with inimitable scorn. 'That's no' kind of a young gentleman.'

'Did he so?' said Michael. 'I bet he didn't offer much.'

'No more he did,' replied Teena; nor could any subsequent questioning elicit from her the sum with which the thrifty leather merchant had attempted to corrupt her. 'But I sent him about his business,' she said gallantly. 'He'll not come here again in a hurry.'

'He mustn't see my father, you know; mind that!' said Michael. 'I'm not going to have any public exhibition to a little beast like him.'

'No fear of me lettin' him,' replied the trusty one. 'But the joke is this, Mr Michael—see, ye're upsettin' the sauce, that's a clean table-cloth—the best of the joke is that he thinks your father's dead and you're keepin' it dark.'

Michael whistled. 'Set a thief to catch a thief,' said he.

'Exac'ly what I told him!' cried the delighted dame.

'I'll make him dance for that,' said Michael.

'Couldn't ye get the law of him some way?' suggested Teena truculently.

'No, I don't think I could, and I'm quite sure I don't want to,' replied Michael. 'But I say, Teena, I really don't believe this claret's wholesome; it's not a sound, reliable wine. Give us a brandy and soda, there's a good soul.' Teena's face became like adamant. 'Well, then,' said the lawyer fretfully, 'I won't eat any more dinner.'

'Ye can please yourself about that, Mr Michael,' said Teena, and began composedly to take away.

'I do wish Teena wasn't a faithful servant!' sighed the lawyer, as he issued into Kings's Road.

The rain had ceased; the wind still blew, but only with a pleasant freshness; the town, in the clear darkness of the night, glittered with street-lamps and shone with glancing rain-pools. 'Come, this is better,' thought the lawyer to himself, and he walked on eastward, lending a pleased ear to the wheels and the million footfalls of the city.

Near the end of the King's Road he remembered his brandy and soda, and entered a flaunting public-house. A good many persons were present, a waterman from a cab-stand, half a dozen of the chronically unemployed, a gentleman (in one corner) trying to sell aesthetic photographs out of a leather case to another and very youthful gentleman with a yellow goatee, and a pair of lovers debating some fine shade (in the other). But the centre-piece and great attraction was a little old man, in a black, ready-made surtout, which was obviously a recent purchase. On the marble table in front of him, beside a sandwich and a glass of beer, there lay a battered forage cap. His hand fluttered abroad with oratorical gestures; his voice, naturally shrill, was plainly tuned to the pitch of the lecture-room; and by arts, comparable to those of the Ancient Mariner, he was now holding spellbound the barmaid, the waterman, and four of the unemployed.

'I have examined all the theatres in London,' he was saying; 'and pacing the principal entrances, I have ascertained them to be ridiculously disproportionate to the requirements of their audiences. The doors opened the wrong way—I forget at this moment which it is, but have a note of it at home; they were frequently locked during the performance, and when the auditorium was literally thronged with English people. You have probably not had my opportunities of comparing distant lands; but I can assure you this has been long ago recognized as a mark of aristocratic government. Do you suppose, in a country really self-governed, such abuses could exist? Your own intelligence, however uncultivated, tells you they could not. Take Austria, a country even possibly more enslaved than England. I have myself conversed with one of the survivors of the Ring Theatre, and though his colloquial German was not very good, I succeeded in gathering a pretty clear idea of his opinion of the case. But, what will perhaps interest you still more, here is a cutting on the subject from a Vienna newspaper, which I will now read to you, translating as I go. You can see for yourselves; it is printed in the German character.' And he held the cutting out for verification, much as a conjuror passes a trick orange along the front bench.

'Hullo, old gentleman! Is this you?' said Michael, laying his hand upon the orator's shoulder.

The figure turned with a convulsion of alarm, and showed the countenance of Mr Joseph Finsbury.

'You, Michael!' he cried. 'There's no one with you, is there?'

'No,' replied Michael, ordering a brandy and soda, 'there's nobody with me; whom do you expect?'

'I thought of Morris or John,' said the old gentleman, evidently greatly relieved.

'What the devil would I be doing with Morris or John?' cried the nephew.

'There is something in that,' returned Joseph. 'And I believe I can trust you. I believe you will stand by me.'

'I hardly know what you mean,' said the lawyer, 'but if you are in need of money I am flush.'

'It's not that, my dear boy,' said the uncle, shaking him by the hand. 'I'll tell you all about it afterwards.'

'All right,' responded the nephew. 'I stand treat, Uncle Joseph; what will you have?'

'In that case,' replied the old gentleman, 'I'll take another sandwich. I daresay I surprise you,' he went on, 'with my presence in a public-house; but the fact is, I act on a sound but little-known principle of my own——'

'O, it's better known than you suppose,' said Michael sipping his brandy and soda. 'I always act on it myself when I want a drink.'

The old gentleman, who was anxious to propitiate Michael, laughed a cheerless laugh. 'You have such a flow of spirits,' said he, 'I am sure I often find it quite amusing. But regarding this principle of which I was about to speak. It is that of accommodating one's-self to the manners of any land (however humble) in which our lot may be cast. Now, in France, for instance, every one goes to a café for his meals; in America, to what is called a "two-bit house"; in England the people resort to such an institution as the present for refreshment. With sandwiches, tea, and an occasional glass of bitter beer, a man can live luxuriously in London for fourteen pounds twelve shillings per annum.'

'Yes, I know,' returned Michael, 'but that's not including clothes, washing, or boots. The whole thing, with cigars and occasional sprees, costs me over seven hundred a year.'

But this was Michael's last interruption. He listened in good-humoured silence to the remainder of his uncle's lecture, which speedily branched to political reform, thence to the theory of the weather-glass, with an illustrative account of a bora in the Adriatic; thence again to the best manner of teaching arithmetic to the deaf-and-dumb; and with that, the sandwich being then no more, *explicuit valde feliciter*. A moment later the pair issued forth on the King's Road.

'Michael,' said his uncle, 'the reason that I am here is because I cannot endure those nephews of mine. I find them intolerable.'

'I daresay you do,' assented Michael, 'I never could stand them for a moment.'

'They wouldn't let me speak,' continued the old gentleman bitterly; 'I never was allowed to get a word in edgewise; I was shut up at once with some impertinent remark. They kept me on short allowance of pencils, when I wished to make notes of the most absorbing interest; the daily newspaper was guarded from me like a young baby from a gorilla. Now, you know me, Michael. I live for my calculations;

I live for my manifold and ever-changing views of life; pens and paper and the productions of the popular press are to me as important as food and drink; and my life was growing quite intolerable when, in the confusion of that fortunate railway accident at Browndean, I made my escape. They must think me dead, and are trying to deceive the world for the chance of the tontine.'

'By the way, how do you stand for money?' asked Michael kindly.

'Pecuniarily speaking, I am rich,' returned the old man with cheerfulness. 'I am living at present at the rate of one hundred a year, with unlimited pens and paper; the British Museum at which to get books; and all the newspapers I choose to read. But it's extraordinary how little a man of intellectual interest requires to bother with books in a progressive age. The newspapers supply all the conclusions.'

'I'll tell you what,' said Michael, 'come and stay with me.'

'Michael,' said the old gentleman, 'it's very kind of you, but you scarcely understand what a peculiar position I occupy. There are some little financial complications; as a guardian, my efforts were not altogether blessed; and not to put too fine a point upon the matter, I am absolutely in the power of that vile fellow, Morris.'

'You should be disguised,' cried Michael eagerly; 'I will lend you a pair of window-glass spectacles and some red side-whiskers.'

'I had already canvassed that idea,' replied the old gentleman, 'but feared to awaken remark in my unpretentious lodgings. The aristocracy, I am well aware——'

'But see here,' interrupted Michael, 'how do you come to have any money at all? Don't make a stranger of me, Uncle Joseph; I know all about the trust, and the hash you made of it, and the assignment you were forced to make to Morris.'

Joseph narrated his dealings with the bank.

'O, but I say, this won't do,' cried the lawyer. 'You've put your foot in it. You had no right to do what you did.'

'The whole thing is mine, Michael,' protested the old gentleman. 'I founded and nursed that business on principles entirely of my own.'

'That's all very fine,' said the lawyer; 'but you made an assignment, you were forced to make it, too; even then your position was extremely shaky; but now, my dear sir, it means the dock.'

'It isn't possible,' cried Joseph; 'the law cannot be so unjust as that?'

'And the cream of the thing,' interrupted Michael, with a sudden shout of laughter, 'the cream of the thing is this, that of course you've downed the leather business! I must say, Uncle Joseph, you have strange ideas of law, but I like your taste in humour.'

'I see nothing to laugh at,' observed Mr Finsbury tartly.

'And talking of that, has Morris any power to sign for the firm?' asked Michael.

'No one but myself,' replied Joseph.

'Poor devil of a Morris! O, poor devil of a Morris!' cried the lawyer in delight. 'And his keeping up the farce that you're at home! O, Morris, the Lord has delivered you into my hands! Let me see, Uncle Joseph, what do you suppose the leather business worth?'

'It *was* worth a hundred thousand,' said Joseph bitterly, 'when it was in my hands. But then there came a Scotsman—it is supposed he had a certain talent—it was entirely directed to bookkeeping—no accountant in London could understand a word of any of his books; and then there was Morris, who is perfectly incompetent. And now it is worth very little. Morris tried to sell it last year; and Pogram and Jarris offered only four thousand.'

'I shall turn my attention to leather,' said Michael with decision.

'You?' asked Joseph. 'I advise you not. There is nothing in the whole field of commerce more surprising than the fluctuations of the leather market. Its sensitiveness may be described as morbid.'

'And now, Uncle Joseph, what have you done with all that money?' asked the lawyer.

'Paid it into a bank and drew twenty pounds,' answered Mr Finsbury promptly. 'Why?'

'Very well,' said Michael. 'Tomorrow I shall send down a clerk with a cheque for a hundred, and he'll draw out the original sum and return it to the Anglo-Patagonian, with some sort of explanation which I will try to invent for you. That will clear your feet, and as Morris can't touch a penny of it without forgery, it will do no harm to my little scheme.'

'But what am I to do?' asked Joseph; 'I cannot live upon nothing.'

'Don't you hear?' returned Michael. 'I send you a cheque for a hundred; which leaves you eighty to go along upon; and when that's done, apply to me again.'

'I would rather not be beholden to your bounty all the same,' said Joseph, biting at his white moustache. 'I would rather live on my own money, since I have it.'

Michael grasped his arm. 'Will nothing make you believe,' he cried, 'that I am trying to save you from Dartmoor?'

His earnestness staggered the old man. 'I must turn my attention to law,' he said; 'it will be a new field; for though, of course, I understand its general principles, I have never really applied my mind to the details, and this view of yours, for example, comes on me entirely by surprise. But you may be right, and of course at my time of life—for I am no longer young—any really long term of imprisonment would be highly prejudicial. But, my dear nephew, I have no claim on you; you have no call to support me.'

'That's all right,' said Michael; 'I'll probably get it out of the leather business.'

And having taken down the old gentleman's address, Michael left him at the corner of a street.

'What a wonderful old muddler!' he reflected, 'and what a singular thing is life! I seem to be condemned to be the instrument of Providence. Let me see; what have I done today? Disposed of a dead body, saved Pitman, saved my Uncle Joseph, brightened up Forsyth, and drunk a devil of a lot of most indifferent liquor. Let's top off with a visit to my cousins, and be the instrument of Providence in earnest. Tomorrow I can turn my attention to leather; tonight I'll just make it lively for 'em in a friendly spirit.'

About a quarter of an hour later, as the clocks were striking eleven, the instrument of Providence descended from a hansom, and, bidding the driver wait, rapped at the door of No. 16 John Street.

It was promptly opened by Morris.

'O, it's you, Michael,' he said, carefully blocking up the narrow opening: 'it's very late.'

Michael without a word reached forth, grasped Morris warmly by the hand, and gave it so extreme a squeeze that the sullen householder fell back. Profiting by this movement, the lawyer obtained a footing in the lobby and marched into the dining-room, with Morris at his heels.

'Where's my Uncle Joseph?' demanded Michael, sitting down in the most comfortable chair.

'He's not been very well lately,' replied Morris; 'he's staying at Browndean; John is nursing him; and I am alone, as you see.'

Michael smiled to himself. 'I want to see him on particular business,' he said.

'You can't expect to see my uncle when you won't let me see your father,' returned Morris.

'Fiddlestick,' said Michael. 'My father is my father; but Joseph is just as much my uncle as he's yours; and you have no right to sequestrate his person.'

'I do no such thing,' said Morris doggedly. 'He is not well, he is dangerously ill and nobody can see him.'

'I'll tell you what, then,' said Michael. 'I'll make a clean breast of it. I have come down like the opossum, Morris; I have come to compromise.'

Poor Morris turned as pale as death, and then a flush of wrath against the injustice of man's destiny dyed his very temples. 'What do you mean?' he cried, 'I don't believe a word of it!' And when Michael had assured him of his seriousness, 'Well, then,' he cried, with another deep flush, 'I won't; so you can put that in your pipe and smoke it.'

'Oho!' said Michael queerly. 'You say your uncle is dangerously ill, and you won't compromise? There's something very fishy about that.'

'What do you mean?' cried Morris hoarsely.

'I only say it's fishy,' returned Michael, 'that is, pertaining to the finny tribe.'

'Do you mean to insinuate anything?' cried Morris stormily, trying the high hand.

'Insinuate?' repeated Michael. 'O, don't let's begin to use awkward expressions! Let us drown our differences in a bottle, like two affable kinsmen. *The Two Affable Kinsmen*, sometimes attributed to Shakespeare,' he added.

Morris's mind was labouring like a mill. 'Does he suspect? or is this chance and stuff? Should I soap, or should I bully? Soap,' he concluded. 'It gains time. Well,' said he aloud, and with rather a painful affectation of heartiness, 'it's long since we have had an evening together, Michael; and though my habits (as you know) are very temperate, I may as well make an exception. Excuse me one moment till I fetch a bottle of whisky from the cellar.'

'No whisky for me,' said Michael; 'a little of the old still champagne or nothing.'

For a moment Morris stood irresolute, for the wine was very valuable: the next he had quitted the room without a word. His quick mind had perceived his advantage; in thus dunning him for the cream of the cellar, Michael was playing into his hand. 'One bottle?' he thought. 'By George, I'll give him two! this is no moment for economy; and once the beast is drunk, it's strange if I don't wring his secret out of him.'

With two bottles, accordingly, he returned. Glasses were produced, and Morris filled them with hospitable grace.

'I drink to you, cousin!' he cried gaily. 'Don't spare the wine-cup in my house.'

Michael drank his glass deliberately, standing at the table; filled it again, and returned to his chair, carrying the bottle along with him.

'The spoils of war!' he said apologetically. 'The weakest goes to the wall. Science, Morris, science.' Morris could think of no reply, and for an appreciable interval silence reigned. But two glasses of the still champagne produced a rapid change in Michael.

'There's a want of vivacity about you, Morris,' he observed. 'You may be deep; but I'll be hanged if you're vivacious!'

'What makes you think me deep?' asked Morris with an air of pleased simplicity.

'Because you won't compromise,' said the lawyer. 'You're deep dog, Morris, very deep dog, not t' compromise—remarkable deep dog. And a very good glass of wine; it's the only respectable feature in the Finsbury family, this wine; rarer thing than a title—much rarer. Now a man with glass wine like this in cellar, I wonder why won't compromise?'

'Well, *you* wouldn't compromise before, you know,' said the smiling Morris. 'Turn about is fair play.'

'I wonder why *I* wouldn' compromise? I wonder why *you* wouldn'?' enquired Michael. 'I wonder why we each think the other wouldn'? 'S quite a remarrable—remarkable problem,' he added, triumphing over oral obstacles, not without obvious pride. 'Wonder what we each think—don't you?'

'What do you suppose to have been my reason?' asked Morris adroitly.

Michael looked at him and winked. 'That's cool,' said he. 'Next thing, you'll ask me to help you out of the muddle. I know I'm emissary of Providence, but not that kind! You get out of it yourself, like Aesop and the other fellow. Must be dreadful muddle for young orphan o' forty; leather business and all!'

'I am sure I don't know what you mean,' said Morris.

'Not sure I know myself,' said Michael. 'This is exc'lent vintage, sir—exc'lent vintage. Nothing against the tipple. Only thing: here's a valuable uncle disappeared. Now, what I want to know: where's valuable uncle?'

'I have told you: he is at Browndean,' answered Morris, furtively wiping his brow, for these repeated hints began to tell upon him cruelly.

'Very easy say Brown—Browndee—no' so easy after all!' cried Michael. 'Easy say; anything's easy say, when you can say it. What I don' like's total disappearance of an uncle. Not businesslike.' And he wagged his head.

'It is all perfectly simple,' returned Morris, with laborious calm. 'There is no mystery. He stays at Browndean, where he got a shake in the accident.'

'Ah!' said Michael, 'got devil of a shake!'

'Why do you say that?' cried Morris sharply.

'Best possible authority. Told me so yourself,' said the lawyer. 'But if you tell me contrary now, of course I'm bound to believe either the one story or the other. Point is—I've upset this bottle, still champagne's exc'lent thing carpet—point is, is valuable uncle dead—an'—bury?'

Morris sprang from his seat. 'What's that you say?' he gasped.

'I say it's exc'lent thing carpet,' replied Michael, rising. 'Exc'lent thing promote healthy action of the skin. Well, it's all one, anyway. Give my love to Uncle Champagne.'

'You're not going away?' said Morris.

'Awf'ly sorry, ole man. Got to sit up sick friend,' said the wavering Michael.

'You shall not go till you have explained your hints,' returned Morris fiercely. 'What do you mean? What brought you here?'

'No offence, I trust,' said the lawyer, turning round as he opened the door; 'only doing my duty as shemishery of Providence.'

Groping his way to the front-door, he opened it with some difficulty, and descended the steps to the hansom. The tired driver looked up as he approached, and asked where he was to go next.

Michael observed that Morris had followed him to the steps; a brilliant inspiration came to him. 'Anything t' give pain,' he reflected. ... 'Drive Shcotlan' Yard,' he added aloud, holding to the wheel to steady himself; 'there's something devilish fishy, cabby, about those cousins. Mush' be cleared up! Drive Shcotlan' Yard.'

'You don't mean that, sir,' said the man, with the ready sympathy of the lower orders for an intoxicated gentleman. 'I had better take you home, sir; you can go to Scotland Yard tomorrow.'

'Is it as friend or as perfessional man you advise me not to go Shcotlan' Yard t'night?' enquired Michael. 'All righ', never min' Shcotlan' Yard, drive Gaiety bar.'

'The Gaiety bar is closed,' said the man.

'Then home,' said Michael, with the same cheerfulness.

'Where to, sir?'

'I don't remember, I'm sure,' said Michael, entering the vehicle, 'drive Shcotlan' Yard and ask.'

'But you'll have a card,' said the man, through the little aperture in the top, 'give me your card-case.'

'What imagi—imagination in a cabby!' cried the lawyer, producing his card-case, and handing it to the driver.

The man read it by the light of the lamp. 'Mr Michael Finsbury, 233 King's Road, Chelsea. Is that it, sir?'

'Right you are,' cried Michael, 'drive there if you can see way.'

CHAPTER X

Gideon Forsyth and the Broadwood Grand

The reader has perhaps read that remarkable work, *Who Put Back the Clock?* by E. H. B., which appeared for several days upon the railway bookstalls and then vanished entirely from the face of the earth. Whether eating Time makes the chief of his diet out of old editions; whether Providence has passed a special enactment on behalf of authors; or whether these last have taken the law into their own hand, bound themselves into a dark conspiracy with a password, which I would die rather than reveal, and night after night sally forth under some vigorous leader, such as Mr James Payn or Mr Walter Besant, on their task of secret spoliation—certain it is, at least, that the old editions pass, giving place to new. To the proof, it is believed there are now only three copies extant of *Who Put Back the Clock?* one in the British Museum, successfully concealed by a wrong entry in the catalogue; another in one of the cellars (the cellar where the music accumulates) of the Advocates' Library at Edinburgh; and a third, bound in morocco, in the possession of Gideon Forsyth. To account for the very different fate attending this third exemplar, the readiest theory is to suppose that Gideon admired the tale. How to explain that admiration might appear (to those who have perused the work) more difficult; but the weakness of a parent is extreme, and Gideon (and not his uncle, whose initials he had humorously borrowed) was the author of *Who Put Back the Clock?* He had never acknowledged it, or only to some intimate friends while it was still in proof; after its appearance and alarming failure, the modesty of the novelist had become more pressing, and the secret was now likely to be better kept than that of the authorship of *Waverley*.

A copy of the work (for the date of my tale is already yesterday) still figured in dusty solitude in the bookstall at Waterloo; and Gideon, as he passed with his ticket for Hampton Court, smiled contemptuously at the creature of his thoughts. What an idle ambition was the author's! How far beneath him was the practice of that childish art! With his hand closing on his first brief, he felt himself a man at last;

and the muse who presides over the police romance, a lady presumably of French extraction, fled his neighbourhood, and returned to join the dance round the springs of Helicon, among her Grecian sisters.

Robust, practical reflection still cheered the young barrister upon his journey. Again and again he selected the little country-house in its islet of great oaks, which he was to make his future home. Like a prudent householder, he projected improvements as he passed; to one he added a stable, to another a tennis-court, a third he supplied with a becoming rustic boat-house.

'How little a while ago,' he could not but reflect, 'I was a careless young dog with no thought but to be comfortable! I cared for nothing but boating and detective novels. I would have passed an old-fashioned country-house with large kitchen-garden, stabling, boat-house, and spacious offices, without so much as a look, and certainly would have made no enquiry as to the drains. How a man ripens with the years!'

The intelligent reader will perceive the ravages of Miss Hazeltine. Gideon had carried Julia straight to Mr Bloomfield's house; and that gentleman, having been led to understand she was the victim of oppression, had noisily espoused her cause. He worked himself into a fine breathing heat; in which, to a man of his temperament, action became needful.

'I do not know which is the worse,' he cried, 'the fraudulent old villain or the unmanly young cub. I will write to the *Pall Mall* and expose them. Nonsense, sir; they must be exposed! It's a public duty. Did you not tell me the fellow was a Tory? O, the uncle is a Radical lecturer, is he? No doubt the uncle has been grossly wronged. But of course, as you say, that makes a change; it becomes scarce so much a public duty.'

And he sought and instantly found a fresh outlet for his alacrity. Miss Hazeltine (he now perceived) must be kept out of the way; his houseboat was lying ready—he had returned but a day or two before from his usual cruise; there was no place like a houseboat for concealment; and that very morning, in the teeth of the easterly gale, Mr and Mrs Bloomfield and Miss Julia Hazeltine had started forth on their untimely voyage. Gideon pled in vain to be allowed to join the party. 'No, Gid,' said his uncle. 'You will be watched; you must keep away from us.' Nor had the barrister ventured to contest this strange illusion; for he feared if he rubbed off any of the romance, that Mr Bloomfield might weary of the whole affair. And his discretion was rewarded; for the Squirradical, laying a heavy hand upon his nephew's shoulder, had added these notable expressions: 'I see what you are after, Gid. But if you're going to get the girl, you have to work, sir.'

These pleasing sounds had cheered the barrister all day, as he sat reading in chambers; they continued to form the ground-base of his manly musings as he was whirled to Hampton Court; even when he landed at the station, and began to pull himself together for his delicate interview, the voice of Uncle Ned and the eyes of Julia were not forgotten.

But now it began to rain surprises: in all Hampton Court there was no Kurnaul Villa, no Count Tarnow, and no count. This was strange; but, viewed in the light of the incoherency of his instructions, not perhaps inexplicable; Mr Dickson had been lunching, and he might have made some fatal oversight in the address. What was the thoroughly prompt, manly, and businesslike step? thought Gideon; and he answered himself at once: 'A telegram, very laconic.' Speedily the wires were flashing the following very important missive: 'Dickson, Langham Hotel. Villa and persons both unknown here, suppose erroneous address; follow self next train.—Forsyth.' And at the Langham Hotel, sure enough, with a brow expressive of dispatch and intellectual effort, Gideon descended not long after from a smoking hansom.

I do not suppose that Gideon will ever forget the Langham Hotel. No Count Tarnow was one thing; no John Dickson and no Ezra Thomas, quite another. How, why, and what next, danced in his bewildered brain; from every centre of what we playfully call the human intellect incongruous messages were telegraphed; and before the hubbub of dismay had quite subsided, the barrister found himself driving furiously for his chambers. There was at least a cave of refuge; it was at least a place to think in; and he climbed the stair, put his key in the lock and opened the door, with some approach to hope.

It was all dark within, for the night had some time fallen; but Gideon knew his room, he knew where the matches stood on the end of the chimney-piece; and he advanced boldly, and in so doing dashed himself against a heavy body; where (slightly altering the expressions of the song) no heavy body should have been. There had been nothing there when Gideon went out; he had locked the door behind him, he had found it locked on his return, no one could have entered, the furniture could not have changed its own position. And yet undeniably there was a something there. He thrust out his hands in the darkness. Yes, there was something, something large, something smooth, something cold.

'Heaven forgive me!' said Gideon, 'it feels like a piano.'

And the next moment he remembered the vestas in his waistcoat-pocket and had struck a light.

It was indeed a piano that met his doubtful gaze; a vast and costly instrument, stained with the rains of the afternoon and defaced with recent scratches. The light of the vesta was reflected from the varnished sides, like a star in quiet water; and in the farther end of the room the shadow of that strange visitor loomed bulkily and wavered on the wall.

Gideon let the match burn to his fingers, and the darkness closed once more on his bewilderment. Then with trembling hands he lit the lamp and drew near. Near or far, there was no doubt of the fact: the thing was a piano. There, where by all the laws of God and man it was impossible that it should be—there the thing impudently stood. Gideon threw open the keyboard and struck a chord. Not a sound disturbed the quiet of the room. 'Is there anything wrong with me?' he thought, with a pang; and drawing in a seat, obstinately persisted in his attempts to ravish silence, now with sparkling arpeggios, now with a sonata of Beethoven's which (in happier days) he knew to be one of the loudest pieces of that powerful composer. Still not a sound. He gave the Broadwood two great bangs with his clenched first. All was still as the grave.

The young barrister started to his feet.

'I am stark-staring mad,' he cried aloud, 'and no one knows it but myself. God's worst curse has fallen on me.'

His fingers encountered his watch-chain; instantly he had plucked forth his watch and held it to his ear. He could hear it ticking.

'I am not deaf,' he said aloud. 'I am only insane. My mind has quitted me for ever.'

He looked uneasily about the room, and gazed with lacklustre eyes at the chair in which Mr Dickson had installed himself. The end of a cigar lay near on the fender.

'No,' he thought, 'I don't believe that was a dream; but God knows my mind is failing rapidly. I seem to be hungry, for instance; it's probably another hallucination. Still I might try. I shall have one more good meal; I shall go to the Café Royal, and may possibly be removed from there direct to the asylum.'

He wondered with morbid interest, as he descended the stairs, how he would first betray his terrible condition—would he attack a waiter? or eat glass?—and when he had mounted into a cab, he bade the man drive to Nichol's, with a lurking fear that there was no such place.

The flaring, gassy entrance of the café speedily set his mind at rest; he was cheered besides to recognize his favourite waiter; his orders appeared to be coherent; the dinner, when it came, was quite a sensible meal, and he ate it with enjoyment. 'Upon my word,' he reflected, 'I am about tempted to indulge a hope. Have I been hasty? Have I done what Robert Skill would have done?' Robert Skill (I need scarcely mention) was the name of the principal character in *Who Put Back the Clock?* It had occurred to the author as a brilliant and probable invention; to readers of a critical turn, Robert appeared scarce upon a level with his surname; but it is the difficulty of the police romance, that the reader is always a man of such vastly greater ingenuity than the writer. In the eyes of his creator, however, Robert Skill was a word to conjure with; the thought braced and spurred him; what that brilliant creature would have done Gideon would do also. This frame of mind is not uncommon; the distressed general, the baited divine, the hesitating author, decide severally to do what Napoleon, what St Paul, what Shakespeare would have done; and there remains only the minor question, What is that? In Gideon's case one thing was clear: Skill was a man of singular decision, he would have taken some step (whatever it was) at once; and the only step that Gideon could think of was to return to his chambers.

This being achieved, all further inspiration failed him, and he stood pitifully staring at the instrument of his confusion. To touch the keys again was more than he durst venture on; whether they had maintained their former silence, or responded with the tones of the last trump, it would have equally dethroned his resolution. 'It may be a practical jest,' he reflected, 'though it seems elaborate and costly. And yet what else can it be? It *must* be a practical jest.' And just then his eye fell upon a feature which seemed corroborative of that view: the pagoda of cigars which Michael had erected ere he left the chambers.

'Why that?' reflected Gideon. 'It seems entirely irresponsible.' And drawing near, he gingerly demolished it. 'A key,' he thought. 'Why that? And why so conspicuously placed?' He made the circuit of the instrument, and perceived the keyhole at the back. 'Aha! this is what the key is for,' said he. 'They wanted me to look inside. Stranger and stranger.' And with that he turned the key and raised the lid.

In what antics of agony, in what fits of flighty resolution, in what collapses of despair, Gideon consumed the night, it would be ungenerous to enquire too closely.

That trill of tiny song with which the eaves-birds of London welcome the approach of day found him limp and rumpled and bloodshot, and with a mind still vacant of resource. He rose and looked forth unrejoicingly on blinded windows, an empty street, and the grey daylight dotted with the yellow lamps. There are mornings when the city seems to awake with a sick headache; this was one of them; and still the twittering reveille of the sparrows stirred in Gideon's spirit.

'Day here,' he thought, 'and I still helpless! This must come to an end.' And he locked up the piano, put the key in his pocket, and set forth in quest of coffee. As he went, his mind trudged for the hundredth time a certain mill-road of terrors, misgivings, and regrets. To call in the police, to give up the body, to cover London with handbills describing John Dickson and Ezra Thomas, to fill the papers with paragraphs, *Mysterious Occurrence in the Temple—Mr Forsyth admitted to bail*, this was one course, an easy course, a safe course; but not, the more he reflected on it, not a pleasant one. For, was it not to publish abroad a number of singular facts about himself? A child ought to have seen through the story of these adventurers, and he had gaped and swallowed it. A barrister of the least self-respect should have refused to listen to clients who came before him in a manner so irregular, and he had listened. And O, if he had only listened; but he had gone upon their errand—he, a barrister, uninstructed even by the shadow of a solicitor—upon an errand fit only for a private detective; and alas!—and for the hundredth time the blood surged to his brow— he had taken their money! 'No,' said he, 'the thing is as plain as St Paul's. I shall be dishonoured! I have smashed my career for a five-pound note.'

Between the possibility of being hanged in all innocence, and the certainty of a public and merited disgrace, no gentleman of spirit could long hesitate. After three gulps of that hot, snuffy, and muddy beverage, that passes on the streets of London for a decoction of the coffee berry, Gideon's mind was made up. He would do without the police. He must face the other side of the dilemma, and be Robert Skill in earnest. What would Robert Skill have done? How does a gentleman dispose of a dead body, honestly come by? He remembered the inimitable story of the hunchback; reviewed its course, and dismissed it for a worthless guide. It was impossible to prop a corpse on the corner of Tottenham Court Road without arousing fatal curiosity in the bosoms of the passers-by; as for lowering it down a London chimney, the physical obstacles were insurmountable. To get it on board a train and drop it out, or on the top of an omnibus and drop it off, were equally out of the question. To get it on a yacht and drop it overboard, was more conceivable; but for a man of moderate means it seemed extravagant. The hire of the yacht was in itself a consideration; the subsequent support of the whole crew (which seemed a necessary consequence) was simply not to be thought of. His uncle and the houseboat here occurred in very luminous colours to his mind. A musical composer (say, of the name of Jimson) might very well suffer, like Hogarth's musician before him, from the disturbances of London. He might very well be pressed for time to finish an opera—say the comic opera *Orange Pekoe*—*Orange Pekoe*, music by Jimson—'this young maestro, one of the most promising of our recent English school'—vigorous entrance of the drums, etc.—the whole character of Jimson and his music arose in bulk before the mind of Gideon. What more likely than Jimson's arrival with a grand piano (say, at Padwick), and his residence in a houseboat alone with the unfinished score of *Orange Pekoe*? His subsequent disappearance, leaving nothing behind but an empty piano case, it might be more difficult to account for. And yet even that was susceptible of explanation. For, suppose Jimson had gone mad over a fugal passage, and had thereupon destroyed the accomplice of his infamy, and plunged into the welcome river? What end, on the whole, more probable for a modern musician?

'By Jove, I'll do it,' cried Gideon. 'Jimson is the boy!'

CHAPTER XI

The Maestro Jimson

Mr Edward Hugh Bloomfield having announced his intention to stay in the neighbourhood of Maidenhead, what more probable than that the Maestro Jimson should turn his mind toward Padwick? Near this pleasant riverside village he remembered to have observed an ancient, weedy houseboat lying moored beside a tuft of willows. It had stirred in him, in his careless hours, as he pulled down the river under a more familiar name, a certain sense of the romantic; and when the nice contrivance of his story was already complete in his mind, he had come near pulling it all down again, like an ungrateful clock, in order to introduce a chapter in which Richard Skill (who was always being decoyed somewhere) should be decoyed on board that lonely hulk by Lord Bellew and the American desperado Gin Sling. It was fortunate he had not done so, he reflected, since the hulk was now required for very different purposes.

Jimson, a man of inconspicuous costume, but insinuating manners, had little difficulty in finding the hireling who had charge of the houseboat, and still less in persuading him to resign his care. The rent was almost nominal, the entry immediate, the key was exchanged against a suitable advance in money, and Jimson returned to town by the afternoon train to see about dispatching his piano.

'I will be down tomorrow,' he had said reassuringly. 'My opera is waited for with such impatience, you know.'

And, sure enough, about the hour of noon on the following day, Jimson might have been observed ascending the riverside road that goes from Padwick to Great Haverham, carrying in one hand a basket of provisions, and under the other arm a leather case containing (it is to be conjectured) the score of *Orange Pekoe*. It was October weather; the stone-grey sky was full of larks, the leaden mirror of the Thames brightened with autumnal foliage, and the fallen leaves of the chestnuts chirped under the composer's footing. There is no time of the year in England more courageous; and Jimson, though he was not without his troubles, whistled as he went.

A little above Padwick the river lies very solitary. On the opposite shore the trees of a private park enclose the view, the chimneys of the mansion just pricking forth above their clusters; on the near side the path is bordered by willows. Close among these lay the houseboat, a thing so soiled by the tears of the overhanging willows, so grown upon with parasites, so decayed, so battered, so neglected, such a haunt of rats, so advertised a storehouse of rheumatic agonies, that the heart of an intending occupant might well recoil. A plank, by way of flying drawbridge, joined it to the shore. And it was a dreary moment for Jimson when he pulled this after him and found himself alone on this unwholesome fortress. He could hear the rats scuttle and flop in the abhorred interior; the key cried among the wards like a thing in pain; the sitting-room was deep in dust, and smelt strong of bilge-water. It could not be called a cheerful spot, even for a composer absorbed in beloved toil; how much less for a young gentleman haunted by alarms and awaiting the arrival of a corpse!

He sat down, cleared away a piece of the table, and attacked the cold luncheon in his basket. In case of any subsequent inquiry into the fate of Jimson, it was desirable he should be little seen: in other words, that he should spend the day entirely in the house. To this end, and further to corroborate his fable, he had brought in the leather case not only writing materials, but a ream of large-size music paper, such as he considered suitable for an ambitious character like Jimson's.

'And now to work,' said he, when he had satisfied his appetite. 'We must leave traces of the wretched man's activity.' And he wrote in bold characters:

ORANGE PEKOE.
Op. 17.
J. B. JIMSON.
Vocal and p. f. score.

'I suppose they never do begin like this,' reflected Gideon; 'but then it's quite out of the question for me to tackle a full score, and Jimson was so unconventional. A dedication would be found convincing, I believe. "Dedicated to" (let me see) "to William Ewart Gladstone, by his obedient servant the composer." And now some music: I had better avoid the overture; it seems to present difficulties. Let's give an air for the tenor: key—O, something modern!—seven sharps.' And he made a businesslike signature across the staves, and then paused and browsed for a while on the handle of his pen. Melody, with no better inspiration than a sheet of paper, is not usually found to spring unbidden in the mind of the amateur; nor is the key of seven sharps a place of much repose to the untried. He cast away that sheet. 'It will help to build up the character of Jimson,' Gideon remarked, and again waited on the muse, in various keys and on divers sheets of paper, but all with results so inconsiderable that he stood aghast. 'It's very odd,' thought he. 'I seem to have less fancy than I thought, or this is an off-day with me; yet Jimson must leave something.' And again he bent himself to the task.

Presently the penetrating chill of the houseboat began to attack the very seat of life. He desisted from his unremunerative trial, and, to the audible annoyance of the rats, walked briskly up and down the cabin. Still he was cold. 'This is all nonsense,' said he. 'I don't care about the risk, but I will not catch a catarrh. I must get out of this den.'

He stepped on deck, and passing to the bow of his embarkation, looked for the first time up the river. He started. Only a few hundred yards above another houseboat lay moored among the willows. It was very spick-and-span, an elegant canoe hung at the stern, the windows were concealed by snowy curtains, a flag floated from a staff. The more Gideon looked at it, the more there mingled with his disgust a sense of impotent surprise. It was very like his uncle's houseboat; it was exceedingly like—it was identical. But for two circumstances, he could have sworn it was the same. The first, that his uncle had gone to Maidenhead, might be explained away by that flightiness of purpose which is so common a trait among the more than usually manly. The second, however, was conclusive: it was not in the least like Mr Bloomfield to display a banner on his floating residence; and if he ever did, it would certainly be dyed in hues of emblematical propriety. Now the Squirradical, like the vast majority of the more manly, had drawn knowledge at the wells of Cambridge—he was wooden spoon in the year 1850; and the flag upon the houseboat streamed on the afternoon air with the colours of that seat of Toryism, that cradle of Puseyism, that home of the inexact and the effete—Oxford.

Still it was strangely like, thought Gideon.

And as he thus looked and thought, the door opened, and a young lady stepped forth on deck. The barrister dropped and fled into his cabin—it was Julia Hazeltine! Through the window he watched her draw in the canoe, get on board of it, cast off, and come dropping downstream in his direction.

'Well, all is up now,' said he, and he fell on a seat.

'Good-afternoon, miss,' said a voice on the water. Gideon knew it for the voice of his landlord.

'Good-afternoon,' replied Julia, 'but I don't know who you are; do I? O yes, I do though. You are the nice man that gave us leave to sketch from the old houseboat.'

Gideon's heart leaped with fear.

'That's it,' returned the man. 'And what I wanted to say was as you couldn't do it any more. You see I've let it.'

'Let it!' cried Julia.

'Let it for a month,' said the man. 'Seems strange, don't it? Can't see what the party wants with it!'

'It seems very romantic of him, I think,' said Julia, 'What sort of a person is he?'

Julia in her canoe, the landlord in his wherry, were close alongside, and holding on by the gunwale of the houseboat; so that not a word was lost on Gideon.

'He's a music-man,' said the landlord, 'or at least that's what he told me, miss; come down here to write an op'ra.'

'Really!' cried Julia, 'I never heard of anything so delightful! Why, we shall be able to slip down at night and hear him improvise! What is his name?'

'Jimson,' said the man.

'Jimson?' repeated Julia, and interrogated her memory in vain. But indeed our rising school of English music boasts so many professors that we rarely hear of one till he is made a baronet. 'Are you sure you have it right?'

'Made him spell it to me,' replied the landlord. 'J-I-M-S-O-N—Jimson; and his op'ra's called—some kind of tea.'

'*Some kind of tea!*' cried the girl. 'What a very singular name for an opera! What can it be about?' And Gideon heard her pretty laughter flow abroad. 'We must try to get acquainted with this Mr Jimson; I feel sure he must be nice.'

'Well, miss, I'm afraid I must be going on. I've got to be at Haverham, you see.'

'O, don't let me keep you, you kind man!' said Julia. 'Good-afternoon.'

'Good-afternoon to you, miss.'

Gideon sat in the cabin a prey to the most harrowing thoughts. Here he was anchored to a rotting houseboat, soon to be anchored to it still more emphatically by the presence of the corpse, and here was the country buzzing about him, and young ladies already proposing pleasure parties to surround his house at night. Well, that meant the gallows; and much he cared for that. What troubled him now was Julia's indescribable levity. That girl would scrape acquaintance with anybody; she had no reserve, none of the enamel of the lady. She was familiar with a brute like his landlord; she took an immediate interest (which she lacked even the delicacy to conceal) in a creature like Jimson! He could conceive her asking Jimson to have tea with her! And it was for a girl like this that a man like Gideon—— Down, manly heart!

He was interrupted by a sound that sent him whipping behind the door in a trice. Miss Hazeltine had stepped on board the houseboat. Her sketch was promising; judging from the stillness, she supposed Jimson not yet come; and she had decided to seize occasion and complete the work of art. Down she sat therefore in the bow, produced her block and water-colours, and was soon singing over (what used to be called) the ladylike accomplishment. Now and then indeed her song was interrupted, as she searched in her memory for some of the odious little receipts by means of which the game is practised—or used to be practised—in the brave days of old; they say the world, and those ornaments of the world, young ladies, are become more sophisticated now; but Julia had probably studied under Pitman, and she stood firm in the old ways.

Gideon, meanwhile, stood behind the door, afraid to move, afraid to breathe, afraid to think of what must follow, racked by confinement and borne to the ground with tedium. This particular phase, he felt with gratitude, could not last for ever; whatever impended (even the gallows, he bitterly and perhaps erroneously reflected) could not fail to be a relief. To calculate cubes occurred to him as an ingenious and even profitable refuge from distressing thoughts, and he threw his manhood into that dreary exercise.

Thus, then, were these two young persons occupied—Gideon attacking the perfect number with resolution; Julia vigorously stippling incongruous colours on her block, when Providence dispatched into these waters a steam-launch asthmatically panting up the Thames. All along the banks the water swelled and fell, and the reeds rustled. The houseboat itself, that ancient stationary creature, became suddenly imbued with life, and rolled briskly at her moorings, like a sea-going ship when she begins to smell the harbour bar. The wash had nearly died away, and the quick panting of the launch sounded already faint and far off, when Gideon was startled by a cry from Julia. Peering through the window, he beheld her staring disconsolately downstream at the fast-vanishing canoe. The barrister (whatever were his faults) displayed on this occasion a promptitude worthy of his hero, Robert Skill; with one effort of his mind he foresaw what was about to follow; with one movement of his body he dropped to the floor and crawled under the table.

Julia, on her part, was not yet alive to her position. She saw she had lost the canoe, and she looked forward with something less than avidity to her next interview with Mr Bloomfield; but she had no idea that she was imprisoned, for she knew of the plank bridge.

She made the circuit of the house, and found the door open and the bridge withdrawn. It was plain, then, that Jimson must have come; plain, too, that he must be on board. He must be a very shy man to have suffered this invasion of his residence, and made no sign; and her courage rose higher at the thought. He must come now, she must force him from his privacy, for the plank was too heavy for her single strength; so she tapped upon the open door. Then she tapped again.

'Mr Jimson,' she cried, 'Mr Jimson! here, come!—you *must* come, you know, sooner or later, for I can't get off without you. O, don't be so exceedingly silly! O, please, come!'

Still there was no reply.

'If he *is* here he must be mad,' she thought, with a little fear. And the next moment she remembered he had probably gone aboard like herself in a boat. In that case she might as well see the houseboat, and she pushed open the door and stepped in. Under the table, where he lay smothered with dust, Gideon's heart stood still.

There were the remains of Jimson's lunch. 'He likes rather nice things to eat,' she thought. 'O, I am sure he is quite a delightful man. I wonder if he is as good-looking as Mr Forsyth. Mrs Jimson—I don't believe it sounds as nice as Mrs Forsyth; but then "Gideon" is so really odious! And here is some of his music too; this is delightful. *Orange Pekoe*—O, that's what he meant by some kind of tea.' And she trilled with laughter. '*Adagio molto espressivo, sempre legato,*' she read next. (For the literary part of a composer's business Gideon was well equipped.) 'How very strange to have all these directions, and only three or four notes! O, here's another with some more. *Andante patetico.*' And she began to glance over the music. 'O dear me,' she thought, 'he must be terribly modern! It all seems discords to me. Let's try the air. It is very strange, it seems familiar.' She began to sing it, and suddenly broke off with laughter. 'Why, it's "Tommy make room for your Uncle!"' she cried aloud, so that the soul of Gideon was filled with bitterness. '*Andante patetico*, indeed! The man must be a mere impostor.'

And just at this moment there came a confused, scuffling sound from underneath the table; a strange note, like that of a barn-door fowl, ushered in a most explosive sneeze; the head of the sufferer was at the same time brought smartly in contact with the boards above; and the sneeze was followed by a hollow groan.

Julia fled to the door, and there, with the salutary instinct of the brave, turned and faced the danger. There was no pursuit. The sounds continued; below the table a crouching figure was indistinctly to be seen jostled by the throes of a sneezing-fit; and that was all.

'Surely,' thought Julia, 'this is most unusual behaviour. He cannot be a man of the world!'

Meanwhile the dust of years had been disturbed by the young barrister's convulsions; and the sneezing-fit was succeeded by a passionate access of coughing.

Julia began to feel a certain interest. 'I am afraid you are really quite ill,' she said, drawing a little nearer. 'Please don't let me put you out, and do not stay under that table, Mr Jimson. Indeed it cannot be good for you.'

Mr Jimson only answered by a distressing cough; and the next moment the girl was on her knees, and their faces had almost knocked together under the table.

'O, my gracious goodness!' exclaimed Miss Hazeltine, and sprang to her feet. 'Mr Forsyth gone mad!'

'I am not mad,' said the gentleman ruefully, extricating himself from his position. 'Dearest Miss Hazeltine, I vow to you upon my knees I am not mad!'

'You are not!' she cried, panting.

'I know,' he said, 'that to a superficial eye my conduct may appear unconventional.'

'If you are not mad, it was no conduct at all,' cried the girl, with a flash of colour, 'and showed you did not care one penny for my feelings!'

'This is the very devil and all. I know—I admit that,' cried Gideon, with a great effort of manly candour.

'It was abominable conduct!' said Julia, with energy.

'I know it must have shaken your esteem,' said the barrister. 'But, dearest Miss Hazeltine, I beg of you to hear me out; my behaviour, strange as it may seem, is not unsusceptible of explanation; and I positively cannot and will not consent to continue to try to exist without—without the esteem of one whom I admire—the moment is ill chosen, I am well aware of that; but I repeat the expression—one whom I admire.'

A touch of amusement appeared on Miss Hazeltine's face. 'Very well,' said she, 'come out of this dreadfully cold place, and let us sit down on deck.' The barrister dolefully followed her. 'Now,' said she, making herself comfortable against the end of the house, 'go on. I will hear you out.' And then, seeing him stand before her with so much obvious disrelish to the task, she was suddenly overcome with laughter. Julia's laugh was a thing to ravish lovers; she rolled her mirthful descant with the freedom and the melody of a blackbird's song upon the river, and repeated by the echoes of the farther bank. It seemed a thing in its own place and a sound native to the open air. There was only one creature who heard it without joy, and that was her unfortunate admirer.

'Miss Hazeltine,' he said, in a voice that tottered with annoyance, 'I speak as your sincere well-wisher, but this can only be called levity.'

Julia made great eyes at him.

'I can't withdraw the word,' he said: 'already the freedom with which I heard you hobnobbing with a boatman gave me exquisite pain. Then there was a want of reserve about Jimson——'

'But Jimson appears to be yourself,' objected Julia.

'I am far from denying that,' cried the barrister, 'but you did not know it at the time. What could Jimson be to you? Who was Jimson? Miss Hazeltine, it cut me to the heart.'

'Really this seems to me to be very silly,' returned Julia, with severe decision. 'You have behaved in the most extraordinary manner; you pretend you are able to explain your conduct, and instead of doing so you begin to attack me.'

'I am well aware of that,' replied Gideon. 'I—I will make a clean breast of it. When you know all the circumstances you will be able to excuse me.'

And sitting down beside her on the deck, he poured forth his miserable history.

'O, Mr Forsyth,' she cried, when he had done, 'I am—so—sorry! I wish I hadn't laughed at you—only you know you really were so exceedingly funny. But I wish I hadn't, and I wouldn't either if I had only known.' And she gave him her hand.

Gideon kept it in his own. 'You do not think the worse of me for this?' he asked tenderly.

'Because you have been so silly and got into such dreadful trouble? you poor boy, no!' cried Julia; and, in the warmth of the moment, reached him her other hand; 'you may count on me,' she added.

'Really?' said Gideon.

'Really and really!' replied the girl.

'I do then, and I will,' cried the young man. 'I admit the moment is not well chosen; but I have no friends—to speak of.'

'No more have I,' said Julia. 'But don't you think it's perhaps time you gave me back my hands?'

'*La ci darem la mano*,' said the barrister, 'the merest moment more! I have so few friends,' he added.

'I thought it was considered such a bad account of a young man to have no friends,' observed Julia.

'O, but I have crowds of *friends*!' cried Gideon. 'That's not what I mean. I feel the moment is ill chosen; but O, Julia, if you could only see yourself!'

'Mr Forsyth——'

'Don't call me by that beastly name!' cried the youth. 'Call me Gideon!'

'O, never that!' from Julia. 'Besides, we have known each other such a short time.'

'Not at all!' protested Gideon. 'We met at Bournemouth ever so long ago. I never forgot you since. Say you never forgot me. Say you never forgot me, and call me Gideon!'

'Isn't this rather—a want of reserve about Jimson?' enquired the girl.

'O, I know I am an ass,' cried the barrister, 'and I don't care a halfpenny! I know I'm an ass, and you may laugh at me to your heart's delight.' And as Julia's lips opened with a smile, he once more dropped into music. 'There's the Land of Cherry Isle!' he sang, courting her with his eyes.

'It's like an opera,' said Julia, rather faintly.

'What should it be?' said Gideon. 'Am I not Jimson? It would be strange if I did not serenade my love. O yes, I mean the word, my Julia; and I mean to win you. I am in dreadful trouble, and I have not a penny of my own, and I have cut the silliest figure; and yet I mean to win you, Julia. Look at me, if you can, and tell me no!'

She looked at him; and whatever her eyes may have told him, it is to be supposed he took a pleasure in the message, for he read it a long while.

'And Uncle Ned will give us some money to go on upon in the meanwhile,' he said at last.

'Well, I call that cool!' said a cheerful voice at his elbow.

Gideon and Julia sprang apart with wonderful alacrity; the latter annoyed to observe that although they had never moved since they sat down, they were now quite close together; both presenting faces of a very heightened colour to the eyes of Mr Edward Hugh Bloomfield. That gentleman, coming up the river in his boat, had captured the truant canoe, and divining what had happened, had thought to steal a march upon Miss Hazeltine at her sketch. He had unexpectedly brought down two birds with one stone; and as he looked upon the pair of flushed and breathless culprits, the pleasant human instinct of the matchmaker softened his heart.

'Well, I call that cool,' he repeated; 'you seem to count very securely upon Uncle Ned. But look here, Gid, I thought I had told you to keep away?'

'To keep away from Maidenhead,' replied Gid. 'But how should I expect to find you here?'

'There is something in that,' Mr Bloomfield admitted. 'You see I thought it better that even you should be ignorant of my address; those rascals, the Finsburys, would have wormed it out of you. And just to put them off the scent I hoisted these abominable colours. But that is not all, Gid; you promised me to work, and here I find you playing the fool at Padwick.'

'Please, Mr Bloomfield, you must not be hard on Mr Forsyth,' said Julia. 'Poor boy, he is in dreadful straits.'

'What's this, Gid?' enquired the uncle. 'Have you been fighting? or is it a bill?'

These, in the opinion of the Squirradical, were the two misfortunes incident to gentlemen; and indeed both were culled from his own career. He had once put his name (as a matter of form) on a friend's paper; it had cost him a cool thousand; and the friend had gone about with the fear of death upon him ever since, and never turned a corner without scouting in front of him for Mr Bloomfield and the oaken staff. As for fighting, the Squirradical was always on the brink of it; and once, when (in the character of president of a Radical club) he had cleared out the hall of his opponents, things had gone even further. Mr Holtum, the Conservative candidate, who lay so long on the bed of sickness, was prepared to swear to Mr Bloomfield. 'I will swear to it in any court—it was the hand of that brute that struck me down,' he was reported to have said; and when he was thought to be sinking, it was known that he had made an *ante-mortem* statement in that sense. It was a cheerful day for the Squirradical when Holtum was restored to his brewery.

'It's much worse than that,' said Gideon; 'a combination of circumstances really providentially unjust—a—in fact, a syndicate of murderers seem to have perceived my latent ability to rid them of the traces of their crime. It's a legal study after all, you see!' And with these words, Gideon, for the second time that day, began to describe the adventures of the Broadwood Grand.

'I must write to *The Times*,' cried Mr Bloomfield.

'Do you want to get me disbarred?' asked Gideon.

'Disbarred! Come, it can't be as bad as that,' said his uncle. 'It's a good, honest, Liberal Government that's in, and they would certainly move at my request. Thank God, the days of Tory jobbery are at an end.'

'It wouldn't do, Uncle Ned,' said Gideon.

'But you're not mad enough,' cried Mr Bloomfield, 'to persist in trying to dispose of it yourself?'

'There is no other path open to me,' said Gideon.

'It's not common sense, and I will not hear of it,' cried Mr Bloomfield. 'I command you, positively, Gid, to desist from this criminal interference.'

'Very well, then, I hand it over to you,' said Gideon, 'and you can do what you like with the dead body.'

'God forbid!' ejaculated the president of the Radical Club, 'I'll have nothing to do with it.'

'Then you must allow me to do the best I can,' returned his nephew. 'Believe me, I have a distinct talent for this sort of difficulty.'

'We might forward it to that pest-house, the Conservative Club,' observed Mr Bloomfield. 'It might damage them in the eyes of their constituents; and it could be profitably worked up in the local journal.'

'If you see any political capital in the thing,' said Gideon, 'you may have it for me.'

'No, no, Gid—no, no, I thought *you* might. I will have no hand in the thing. On reflection, it's highly undesirable that either I or Miss Hazeltine should linger here. We might be observed,' said the president, looking up and down the river; 'and in my public position the consequences would be painful for the party. And, at any rate, it's dinner-time.'

'What?' cried Gideon, plunging for his watch. 'And so it is! Great heaven, the piano should have been here hours ago!'

Mr Bloomfield was clambering back into his boat; but at these words he paused.

'I saw it arrive myself at the station; I hired a carrier man; he had a round to make, but he was to be here by four at the latest,' cried the barrister. 'No doubt the piano is open, and the body found.'

'You must fly at once,' cried Mr Bloomfield, 'it's the only manly step.'

'But suppose it's all right?' wailed Gideon. 'Suppose the piano comes, and I am not here to receive it? I shall have hanged myself by my cowardice. No, Uncle Ned, enquiries must be made in Padwick; I dare not go, of course; but you may—you could hang about the police office, don't you see?'

'No, Gid—no, my dear nephew,' said Mr Bloomfield, with the voice of one on the rack. 'I regard you with the most sacred affection; and I thank God I am an Englishman—and all that. But not—not the police, Gid.'

'Then you desert me?' said Gideon. 'Say it plainly.'

'Far from it! far from it!' protested Mr Bloomfield. 'I only propose caution. Common sense, Gid, should always be an Englishman's guide.'

'Will you let me speak?' said Julia. 'I think Gideon had better leave this dreadful houseboat, and wait among the willows over there. If the piano comes, then he could step out and take it in; and if the police come, he could slip into our houseboat, and there needn't be any more Jimson at all. He could go to bed, and we could burn his clothes (couldn't we?) in the steam-launch; and then really it seems as if it would be all right. Mr Bloomfield is so respectable, you know, and such a leading character, it would be quite impossible even to fancy that he could be mixed up with it.'

'This young lady has strong common sense,' said the Squirradical.

'O, I don't think I'm at all a fool,' said Julia, with conviction.

'But what if neither of them come?' asked Gideon; 'what shall I do then?'

'Why then,' said she, 'you had better go down to the village after dark; and I can go with you, and then I am sure you could never be suspected; and even if you were, I could tell them it was altogether a mistake.'

'I will not permit that—I will not suffer Miss Hazeltine to go,' cried Mr Bloomfield.

'Why?' asked Julia.

Mr Bloomfield had not the least desire to tell her why, for it was simply a craven fear of being drawn himself into the imbroglio; but with the usual tactics of a man who is ashamed of himself, he took the high hand. 'God forbid, my dear Miss Hazeltine, that I should dictate to a lady on the question of propriety——' he began.

'O, is that all?' interrupted Julia. 'Then we must go all three.'

'Caught!' thought the Squirradical.

CHAPTER XII

Positively the Last Appearance of the Broadwood Grand

England is supposed to be unmusical; but without dwelling on the patronage extended to the organ-grinder, without seeking to found any argument on the prevalence of the jew's trump, there is surely one instrument that may be said to be national in the fullest acceptance of the word. The herdboy in the broom, already musical in the days of Father Chaucer, startles (and perhaps pains) the lark with this exiguous pipe; and in the hands of the skilled bricklayer,

> 'The thing becomes a trumpet, whence he blows'

(as a general rule) either 'The British Grenadiers' or 'Cherry Ripe'. The latter air is indeed the shibboleth and diploma piece of the penny whistler; I hazard a guess it was originally composed for this instrument. It is singular enough that a man should be able to gain a livelihood, or even to tide over a period of unemployment, by the display of his proficiency upon the penny whistle; still more so, that the professional should almost invariably confine himself to 'Cherry Ripe'. But indeed, singularities surround the subject, thick like blackberries. Why, for instance, should the pipe be called a penny whistle? I think no one ever bought it for a penny. Why should the alternative name be tin whistle? I am grossly deceived if it be made of tin. Lastly, in what deaf catacomb, in what earless desert, does the beginner pass the excruciating interval of his apprenticeship? We have all heard people learning the piano, the fiddle, and the cornet; but the young of the penny whistler (like that of the salmon) is occult from observation; he is never heard until proficient; and providence (perhaps alarmed by the works of Mr Mallock) defends human hearing from his first attempts upon the upper octave.

A really noteworthy thing was taking place in a green lane, not far from Padwick. On the bench of a carrier's cart there sat a tow-headed, lanky, modest-looking youth; the reins were on his lap; the whip lay behind him in the interior of the cart; the horse proceeded without guidance or encouragement; the carrier (or the carrier's man), rapt into a higher sphere than that of his daily occupations, his looks dwelling on the skies, devoted himself wholly to a brand-new D penny whistle, whence he diffidently endeavoured to elicit that pleasing melody 'The Ploughboy'. To any observant person who should have chanced to saunter in that lane, the hour would have been thrilling. 'Here at last,' he would have said, 'is the beginner.'

The tow-headed youth (whose name was Harker) had just encored himself for the nineteenth time, when he was struck into the extreme of confusion by the discovery that he was not alone.

'There you have it!' cried a manly voice from the side of the road. 'That's as good as I want to hear. Perhaps a leetle oilier in the run,' the voice suggested, with meditative gusto. 'Give it us again.'

Harker glanced, from the depths of his humiliation, at the speaker. He beheld a powerful, sun-brown, clean-shaven fellow, about forty years of age, striding beside the cart with a non-commissioned military bearing, and (as he strode) spinning in the air a cane. The fellow's clothes were very bad, but he looked clean and self-reliant.

'I'm only a beginner,' gasped the blushing Harker, 'I didn't think anybody could hear me.'

'Well, I like that!' returned the other. 'You're a pretty old beginner. Come, I'll give you a lead myself. Give us a seat here beside you.'

The next moment the military gentleman was perched on the cart, pipe in hand. He gave the instrument a knowing rattle on the shaft, mouthed it, appeared to commune for a moment with the muse, and dashed into 'The girl I left behind me'. He was a great, rather than a fine, performer; he lacked the bird-like richness; he could scarce have extracted all the honey out of 'Cherry Ripe'; he did not fear—he even ostentatiously displayed and seemed to revel in— the shrillness of the instrument; but in fire, speed, precision, even- ness, and fluency; in linked agility of *jimmy*—a technical expression, by your leave, answering to *warblers* on the bagpipe; and perhaps, above all, in that inspiring side-glance of the eye, with which he followed the effect and (as by a human appeal) eked out the insuffi- ciency of his performance: in these, the fellow stood without a rival. Harker listened: 'The girl I left behind me' filled him with despair; 'The Soldier's Joy' carried him beyond jealousy into generous enthusiasm.

'Turn about,' said the military gentleman, offering the pipe.

'O, not after you!' cried Harker; 'you're a professional.'

'No,' said his companion; 'an amatyure like yourself. That's one style of play, yours is the other, and I like it best. But I began when I was a boy, you see, before my taste was formed. When you're my age you'll play that thing like a cornet-à-piston. Give us that air again; how does it go?' and he affected to endeavour to recall 'The Ploughboy'.

A timid, insane hope sprang in the breast of Harker. Was it possible? Was there something in his playing? It had, indeed, seemed to him at times as if he got a kind of a richness out of it. Was he a genius? Meantime the military gentleman stumbled over the air.

'No,' said the unhappy Harker, 'that's not quite it. It goes this way—just to show you.'

And, taking the pipe between his lips, he sealed his doom. When he had played the air, and then a second time, and a third; when the military gentleman had tried it once more, and once more failed; when it became clear to Harker that he, the blushing débutant, was actually giving a lesson to this full-grown flutist—and the flutist under his care was not very brilliantly progressing—how am I to tell what floods of glory brightened the autumnal countryside; how, unless the reader were an amateur himself, describe the heights of idiotic vanity to which the carrier climbed? One significant fact shall paint the situation: thenceforth it was Harker who played, and the military gentleman listened and approved.

As he listened, however, he did not forget the habit of soldierly precaution, looking both behind and before. He looked behind and computed the value of the carrier's load, divining the contents of the brown-paper parcels and the portly hamper, and briefly setting down the grand piano in the brand-new piano-case as 'difficult to get rid of'. He looked before, and spied at the corner of the green lane a little country public-house embowered in roses. 'I'll have a shy at it,' concluded the military gentleman, and roundly proposed a glass.

'Well, I'm not a drinking man,' said Harker.

'Look here, now,' cut in the other, 'I'll tell you who I am: I'm Colour-Sergeant Brand of the Blankth. That'll tell you if I'm a drinking man or not.' It might and it might not, thus a Greek chorus would have intervened, and gone on to point out how very far it fell short of telling why the sergeant was tramping a country lane in tatters; or even to argue that he must have pretermitted some while ago his labours for the general defence, and (in the interval) possibly turned his attention to oakum. But there was no Greek chorus present; and the man of war went on to contend that drinking was one thing and a friendly glass another.

In the Blue Lion, which was the name of the country public-house, Colour-Sergeant Brand introduced his new friend, Mr Harker, to a number of ingenious mixtures, calculated to prevent the approaches of intoxication. These he explained to be 'rekisite' in the service, so that a self-respecting officer should always appear upon parade in a condition honourable to his corps. The most efficacious of these devices was to lace a pint of mild ale with twopenceworth of London gin. I am pleased to hand in this recipe to the discerning reader, who may find it useful even in civil station; for its effect upon Mr Harker was revolutionary. He must be helped on board his own waggon, where he proceeded to display a spirit entirely given over to mirth and music, alternately hooting with laughter, to which the sergeant hastened to bear chorus, and incoherently tootling on the pipe. The man of war, meantime, unostentatiously possessed himself of the reins. It was plain he had a taste for the secluded beauties of an English landscape; for the cart, although it wandered under his guidance for some time, was never observed to issue on the dusty highway, journeying between hedge and ditch, and for the most part under overhanging boughs. It was plain, besides, he had an eye to the true interests of Mr Harker; for though the cart drew up more than once at the doors of public-houses, it was only the sergeant who set foot to ground, and, being equipped himself with a quart bottle, once more proceeded on his rural drive.

To give any idea of the complexity of the sergeant's course, a map of that part of Middlesex would be required, and my publisher is averse from the expense. Suffice it, that a little after the night had closed, the cart was brought to a standstill in a woody road; where the sergeant lifted from among the parcels, and tenderly deposited upon the wayside, the inanimate form of Harker.

'If you come-to before daylight,' thought the sergeant, 'I shall be surprised for one.'

From the various pockets of the slumbering carrier he gently collected the sum of seventeen shillings and eightpence sterling; and, getting once more into the cart, drove thoughtfully away.

'If I was exactly sure of where I was, it would be a good job,' he reflected. 'Anyway, here's a corner.'

He turned it, and found himself upon the riverside. A little above him the lights of a houseboat shone cheerfully; and already close at hand, so close that it was impossible to avoid their notice, three persons, a lady and two gentlemen, were deliberately drawing near. The sergeant put his trust in the convenient darkness of the night, and drove on to meet them. One of the gentlemen, who was of a portly figure, walked in the midst of the fairway, and presently held up a staff by way of signal.

'My man, have you seen anything of a carrier's cart?' he cried.

Dark as it was, it seemed to the sergeant as though the slimmer of the two gentlemen had made a motion to prevent the other speaking, and (finding himself too late) had skipped aside with some alacrity. At another season, Sergeant Brand would have paid more attention to the fact; but he was then immersed in the perils of his own predicament.

'A carrier's cart?' said he, with a perceptible uncertainty of voice. 'No, sir.'

'Ah!' said the portly gentleman, and stood aside to let the sergeant pass. The lady appeared to bend forward and study the cart with every mark of sharpened curiosity, the slimmer gentleman still keeping in the rear.

'I wonder what the devil they would be at,' thought Sergeant Brand; and, looking fearfully back, he saw the trio standing together in the midst of the way, like folk consulting. The bravest of military heroes are not always equal to themselves as to their reputation; and fear, on some singular provocation, will find a lodgment in the most unfamiliar bosom. The word 'detective' might have been heard to gurgle in the sergeant's throat; and vigorously applying the whip, he fled up the riverside road to Great Haverham, at the gallop of the carrier's horse. The lights of the houseboat flashed upon the flying waggon as it passed; the beat of hoofs and the rattle of the vehicle gradually coalesced and died away; and presently, to the trio on the riverside, silence had redescended.

'It's the most extraordinary thing,' cried the slimmer of the two gentlemen, 'but that's the cart!'

'And I know I saw a piano,' said the girl.

'O, it's the cart, certainly; and the extraordinary thing is, it's not the man,' added the first.

'It must be the man, Gid, it must be,' said the portly one.

'Well, then, why is he running away?' asked Gideon.

'His horse bolted, I suppose,' said the Squirradical.

'Nonsense! I heard the whip going like a flail,' said Gideon. 'It simply defies the human reason.'

'I'll tell you,' broke in the girl, 'he came round that corner. Suppose we went and—what do you call it in books?—followed his trail? There may be a house there, or somebody who saw him, or something.'

'Well, suppose we did, for the fun of the thing,' said Gideon.

The fun of the thing (it would appear) consisted in the extremely close juxtaposition of himself and Miss Hazeltine. To Uncle Ned, who was excluded from these simple pleasures, the excursion appeared hopeless from the first; and when a fresh perspective of darkness opened up, dimly contained between park palings on the one side and a hedge and ditch upon the other, the whole without the smallest signal of human habitation, the Squirradical drew up.

'This is a wild-goose chase,' said he.

With the cessation of the footfalls, another sound smote upon their ears.

'O, what's that?' cried Julia.

'I can't think,' said Gideon.

The Squirradical had his stick presented like a sword. 'Gid,' he began, 'Gid, I——'

'O Mr Forsyth!' cried the girl. 'O don't go forward, you don't know what it might be—it might be something perfectly horrid.'

'It may be the devil itself,' said Gideon, disengaging himself, 'but I am going to see it.'

'Don't be rash, Gid,' cried his uncle.

The barrister drew near to the sound, which was certainly of a portentous character. In quality it appeared to blend the strains of the cow, the fog-horn, and the mosquito; and the startling manner of its enunciation added incalculably to its terrors. A dark object, not unlike the human form divine, appeared on the brink of the ditch.

'It's a man,' said Gideon, 'it's only a man; he seems to be asleep and snoring. Hullo,' he added, a moment after, 'there must be something wrong with him, he won't waken.'

Gideon produced his vestas, struck one, and by its light recognized the tow head of Harker.

'This is the man,' said he, 'as drunk as Belial. I see the whole story'; and to his two companions, who had now ventured to rejoin him, he set forth a theory of the divorce between the carrier and his cart, which was not unlike the truth.

'Drunken brute!' said Uncle Ned, 'let's get him to a pump and give him what he deserves.'

'Not at all!' said Gideon. 'It is highly undesirable he should see us together; and really, do you know, I am very much obliged to him, for this is about the luckiest thing that could have possibly occurred. It seems to me—Uncle Ned, I declare to heaven it seems to me—I'm clear of it!'

'Clear of what?' asked the Squirradical.

'The whole affair!' cried Gideon. 'That man has been ass enough to steal the cart and the dead body; what he hopes to do with it I neither know nor care. My hands are free, Jimson ceases; down with Jimson. Shake hands with me, Uncle Ned—Julia, darling girl, Julia, I——'

'Gideon, Gideon!' said his uncle.

'O, it's all right, uncle, when we're going to be married so soon,' said Gideon. 'You know you said so yourself in the houseboat.'

'Did I?' said Uncle Ned; 'I am certain I said no such thing.'

'Appeal to him, tell him he did, get on his soft side,' cried Gideon. 'He's a real brick if you get on his soft side.'

'Dear Mr Bloomfield,' said Julia, 'I know Gideon will be such a very good boy, and he has promised me to do such a lot of law, and I will see that he does too. And you know it is so very steadying to young men, everybody admits that; though, of course, I know I have no money, Mr Bloomfield,' she added.

'My dear young lady, as this rapscallion told you today on the boat, Uncle Ned has plenty,' said the Squirradical, 'and I can never forget that you have been shamefully defrauded. So as there's nobody looking, you had better give your Uncle Ned a kiss. There, you rogue,' resumed Mr Bloomfield, when the ceremony had been daintily performed, 'this very pretty young lady is yours, and a vast deal more than you deserve. But now, let us get back to the houseboat, get up steam on the launch, and away back to town.'

'That's the thing!' cried Gideon; 'and tomorrow there will be no houseboat, and no Jimson, and no carrier's cart, and no piano; and when Harker awakes on the ditchside, he may tell himself the whole affair has been a dream.'

'Aha!' said Uncle Ned, 'but there's another man who will have a different awakening. That fellow in the cart will find he has been too clever by half.'

'Uncle Ned and Julia,' said Gideon, 'I am as happy as the King of Tartary, my heart is like a threepenny-bit, my heels are like feathers; I am out of all my troubles, Julia's hand is in mine. Is this a time for anything but handsome sentiments? Why, there's not room in me for anything that's not angelic! And when I think of that poor unhappy devil in the cart, I stand here in the night and cry with a single heart— God help him!'

'Amen,' said Uncle Ned.

CHAPTER XIII

The Tribulations of Morris: Part the Second

In a really polite age of literature I would have scorned to cast my eye again on the contortions of Morris. But the study is in the spirit of the day; it presents, besides, features of a high, almost a repulsive, morality; and if it should prove the means of preventing any respectable and inexperienced gentleman from plunging light-heartedly into crime, even political crime, this work will not have been penned in vain.

He rose on the morrow of his night with Michael, rose from the leaden slumber of distress, to find his hand tremulous, his eyes closed with rheum, his throat parched, and his digestion obviously paralysed. 'Lord knows it's not from eating!' Morris thought; and as he dressed he reconsidered his position under several heads. Nothing will so well depict the troubled seas in which he was now voyaging as a review of these various anxieties. I have thrown them (for the reader's convenience) into a certain order; but in the mind of one poor human equal they whirled together like the dust of hurricanes. With the same obliging preoccupation, I have put a name to each of his distresses; and it will be observed with pity that every individual item would have graced and commended the cover of a railway novel.

Anxiety the First: *Where is the Body? or, The Mystery of Bent Pitman*. It was now manifestly plain that Bent Pitman (as was to be looked for from his ominous appellation) belonged to the darker order of the criminal class. An honest man would not have cashed the bill; a humane man would not have accepted in silence the tragic contents of the water-butt; a man, who was not already up to the hilts in gore, would have lacked the means of secretly disposing them. This process of reasoning left a horrid image of the monster, Pitman. Doubtless he had long ago disposed of the body—dropping it through a trapdoor in his back kitchen, Morris supposed, with some hazy recollection of a picture in a penny dreadful; and doubtless the man now lived in wanton splendour on the proceeds of the bill. So far, all was peace. But with the profligate habits of a man like Bent

Pitman (who was no doubt a hunchback in the bargain), eight hundred pounds could be easily melted in a week. When they were gone, what would he be likely to do next? A hell-like voice in Morris's own bosom gave the answer: 'Blackmail me.'

Anxiety the Second: *The Fraud of the Tontine; or, Is my Uncle dead?* This, on which all Morris's hopes depended, was yet a question. He had tried to bully Teena; he had tried to bribe her; and nothing came of it. He had his moral conviction still; but you cannot blackmail a sharp lawyer on a moral conviction. And besides, since his interview with Michael, the idea wore a less attractive countenance. Was Michael the man to be blackmailed? and was Morris the man to do it? Grave considerations. 'It's not that I'm afraid of him,' Morris so far condescended to reassure himself; 'but I must be very certain of my ground, and the deuce of it is, I see no way. How unlike is life to novels! I wouldn't have even begun this business in a novel, but what I'd have met a dark, slouching fellow in the Oxford Road, who'd have become my accomplice, and known all about how to do it, and probably broken into Michael's house at night and found nothing but a waxwork image; and then blackmailed or murdered me. But here, in real life, I might walk the streets till I dropped dead, and none of the criminal classes would look near me. Though, to be sure, there is always Pitman,' he added thoughtfully.

Anxiety the Third: *The Cottage at Browndean; or, The Underpaid Accomplice.* For he had an accomplice, and that accomplice was blooming unseen in a damp cottage in Hampshire with empty pockets. What could be done about that? He really ought to have sent him something; if it was only a post-office order for five bob, enough to prove that he was kept in mind, enough to keep him in hope, beer, and tobacco. 'But what would you have?' thought Morris; and ruefully poured into his hand a half-crown, a florin, and eightpence in small change. For a man in Morris's position, at war with all society, and conducting, with the hand of inexperience, a widely ramified intrigue, the sum was already a derision. John would have to be doing; no mistake of that. 'But then,' asked the hell-like voice, 'how long is John likely to stand it?'

Anxiety the Fourth: *The Leather Business; or, The Shutters at Last: a Tale of the City.* On this head Morris had no news. He had not yet dared to visit the family concern; yet he knew he must delay no longer, and if anything had been wanted to sharpen this conviction, Michael's references of the night before rang ambiguously in his ear. Well and good. To visit the city might be indispensable; but what was he to do when he was there? He had no right to sign in his own name; and, with all the will in the world, he seemed to lack the art of signing with his uncle's. Under these circumstances, Morris could do nothing to procrastinate the crash; and, when it came, when prying eyes began to be applied to every joint of his behaviour, two questions could not fail to be addressed, sooner or later, to a speechless and perspiring insolvent. Where is Mr Joseph Finsbury? and how about your visit to the bank? Questions, how easy to put!—ye gods, how impossible to answer! The man to whom they should be addressed went certainly to gaol, and—eh! what was this?—possibly to the gallows. Morris was trying to shave when this idea struck him, and he laid the razor down. Here (in Michael's words) was the total disappearance of a valuable uncle; here was a time of inexplicable conduct on the part of a nephew who had been in bad blood with the old man any time these seven years; what a chance for a judicial blunder! 'But no,' thought Morris, 'they cannot, they dare not, make it murder. Not that. But honestly, and speaking as a man to a man, I don't see any other crime in the calendar (except arson) that I don't seem somehow to have committed. And yet I'm a perfectly respectable man, and wished nothing but my due. Law is a pretty business.'

With this conclusion firmly seated in his mind, Morris Finsbury descended to the hall of the house in John Street, still half-shaven. There was a letter in the box; he knew the handwriting: John at last!

'Well, I think I might have been spared this,' he said bitterly, and tore it open.

Dear Morris [it ran], what the dickens do you mean by it? I'm in an awful hole down here; I have to go on tick, and the parties on the spot don't cotton to the idea; they couldn't, because it is so plain I'm in a stait of Destitution. I've got no bedclothes, think of that, I must have coins, the hole thing's a Mockry, I wont stand it, nobody would. I would have come away before, only I have no money for the railway fare. Don't be a lunatic, Morris, you don't seem to understand my dredful situation. I have to get the stamp on tick. A fact.—Ever your affte. Brother,

J. FINSBURY

'Can't even spell!' Morris reflected, as he crammed the letter in his pocket, and left the house. 'What can I do for him? I have to go to the expense of a barber, I'm so shattered! How can I send anybody coins? It's hard lines, I daresay; but does he think I'm living on hot muffins? One comfort,' was his grim reflection, 'he can't cut and run—he's got to stay; he's as helpless as the dead.' And then he broke forth again: 'Complains, does he? and he's never even heard of Bent Pitman! If he had what I have on my mind, he might complain with a good grace.'

But these were not honest arguments, or not wholly honest; there was a struggle in the mind of Morris; he could not disguise from himself that his brother John was miserably situated at Browndean, without news, without money, without bedclothes, without society or any entertainment; and by the time he had been shaved and picked a hasty breakfast at a coffee tavern, Morris had arrived at a compromise.

'Poor Johnny,' he said to himself, 'he's in an awful box! I can't send him coins, but I'll tell you what I'll do: I'll send him the *Pink Un*—it'll cheer John up; and besides, it'll do his credit good getting anything by post.'

Accordingly, on his way to the leather business, whither he proceeded (according to his thrifty habit) on foot, Morris purchased and dispatched a single copy of that enlivening periodical, to which (in a sudden pang of remorse) he added at random the *Athenæum*, the *Revivalist*, and the *Penny Pictorial Weekly*. So there was John set up with literature, and Morris had laid balm upon his conscience.

As if to reward him, he was received in his place of business with good news. Orders were pouring in; there was a run on some of the back stock, and the figure had gone up. Even the manager appeared elated. As for Morris, who had almost forgotten the meaning of good news, he longed to sob like a little child; he could have caught the manager (a pallid man with startled eyebrows) to his bosom; he could have found it in his generosity to give a cheque (for a small sum) to every clerk in the counting-house. As he sat and opened his letters a chorus of airy vocalists sang in his brain, to most exquisite music, 'This whole concern may be profitable yet, profitable yet, profitable yet.'

To him, in this sunny moment of relief, enter a Mr Rodgerson, a creditor, but not one who was expected to be pressing, for his connection with the firm was old and regular.

'O, Finsbury,' said he, not without embarrassment, 'it's of course only fair to let you know—the fact is, money is a trifle tight—I have some paper out—for that matter, every one's complaining—and in short——'

'It has never been our habit, Rodgerson,' said Morris, turning pale. 'But give me time to turn round, and I'll see what I can do; I daresay we can let you have something to account.'

'Well, that's just where it is,' replied Rodgerson. 'I was tempted; I've let the credit out of my hands.'

'Out of your hands?' repeated Morris. 'That's playing rather fast and loose with us, Mr Rodgerson.'

'Well, I got cent. for cent. for it,' said the other, 'on the nail, in a certified cheque.'

'Cent. for cent.!' cried Morris. 'Why, that's something like thirty per cent. bonus; a singular thing! Who's the party?'

'Don't know the man,' was the reply. 'Name of Moss.'

'A Jew,' Morris reflected, when his visitor was gone. And what could a Jew want with a claim of—he verified the amount in the books—a claim of three five eight, nineteen, ten, against the house of Finsbury? And why should he pay cent. for cent.? The figure proved the loyalty of Rodgerson—even Morris admitted that. But it proved unfortunately something else—the eagerness of Moss. The claim must have been wanted instantly, for that day, for that morning even. Why? The mystery of Moss promised to be a fit pendant to the mystery of Pitman. 'And just when all was looking well too!' cried Morris, smiting his hand upon the desk. And almost at the same moment Mr Moss was announced.

Mr Moss was a radiant Hebrew, brutally handsome, and offensively polite. He was acting, it appeared, for a third party; he understood nothing of the circumstances; his client desired to have his position regularized; but he would accept an antedated cheque—antedated by two months, if Mr Finsbury chose.

'But I don't understand this,' said Morris. 'What made you pay cent. per cent. for it today?'

Mr Moss had no idea; only his orders.

'The whole thing is thoroughly irregular,' said Morris. 'It is not the custom of the trade to settle at this time of the year. What are your instructions if I refuse?'

'I am to see Mr Joseph Finsbury, the head of the firm,' said Mr Moss. 'I was directed to insist on that; it was implied you had no status here—the expressions are not mine.'

'You cannot see Mr Joseph; he is unwell,' said Morris.

'In that case I was to place the matter in the hands of a lawyer. Let me see,' said Mr Moss, opening a pocket-book with, perhaps, suspicious care, at the right place—'Yes—of Mr Michael Finsbury. A relation, perhaps? In that case, I presume, the matter will be pleasantly arranged.'

To pass into the hands of Michael was too much for Morris. He struck his colours. A cheque at two months was nothing, after all. In two months he would probably be dead, or in a gaol at any rate. He bade the manager give Mr Moss a chair and the paper. 'I'm going over to get a cheque signed by Mr Finsbury,' said he, 'who is lying ill at John Street.'

A cab there and a cab back; here were inroads on his wretched capital! He counted the cost; when he was done with Mr Moss he would be left with twelvepence-halfpenny in the world. What was even worse, he had now been forced to bring his uncle up to Bloomsbury. 'No use for poor Johnny in Hampshire now,' he reflected. 'And how the farce is to be kept up completely passes me. At Browndean it was just possible; in Bloomsbury it seems beyond human ingenuity—though I suppose it's what Michael does. But then he has accomplices—that Scotsman and the whole gang. Ah, if I had accomplices!'

Necessity is the mother of the arts. Under a spur so immediate, Morris surprised himself by the neatness and dispatch of his new forgery, and within three-fourths of an hour had handed it to Mr Moss.

'That is very satisfactory,' observed that gentleman, rising. 'I was to tell you it will not be presented, but you had better take care.'

The room swam round Morris. 'What—what's that!' he cried, grasping the table. He was miserably conscious the next moment of his shrill tongue and ashen face. 'What do you mean—it will not be presented? Why am I to take care? What is all this mummery?'

'I have no idea, Mr Finsbury,' replied the smiling Hebrew. 'It was a message I was to deliver. The expressions were put into my mouth.'

'What is your client's name?' asked Morris.

'That is a secret for the moment,' answered Mr Moss.

Morris bent toward him. 'It's not the bank?' he asked hoarsely.

'I have no authority to say more, Mr Finsbury,' returned Mr Moss. 'I will wish you a good morning, if you please.'

'Wish me a good morning!' thought Morris; and the next moment, seizing his hat, he fled from his place of business like a madman. Three streets away he stopped and groaned. 'Lord! I should have borrowed from the manager!' he cried. 'But it's too late now; it would look dicky to go back; I'm penniless—simply penniless—like the unemployed.'

He went home and sat in the dismantled dining-room with his head in his hands. Newton never thought harder than this victim of circumstances, and yet no clearness came. 'It may be a defect in my intelligence,' he cried, rising to his feet, 'but I cannot see that I am fairly used. The bad luck I've had is a thing to write to *The Times* about; it's enough to breed a revolution. And the plain English of the whole thing is that I must have money at once. I'm done with all morality now; I'm long past that stage; money I must have, and the only chance I see is Bent Pitman. Bent Pitman is a criminal, and therefore his position's weak. He must have some of that eight hundred left; if he has I'll force him to go shares; and even if he hasn't, I'll tell him the tontine affair, and with a desperate man like Pitman at my back, it'll be strange if I don't succeed.'

Well and good. But how to lay hands upon Bent Pitman, except by advertisement, was not so clear. And even so, in what terms to ask a meeting? on what grounds? and where? Not at John Street, for it would never do to let a man like Bent Pitman know your real address; nor yet at Pitman's house, some dreadful place in Holloway, with a trapdoor in the back kitchen; a house which you might enter in a light summer overcoat and varnished boots, to come forth again piecemeal in a market-basket. That was the drawback of a really efficient accomplice, Morris felt, not without a shudder. 'I never dreamed I should come to actually covet such society,' he thought. And then a brilliant idea struck him. Waterloo Station, a public place, yet at certain hours of the day a solitary; a place, besides, the very name of which must knock upon the heart of Pitman, and at once suggest a knowledge of the latest of his guilty secrets. Morris took a piece of paper and sketched his advertisement.

WILLIAM BENT PITMAN, if this should meet the eye of, he will hear of SOMETHING TO HIS ADVANTAGE on the far end of the main line departure platform, Waterloo Station, 2 to 4 P.M., Sunday next.

Morris reperused this literary trifle with approbation. 'Terse,' he reflected. 'Something to his advantage is not strictly true; but it's taking and original, and a man is not on oath in an advertisement. All that I require now is the ready cash for my own meals and for the advertisement, and—no, I can't lavish money upon John, but I'll give him some more papers. How to raise the wind?'

He approached his cabinet of signets, and the collector suddenly revolted in his blood. 'I will not!' he cried; 'nothing shall induce me to massacre my collection—rather theft!' And dashing upstairs to the drawing-room, he helped himself to a few of his uncle's curiosities: a pair of Turkish babooshes, a Smyrna fan, a water-cooler, a musket guaranteed to have been seized from an Ephesian bandit, and a pocketful of curious but incomplete seashells.

CHAPTER XIV

William Bent Pitman Hears of Something to his Advantage

On the morning of Sunday, William Dent Pitman rose at his usual hour, although with something more than the usual reluctance. The day before (it should be explained) an addition had been made to his family in the person of a lodger. Michael Finsbury had acted sponsor in the business, and guaranteed the weekly bill; on the other hand, no doubt with a spice of his prevailing jocularity, he had drawn a depressing portrait of the lodger's character. Mr Pitman had been led to understand his guest was not good company; he had approached the gentleman with fear, and had rejoiced to find himself the entertainer of an angel. At tea he had been vastly pleased; till hard on one in the morning he had sat entranced by eloquence and progressively fortified with information in the studio; and now, as he reviewed over his toilet the harmless pleasures of the evening, the future smiled upon him with revived attractions. 'Mr Finsbury is indeed an acquisition,' he remarked to himself; and as he entered the little parlour, where the table was already laid for breakfast, the cordiality of his greeting would have befitted an acquaintanceship already old.

'I am delighted to see you, sir'—these were his expressions—'and I trust you have slept well.'

'Accustomed as I have been for so long to a life of almost perpetual change,' replied the guest, 'the disturbance so often complained of by the more sedentary, as attending their first night in (what is called) a new bed, is a complaint from which I am entirely free.'

'I am delighted to hear it,' said the drawing-master warmly. 'But I see I have interrupted you over the paper.'

'The Sunday paper is one of the features of the age,' said Mr Finsbury. 'In America, I am told, it supersedes all other literature, the bone and sinew of the nation finding their requirements catered for; hundreds of columns will be occupied with interesting details

of the world's doings, such as water-spouts, elopements, confla-
grations, and public entertainments; there is a corner for politics,
ladies' work, chess, religion, and even literature; and a few spicy
editorials serve to direct the course of public thought. It is difficult
to estimate the part played by such enormous and miscellaneous
repositories in the education of the people. But this (though interesting in itself) partakes of the nature of a digression; and what I
was about to ask you was this: Are you yourself a student of the daily
press?'

'There is not much in the papers to interest an artist,' returned
Pitman.

'In that case,' resumed Joseph, 'an advertisement which has
appeared the last two days in various journals, and reappears this
morning, may possibly have failed to catch your eye. The name, with
a trifling variation, bears a strong resemblance to your own. Ah, here
it is. If you please, I will read it to you:

WILLIAM BENT PITMAN, if this should meet the eye of, he will hear of
SOMETHING TO HIS ADVANTAGE at the far end of the main line departure
platform, Waterloo Station, 2 to 4 P.M. today.

'Is that in print?' cried Pitman. 'Let me see it! Bent? It must be
Dent! *Something to my advantage?* Mr Finsbury, excuse me offering a
word of caution; I am aware how strangely this must sound in your
ears, but there are domestic reasons why this little circumstance
might perhaps be better kept between ourselves. Mrs Pitman—my
dear sir, I assure you there is nothing dishonourable in my secrecy;
the reasons are domestic, merely domestic; and I may set your conscience at rest when I assure you all the circumstances are known to
our common friend, your excellent nephew, Mr Michael, who has not
withdrawn from me his esteem.'

'A word is enough, Mr Pitman,' said Joseph, with one of his
Oriental reverences.

Half an hour later, the drawing-master found Michael in bed and
reading a book, the picture of good-humour and repose.

'Hillo, Pitman,' he said, laying down his book, 'what brings you
here at this inclement hour? Ought to be in church, my boy!'

'I have little thought of church today, Mr Finsbury,' said the
drawing-master. 'I am on the brink of something new, sir.' And he
presented the advertisement.

'Why, what is this?' cried Michael, sitting suddenly up. He studied it for half a minute with a frown. 'Pitman, I don't care about this document a particle,' said he.

'It will have to be attended to, however,' said Pitman.

'I thought you'd had enough of Waterloo,' returned the lawyer. 'Have you started a morbid craving? You've never been yourself anyway since you lost that beard. I believe now it was where you kept your senses.'

'Mr Finsbury,' said the drawing-master, 'I have tried to reason this matter out, and, with your permission, I should like to lay before you the results.'

'Fire away,' said Michael; 'but please, Pitman, remember it's Sunday, and let's have no bad language.'

'There are three views open to us,' began Pitman. 'First this may be connected with the barrel; second, it may be connected with Mr Semitopolis's statue; and third, it may be from my wife's brother, who went to Australia. In the first case, which is of course possible, I confess the matter would be best allowed to drop.'

'The court is with you there, Brother Pitman,' said Michael.

'In the second,' continued the other, 'it is plainly my duty to leave no stone unturned for the recovery of the lost antique.'

'My dear fellow, Semitopolis has come down like a trump; he has pocketed the loss and left you the profit. What more would you have?' enquired the lawyer.

'I conceive, sir, under correction, that Mr Semitopolis's generosity binds me to even greater exertion,' said the drawing-master. 'The whole business was unfortunate; it was—I need not disguise it from you—it was illegal from the first: the more reason that I should try to behave like a gentleman,' concluded Pitman, flushing.

'I have nothing to say to that,' returned the lawyer. 'I have sometimes thought I should like to try to behave like a gentleman myself; only it's such a one-sided business, with the world and the legal profession as they are.'

'Then, in the third,' resumed the drawing-master, 'if it's Uncle Tim, of course, our fortune's made.'

'It's not Uncle Tim, though,' said the lawyer.

'Have you observed that very remarkable expression: *Something to his advantage?*' enquired Pitman shrewdly.

'You innocent mutton,' said Michael, 'it's the seediest common-place in the English language, and only proves the advertiser is an ass. Let me demolish your house of cards for you at once. Would Uncle Tim make that blunder in your name?—in itself, the blunder is delicious, a huge improvement on the gross reality, and I mean to adopt it in the future; but is it like Uncle Tim?'

'No, it's not like him,' Pitman admitted. 'But his mind may have become unhinged at Ballarat.'

'If you come to that, Pitman,' said Michael, 'the advertiser *may* be Queen Victoria, fired with the desire to make a duke of you. I put it to yourself if that's probable; and yet it's not against the laws of nature. But we sit here to consider probabilities; and with your genteel permission, I eliminate her Majesty and Uncle Tim on the threshold. To proceed, we have your second idea, that this has some connection with the statue. Possible; but in that case who is the advertiser? Not Ricardi, for he knows your address; not the person who got the box, for he doesn't know your name. The vanman, I hear you suggest, in a lucid interval. He might have got your name, and got it incorrectly, at the station; and he might have failed to get your address. I grant the vanman. But a question: Do you really wish to meet the vanman?'

'Why should I not?' asked Pitman.

'If he wants to meet you,' replied Michael, 'observe this: it is because he has found his address-book, has been to the house that got the statue, and—mark my words!—is moving at the instigation of the murderer.'

'I should be very sorry to think so,' said Pitman; 'but I still consider it my duty to Mr Semitopolis . . .'

'Pitman,' interrupted Michael, 'this will not do. Don't seek to impose on your legal adviser; don't try to pass yourself off for the Duke of Wellington, for that is not your line. Come, I wager a dinner I can read your thoughts. You still believe it's Uncle Tim.'

'Mr Finsbury,' said the drawing-master, colouring, 'you are not a man in narrow circumstances, and you have no family. Guendolen is growing up, a very promising girl—she was confirmed this year; and I think you will be able to enter into my feelings as a parent when I tell you she is quite ignorant of dancing. The boys are at the board school, which is all very well in its way; at least, I am the last man in the world to criticize the institutions of my native land. But I had fondly hoped that Harold might become a professional musician; and little Otho shows a quite remarkable vocation for the Church. I am not exactly an ambitious man . . .'

'Well, well,' interrupted Michael. 'Be explicit; you think it's Uncle Tim?'

'It might be Uncle Tim,' insisted Pitman, 'and if it were, and I neglected the occasion, how could I ever look my children in the face? I do not refer to Mrs Pitman . . .'

'No, you never do,' said Michael.

'. . . but in the case of her own brother returning from Ballarat . . .' continued Pitman.

'. . . with his mind unhinged,' put in the lawyer.

'. . . returning from Ballarat with a large fortune, her impatience may be more easily imagined than described,' concluded Pitman.

'All right,' said Michael, 'be it so. And what do you propose to do?'

'I am going to Waterloo,' said Pitman, 'in disguise.'

'All by your little self?' enquired the lawyer. 'Well, I hope you think it safe. Mind and send me word from the police cells.'

'O, Mr Finsbury, I had ventured to hope—perhaps you might be induced to—to make one of us,' faltered Pitman.

'Disguise myself on Sunday?' cried Michael. 'How little you understand my principles!'

'Mr Finsbury, I have no means of showing you my gratitude; but let me ask you one question,' said Pitman. 'If I were a very rich client, would you not take the risk?'

'Diamond, Diamond, you know not what you do!' cried Michael. 'Why, man, do you suppose I make a practice of cutting about London with my clients in disguise? Do you suppose money would induce me to touch this business with a stick? I give you my word of honour, it would not. But I own I have a real curiosity to see how you conduct this interview—that tempts me; it tempts me, Pitman, more than gold—it should be exquisitely rich.' And suddenly Michael laughed. 'Well, Pitman,' said he, 'have all the truck ready in the studio. I'll go.'

About twenty minutes after two, on this eventful day, the vast and gloomy shed of Waterloo lay, like the temple of a dead religion, silent and deserted. Here and there at one of the platforms, a train lay becalmed; here and there a wandering footfall echoed; the cab-horses outside stamped with startling reverberations on the stones; or from the neighbouring wilderness of railway an engine snorted forth a whistle. The main-line departure platform slumbered like the rest; the booking-hutches closed; the backs of Mr Haggard's novels, with which upon a weekday the bookstall shines emblazoned, discreetly hidden behind dingy shutters; the rare officials, undisguisedly somnambulant; and the customary loiterers, even to the middle-aged woman with the ulster and the handbag, fled to more congenial scenes. As in the inmost dells of some small tropic island the throbbing of the ocean lingers, so here a faint pervading hum and trepidation told in every corner of surrounding London.

At the hour already named, persons acquainted with John Dickson, of Ballarat, and Ezra Thomas, of the United States of America, would have been cheered to behold them enter through the booking-office.

'What names are we to take?' enquired the latter, anxiously adjusting the window-glass spectacles which he had been suffered on this occasion to assume.

'There's no choice for you, my boy,' returned Michael. 'Bent Pitman or nothing. As for me, I think I look as if I might be called Appleby; something agreeably old-world about Appleby—breathes of Devonshire cider. Talking of which, suppose you wet your whistle? the interview is likely to be trying.'

'I think I'll wait till afterwards,' returned Pitman; 'on the whole, I think I'll wait till the thing's over. I don't know if it strikes you as it does me; but the place seems deserted and silent, Mr Finsbury, and filled with very singular echoes.'

'Kind of Jack-in-the-box feeling?' enquired Michael, 'as if all these empty trains might be filled with policemen waiting for a signal? and Sir Charles Warren perched among the girders with a silver whistle to his lips? It's guilt, Pitman.'

In this uneasy frame of mind they walked nearly the whole length of the departure platform, and at the western extremity became aware of a slender figure standing back against a pillar. The figure was plainly sunk into a deep abstraction; he was not aware of their approach, but gazed far abroad over the sunlit station. Michael stopped.

'Holloa!' said he, 'can that be your advertiser? If so, I'm done with it.' And then, on second thoughts: 'Not so, either,' he resumed more cheerfully. 'Here, turn your back a moment. So. Give me the specs.'

'But you agreed I was to have them,' protested Pitman.

'Ah, but that man knows me,' said Michael.

'Does he? what's his name?' cried Pitman.

'O, he took me into his confidence,' returned the lawyer. 'But I may say one thing: if he's your advertiser (and he may be, for he seems to have been seized with criminal lunacy) you can go ahead with a clear conscience, for I hold him in the hollow of my hand.'

The change effected, and Pitman comforted with this good news, the pair drew near to Morris.

'Are you looking for Mr William Bent Pitman?' enquired the drawing-master. 'I am he.'

Morris raised his head. He saw before him, in the speaker, a person of almost indescribable insignificance, in white spats and a shirt cut indecently low. A little behind, a second and more burly figure offered little to criticism, except ulster, whiskers, spectacles, and deerstalker hat. Since he had decided to call up devils from the underworld of London, Morris had pondered deeply on the probabilities of their appearance. His first emotion, like that of Charoba when she beheld the sea, was one of disappointment; his second did more justice to the case. Never before had he seen a couple dressed like these; he had struck a new stratum.

'I must speak with you alone,' said he.

'You need not mind Mr Appleby,' returned Pitman. 'He knows all.'

'All? Do you know what I am here to speak of?' enquired Morris. 'The barrel.'

Pitman turned pale, but it was with manly indignation. 'You are the man!' he cried. 'You very wicked person.'

'Am I to speak before him?' asked Morris, disregarding these severe expressions.

'He has been present throughout,' said Pitman. 'He opened the barrel; your guilty secret is already known to him, as well as to your Maker and myself.'

'Well, then,' said Morris, 'what have you done with the money?'

'I know nothing about any money,' said Pitman.

'You needn't try that on,' said Morris. 'I have tracked you down; you came to the station sacrilegiously disguised as a clergyman, procured my barrel, opened it, rifled the body, and cashed the bill. I have been to the bank, I tell you! I have followed you step by step, and your denials are childish and absurd.'

'Come, come, Morris, keep your temper,' said Mr Appleby.

'Michael!' cried Morris, 'Michael here too!'

'Here too,' echoed the lawyer; 'here and everywhere, my good fellow; every step you take is counted; trained detectives follow you like your shadow; they report to me every three-quarters of an hour; no expense is spared.'

Morris's face took on a hue of dirty grey. 'Well, I don't care; I have the less reserve to keep,' he cried. 'That man cashed my bill; it's a theft, and I want the money back.'

'Do you think I would lie to you, Morris?' asked Michael.

'I don't know,' said his cousin. 'I want my money.'

'It was I alone who touched the body,' began Michael.

'You? Michael!' cried Morris, starting back. 'Then why haven't you declared the death?'

'What the devil do you mean?' asked Michael.

'Am I mad? or are you?' cried Morris.

'I think it must be Pitman,' said Michael.

The three men stared at each other, wild-eyed.

'This is dreadful,' said Morris, 'dreadful. I do not understand one word that is addressed to me.'

'I give you my word of honour, no more do I,' said Michael.

'And in God's name, why whiskers?' cried Morris, pointing in a ghastly manner at his cousin. 'Does my brain reel? How whiskers?'

'O, that's a matter of detail,' said Michael.

There was another silence, during which Morris appeared to himself to be shot in a trapeze as high as St Paul's, and as low as Baker Street Station.

'Let us recapitulate,' said Michael, 'unless it's really a dream, in which case I wish Teena would call me for breakfast. My friend Pitman, here, received a barrel which, it now appears, was meant for you. The barrel contained the body of a man. How or why you killed him . . .'

'I never laid a hand on him,' protested Morris. 'This is what I have dreaded all along. But think, Michael! I'm not that kind of man; with all my faults, I wouldn't touch a hair of anybody's head, and it was all dead loss to me. He got killed in that vile accident.'

Suddenly Michael was seized by mirth so prolonged and excessive that his companions supposed beyond a doubt his reason had deserted him. Again and again he struggled to compose himself, and again and again laughter overwhelmed him like a tide. In all this maddening interview there had been no more spectral feature than this of Michael's merriment; and Pitman and Morris, drawn together by the common fear, exchanged glances of anxiety.

'Morris,' gasped the lawyer, when he was at last able to articulate, 'hold on, I see it all now. I can make it clear in one word. Here's the key: *I never guessed it was Uncle Joseph till this moment.*'

This remark produced an instant lightening of the tension for Morris. For Pitman it quenched the last ray of hope and daylight. Uncle Joseph, whom he had left an hour ago in Norfolk Street, pasting newspaper cuttings?—it?—the dead body?—then who was he, Pitman? and was this Waterloo Station or Colney Hatch?

'To be sure!' cried Morris; 'it was badly smashed, I know. How stupid not to think of that! Why, then, all's clear; and, my dear Michael, I'll tell you what—we're saved, both saved. You get the tontine—I don't grudge it you the least—and I get the leather business, which is really beginning to look up. Declare the death at once, don't mind me in the smallest, don't consider me; declare the death, and we're all right.'

'Ah, but I can't declare it,' said Michael.

'Why not?' cried Morris.

'I can't produce the corpus, Morris. I've lost it,' said the lawyer.

'Stop a bit,' ejaculated the leather merchant. 'How is this? It's not possible. I lost it.'

'Well, I've lost it too, my son,' said Michael, with extreme serenity. 'Not recognizing it, you see, and suspecting something irregular in its origin, I got rid of—what shall we say?—got rid of the proceeds at once.'

'You got rid of the body? What made you do that?' wailed Morris. 'But you can get it again? You know where it is?'

'I wish I did, Morris, and you may believe me there, for it would be a small sum in my pocket; but the fact is, I don't,' said Michael.

'Good Lord,' said Morris, addressing heaven and earth, 'good Lord, I've lost the leather business!'

Michael was once more shaken with laughter.

'Why do you laugh, you fool?' cried his cousin, 'you lose more than I. You've bungled it worse than even I did. If you had a spark of feeling, you would be shaking in your boots with vexation. But I'll tell you one thing—I'll have that eight hundred pound—I'll have that and go to Swan River—that's mine, anyway, and your friend must have forged to cash it. Give me the eight hundred, here, upon this platform, or I go straight to Scotland Yard and turn the whole disreputable story inside out.'

'Morris,' said Michael, laying his hand upon his shoulder, 'hear reason. It wasn't us, it was the other man. We never even searched the body.'

'The other man?' repeated Morris.

'Yes, the other man. We palmed Uncle Joseph off upon another man,' said Michael.

'You what? You palmed him off? That's surely a singular expression,' said Morris.

'Yes, palmed him off for a piano,' said Michael with perfect simplicity. 'Remarkably full, rich tone,' he added.

Morris carried his hand to his brow and looked at it; it was wet with sweat. 'Fever,' said he.

'No, it was a Broadwood grand,' said Michael. 'Pitman here will tell you if it was genuine or not.'

'Eh? O! O yes, I believe it was a genuine Broadwood; I have played upon it several times myself,' said Pitman. 'The three-letter E was broken.'

'Don't say anything more about pianos,' said Morris, with a strong shudder; 'I'm not the man I used to be! This—this other man—let's come to him, if I can only manage to follow. Who is he? Where can I get hold of him?'

'Ah, that's the rub,' said Michael. 'He's been in possession of the desired article, let me see—since Wednesday, about four o'clock, and is now, I should imagine, on his way to the isles of Javan and Gadire.'

'Michael,' said Morris pleadingly, 'I am in a very weak state, and I beg your consideration for a kinsman. Say it slowly again, and be sure you are correct. When did he get it?'

Michael repeated his statement.

'Yes, that's the worst thing yet,' said Morris, drawing in his breath.

'What is?' asked the lawyer.

'Even the dates are sheer nonsense,' said the leather merchant. 'The bill was cashed on Tuesday. There's not a gleam of reason in the whole transaction.'

A young gentleman, who had passed the trio and suddenly started and turned back, at this moment laid a heavy hand on Michael's shoulder.

'Aha! so this is Mr Dickson?' said he.

The trump of judgement could scarce have rung with a more dreadful note in the ears of Pitman and the lawyer. To Morris this erroneous name seemed a legitimate enough continuation of the nightmare in which he had so long been wandering. And when Michael, with his brand-new bushy whiskers, broke from the grasp of the stranger and turned to run, and the weird little shaven creature in the low-necked shirt followed his example with a bird-like screech, and the stranger (finding the rest of his prey escape him) pounced with a rude grasp on Morris himself, that gentleman's frame of mind might be very nearly expressed in the colloquial phrase: 'I told you so!'

'I have one of the gang,' said Gideon Forsyth.

'I do not understand,' said Morris dully.

'O, I will make you understand,' returned Gideon grimly.

'You will be a good friend to me if you can make me understand anything,' cried Morris, with a sudden energy of conviction.

'I don't know you personally, do I?' continued Gideon, examining his unresisting prisoner. 'Never mind, I know your friends. They are your friends, are they not?'

'I do not understand you,' said Morris.

'You had possibly something to do with a piano?' suggested Gideon.

'A piano!' cried Morris, convulsively clasping Gideon by the arm. 'Then you're the other man! Where is it? Where is the body? And did you cash the draft?'

'Where is the body? This is very strange,' mused Gideon. 'Do you want the body?'

'Want it?' cried Morris. 'My whole fortune depends upon it! I lost it. Where is it? Take me to it!'

'O, you want it, do you? And the other man, Dickson—does he want it?' enquired Gideon.

'Who do you mean by Dickson? O, Michael Finsbury! Why, of course he does! He lost it too. If he had it, he'd have won the tontine tomorrow.'

'Michael Finsbury! Not the solicitor?' cried Gideon.

'Yes, the solicitor,' said Morris. 'But where is the body?'

'Then that is why he sent the brief! What is Mr Finsbury's private address?' asked Gideon.

'233 King's Road. What brief? Where are you going? Where is the body?' cried Morris, clinging to Gideon's arm.

'I have lost it myself,' returned Gideon, and ran out of the station.

CHAPTER XV

The Return of the Great Vance

Morris returned from Waterloo in a frame of mind that baffles description. He was a modest man; he had never conceived an overweening notion of his own powers; he knew himself unfit to write a book, turn a table napkin-ring, entertain a Christmas party with legerdemain—grapple (in short) any of those conspicuous accomplishments that are usually classed under the head of genius. He knew—he admitted—his parts to be pedestrian, but he had considered them (until quite lately) fully equal to the demands of life. And today he owned himself defeated: life had the upper hand; if there had been any means of flight or place to flee to, if the world had been so ordered that a man could leave it like a place of entertainment, Morris would have instantly resigned all further claim on its rewards and pleasures, and, with inexpressible contentment, ceased to be. As it was, one aim shone before him: he could get home. Even as the sick dog crawls under the sofa, Morris could shut the door of John Street and be alone.

The dusk was falling when he drew near this place of refuge; and the first thing that met his eyes was the figure of a man upon the step, alternately plucking at the bell-handle and pounding on the panels. The man had no hat, his clothes were hideous with filth, he had the air of a hop-picker. Yet Morris knew him; it was John.

The first impulse of flight was succeeded, in the elder brother's bosom, by the empty quiescence of despair. 'What does it matter now?' he thought, and drawing forth his latchkey ascended the steps.

John turned about; his face was ghastly with weariness and dirt and fury; and as he recognized the head of his family, he drew in a long rasping breath, and his eyes glittered.

'Open that door,' he said, standing back.

'I am going to,' said Morris, and added mentally, 'He looks like murder!'

The brothers passed into the hall, the door closed behind them; and suddenly John seized Morris by the shoulders and shook him as a terrier shakes a rat. 'You mangy little cad,' he said, 'I'd serve you right to smash your skull!' And shook him again, so that his teeth rattled and his head smote upon the wall.

'Don't be violent, Johnny,' said Morris. 'It can't do any good now.'

'Shut your mouth,' said John, 'your time's come to listen.'

He strode into the dining-room, fell into the easy-chair, and taking off one of his burst walking-shoes, nursed for a while his foot like one in agony. 'I'm lame for life,' he said. 'What is there for dinner?'

'Nothing, Johnny,' said Morris.

'Nothing? What do you mean by that?' enquired the Great Vance. 'Don't set up your chat to me!'

'I mean simply nothing,' said his brother. 'I have nothing to eat, and nothing to buy it with. I've only had a cup of tea and a sandwich all this day myself.'

'Only a sandwich?' sneered Vance. 'I suppose *you*'re going to complain next. But you had better take care: I've had all I mean to take; and I can tell you what it is, I mean to dine and to dine well. Take your signets and sell them.'

'I can't today,' objected Morris; 'it's Sunday.'

'I tell you I'm going to dine!' cried the younger brother.

'But if it's not possible, Johnny?' pleaded the other.

'You nincompoop!' cried Vance. 'Ain't we householders? Don't they know us at that hotel where Uncle Parker used to come. Be off with you; and if you ain't back in half an hour, and if the dinner ain't good, first I'll lick you till you don't want to breathe, and then I'll go straight to the police and blow the gaff. Do you understand that, Morris Finsbury? Because if you do, you had better jump.'

The idea smiled even upon the wretched Morris, who was sick with famine. He sped upon his errand, and returned to find John still nursing his foot in the armchair.

'What would you like to drink, Johnny?' he enquired soothingly.

'Fizz,' said John. 'Some of the poppy stuff from the end bin; a bottle of the old port that Michael liked, to follow; and see and don't shake the port. And look here, light the fire—and the gas, and draw down the blinds; it's cold and it's getting dark. And then you can lay the cloth. And, I say—here, you! bring me down some clothes.'

The room looked comparatively habitable by the time the dinner came; and the dinner itself was good: strong gravy soup, fillets of sole, mutton chops and tomato sauce, roast beef done rare with roast potatoes, cabinet pudding, a piece of Chester cheese, and some early celery: a meal uncompromisingly British, but supporting.

'Thank God!' said John, his nostrils sniffing wide, surprised by joy into the unwonted formality of grace. 'Now I'm going to take this chair with my back to the fire—there's been a strong frost these two last nights, and I can't get it out of my bones; the celery will be just the ticket—I'm going to sit here, and you are going to stand there, Morris Finsbury, and play butler.'

'But, Johnny, I'm so hungry myself,' pleaded Morris.

'You can have what I leave,' said Vance. 'You're just beginning to pay your score, my daisy; I owe you one-pound-ten; don't you rouse the British lion!' There was something indescribably menacing in the face and voice of the Great Vance as he uttered these words, at which the soul of Morris withered. 'There!' resumed the feaster, 'give us a glass of the fizz to start with. Gravy soup! And I thought I didn't like gravy soup! Do you know how I got here?' he asked, with another explosion of wrath.

'No, Johnny; how could I?' said the obsequious Morris.

'I walked on my ten toes!' cried John; 'tramped the whole way from Browndean; and begged! I would like to see you beg. It's not so easy as you might suppose. I played it on being a shipwrecked mariner from Blyth; I don't know where Blyth is, do you? but I thought it sounded natural. I begged from a little beast of a schoolboy, and he forked out a bit of twine, and asked me to make a clove hitch; I did, too, I know I did, but he said it wasn't, he said it was a granny's knot, and I was a what-d'ye-call-'em, and he would give me in charge. Then I begged from a naval officer—he never bothered me with knots, but he only gave me a tract; there's a nice account of the British navy!—and then from a widow woman that sold lollipops, and I got a hunch of bread from her. Another party I fell in with said you could generally always get bread; and the thing to do was to break a plate-glass window and get into gaol; seemed rather a brilliant scheme.—Pass the beef.'

'Why didn't you stay at Browndean?' Morris ventured to enquire.

'Skittles!' said John. 'On what? The *Pink Un* and a measly religious paper? I had to leave Browndean; I had to, I tell you. I got tick at a public, and set up to be the Great Vance; so would you, if you were leading such a beastly existence! And a card stood me a lot of ale and stuff, and we got swipey, talking about music-halls and the piles of tin

I got for singing; and then they got me on to sing "Around her splendid form I weaved the magic circle," and then he said I couldn't be Vance, and I stuck to it like grim death I was. It was rot of me to sing, of course, but I thought I could brazen it out with a set of yokels. It settled my hash at the public,' said John, with a sigh. 'And then the last thing was the carpenter——'

'Our landlord?' enquired Morris.

'That's the party,' said John. 'He came nosing about the place, and then wanted to know where the water-butt was, and the bedclothes. I told him to go to the devil; so would you too, when there was no possible thing to say! And then he said I had pawned them, and did I know it was felony? Then I made a pretty neat stroke. I remembered he was deaf, and talked a whole lot of rot, very politely, just so low he couldn't hear a word. "I don't hear you," says he. "I know you don't, my buck, and I don't mean you to," says I, smiling away like a haberdasher. "I'm hard of hearing," he roars. "I'd be in a pretty hot corner if you weren't," says I, making signs as if I was explaining everything. It was tip-top as long as it lasted. "Well," he said, "I'm deaf, worse luck, but I bet the constable can hear you." And off he started one way, and I the other. They got a spirit-lamp and the *Pink Un*, and that old religious paper, and another periodical you sent me. I think you must have been drunk—it had a name like one of those spots that Uncle Joseph used to hold forth at, and it was all full of the most awful swipes about poetry and the use of the globes. It was the kind of thing that nobody could read out of a lunatic asylum. The *Athæneum*, that was the name! Golly, what a paper!'

'*Athenæum*, you mean,' said Morris.

'I don't care what you call it,' said John, 'so as I don't require to take it in! There, I feel better. Now I'm going to sit by the fire in the easy-chair; pass me the cheese, and the celery, and the bottle of port—no, a champagne glass, it holds more. And now you can pitch in; there's some of the fish left and a chop, and some fizz. Ah,' sighed the refreshed pedestrian, 'Michael was right about that port; there's old and vatted for you! Michael's a man I like; he's clever and reads books, and the *Athæneum*, and all that; but he's not dreary to meet, he don't talk *Athæneum* like the other parties; why, the most of them would throw a blight over a skittle alley! Talking of Michael, I ain't bored myself to put the question, because of course I knew it from the first. You've made a hash of it, eh?'

'Michael made a hash of it,' said Morris, flushing dark.

'What have we got to do with that?' enquired John.

'He has lost the body, that's what we have to do with it,' cried Morris. 'He has lost the body, and the death can't be established.'

'Hold on,' said John. 'I thought you didn't want to?'

'O, we're far past that,' said his brother. 'It's not the tontine now, it's the leather business, Johnny; it's the clothes upon our back.'

'Stow the slow music,' said John, 'and tell your story from beginning to end.'

Morris did as he was bid.

'Well, now, what did I tell you?' cried the Great Vance, when the other had done. 'But I know one thing: I'm not going to be humbugged out of my property.'

'I should like to know what you mean to do,' said Morris.

'I'll tell you that,' responded John with extreme decision. 'I'm going to put my interests in the hands of the smartest lawyer in London; and whether you go to quod or not is a matter of indifference to me.'

'Why, Johnny, we're in the same boat!' expostulated Morris.

'Are we?' cried his brother. 'I bet we're not! Have I committed forgery? have I lied about Uncle Joseph? have I put idiotic advertisements in the comic papers? have I smashed other people's statues? I like your cheek, Morris Finsbury. No, I've let you run my affairs too long; now they shall go to Michael. I like Michael, anyway; and it's time I understood my situation.'

At this moment the brethren were interrupted by a ring at the bell, and Morris, going timorously to the door, received from the hands of a commissionaire a letter addressed in the hand of Michael. Its contents ran as follows:

MORRIS FINSBURY, if this should meet the eye of, he will hear of SOMETHING TO HIS ADVANTAGE at my office, in Chancery Lane, at 10 A.M. tomorrow.

MICHAEL FINSBURY

So utter was Morris's subjection that he did not wait to be asked, but handed the note to John as soon as he had glanced at it himself.

'That's the way to write a letter,' cried John. 'Nobody but Michael could have written that.'

And Morris did not even claim the credit of priority.

CHAPTER XVI

Final Adjustment of the Leather Business

Finsbury brothers were ushered, at ten the next morning, into a large apartment in Michael's office; the Great Vance, somewhat restored from yesterday's exhaustion, but with one foot in a slipper; Morris, not positively damaged, but a man ten years older than he who had left Bournemouth eight days before, his face ploughed full of anxious wrinkles, his dark hair liberally grizzled at the temples.

Three persons were seated at a table to receive them: Michael in the midst, Gideon Forsyth on his right hand, on his left an ancient gentleman with spectacles and silver hair.

'By Jingo, it's Uncle Joe!' cried John.

But Morris approached his uncle with a pale countenance and glittering eyes.

'I'll tell you what you did!' he cried. 'You absconded!'

'Good-morning, Morris Finsbury,' returned Joseph, with no less asperity; 'you are looking seriously ill.'

'No use making trouble now,' remarked Michael. 'Look the facts in the face. Your uncle, as you see, was not so much as shaken in the accident; a man of your humane disposition ought to be delighted.'

'Then, if that's so,' Morris broke forth, 'how about the body? You don't mean to insinuate that thing I schemed and sweated for, and colported with my own hands, was the body of a total stranger?'

'O no, we can't go as far as that,' said Michael soothingly; 'you may have met him at the club.'

Morris fell into a chair. 'I would have found it out if it had come to the house,' he complained. 'And why didn't it? why did it go to Pitman? what right had Pitman to open it?'

'If you come to that, Morris, what have you done with the colossal Hercules?' asked Michael.

'He went through it with the meat-axe,' said John. 'It's all in spillikins in the back garden.'

'Well, there's one thing,' snapped Morris; 'there's my uncle again, my fraudulent trustee. He's mine, anyway. And the tontine too. I claim the tontine; I claim it now. I believe Uncle Masterman's dead.'

'I must put a stop to this nonsense,' said Michael, 'and that for ever. You say too near the truth. In one sense your uncle is dead, and has been so long; but not in the sense of the tontine, which it is even on the cards he may yet live to win. Uncle Joseph saw him this morning; he will tell you he still lives, but his mind is in abeyance.'

'He did not know me,' said Joseph; to do him justice, not without emotion.

'So you're out again there, Morris,' said John. 'My eye! what a fool you've made of yourself!'

'And that was why you wouldn't compromise,' said Morris.

'As for the absurd position in which you and Uncle Joseph have been making yourselves an exhibition,' resumed Michael, 'it is more than time it came to an end. I have prepared a proper discharge in full, which you shall sign as a preliminary.'

'What!' cried Morris, 'and lose my seven thousand eight hundred pounds, and the leather business, and the contingent interest, and get nothing? Thank you.'

'It's like you to feel gratitude, Morris,' began Michael.

'O, I know it's no good appealing to you, you sneering devil!' cried Morris. 'But there's a stranger present, I can't think why, and I appeal to him. I was robbed of that money when I was an orphan, a mere child, at a commercial academy. Since then, I've never had a wish but to get back my own. You may hear a lot of stuff about me; and there's no doubt at times I have been ill-advised. But it's the pathos of my situation; that's what I want to show you.'

'Morris,' interrupted Michael, 'I do wish you would let me add one point, for I think it will affect your judgement. It's pathetic too—since that's your taste in literature.'

'Well, what is it?' said Morris.

'It's only the name of one of the persons who's to witness your signature, Morris,' replied Michael. 'His name's Moss, my dear.'

There was a long silence. 'I might have been sure it was you!' cried Morris.

'You'll sign, won't you?' said Michael.

'Do you know what you're doing?' cried Morris. 'You're compounding a felony.'

'Very well, then, we won't compound it, Morris,' returned Michael. 'See how little I understood the sterling integrity of your character! I thought you would prefer it so.'

'Look here, Michael,' said John, 'this is all very fine and large; but how about me? Morris is gone up, I see that; but I'm not. And I was robbed, too, mind you; and just as much an orphan, and at the blessed same academy as himself.'

'Johnny,' said Michael, 'don't you think you'd better leave it to me?'

'I'm your man,' said John. 'You wouldn't deceive a poor orphan, I'll take my oath. Morris, you sign that document, or I'll start in and astonish your weak mind.'

With a sudden alacrity, Morris proffered his willingness. Clerks were brought in, the discharge was executed, and there was Joseph a free man once more.

'And now,' said Michael, 'hear what I propose to do. Here, John and Morris, is the leather business made over to the pair of you in partnership. I have valued it at the lowest possible figure, Pogram and Jarris's. And here is a cheque for the balance of your fortune. Now, you see, Morris, you start fresh from the commercial academy; and, as you said yourself the leather business was looking up, I suppose you'll probably marry before long. Here's your marriage present—from a Mr Moss.'

Morris bounded on his cheque with a crimsoned countenance.

'I don't understand the performance,' remarked John. 'It seems too good to be true.'

'It's simply a readjustment,' Michael explained. 'I take up Uncle Joseph's liabilities; and if he gets the tontine, it's to be mine; if my father gets it, it's mine anyway, you see. So that I'm rather advantageously placed.'

'Morris, my unconverted friend, you've got left,' was John's comment.

'And now, Mr Forsyth,' resumed Michael, turning to his silent guest, 'here are all the criminals before you, except Pitman. I really didn't like to interrupt his scholastic career; but you can have him arrested at the seminary—I know his hours. Here we are then; we're not pretty to look at: what do you propose to do with us?'

'Nothing in the world, Mr Finsbury,' returned Gideon. 'I seem to understand that this gentleman'—indicating Morris—'is the *fons et origo* of the trouble; and, from what I gather, he has already paid through the nose. And really, to be quite frank, I do not see who is to gain by any scandal; not me, at least. And besides, I have to thank you for that brief.'

Michael blushed. 'It was the least I could do to let you have some business,' he said. 'But there's one thing more. I don't want you to misjudge poor Pitman, who is the most harmless being upon earth. I wish you would dine with me tonight, and see the creature on his native heath—say at Verrey's?'

'I have no engagement, Mr Finsbury,' replied Gideon. 'I shall be delighted. But subject to your judgement, can we do nothing for the man in the cart? I have qualms of conscience.'

'Nothing but sympathize,' said Michael.

OXFORD

MORE OXFORD PAPERBACKS

This book is just one of nearly 1000 Oxford Paperbacks currently in print. If you would like details of other Oxford Paperbacks, including titles in the World's Classics, Oxford Reference, Oxford Books, OPUS, Past Masters, Oxford Authors, and Oxford Shakespeare series, please write to:

UK and Europe: Oxford Paperbacks Publicity Manager, Arts and Reference Publicity Department, Oxford University Press, Walton Street, Oxford OX2 6DP.

Customers in UK and Europe will find Oxford Paperbacks available in all good bookshops. But in case of difficulty please send orders to the Cash-with-Order Department, Oxford University Press Distribution Services, Saxon Way West, Corby, Northants NN18 9ES. Tel: 01536 741519; Fax: 01536 746337. Please send a cheque for the total cost of the books, plus £1.75 postage and packing for orders under £20; £2.75 for orders over £20. Customers outside the UK should add 10% of the cost of the books for postage and packing.

USA: Oxford Paperbacks Marketing Manager, Oxford University Press, Inc., 200 Madison Avenue, New York, N.Y. 10016.

Canada: Trade Department, Oxford University Press, 70 Wynford Drive, Don Mills, Ontario M3C 1J9.

Australia: Trade Marketing Manager, Oxford University Press, G.P.O. Box 2784Y, Melbourne 3001, Victoria.

South Africa: Oxford University Press, P.O. Box 1141, Cape Town 8000.

OXFORD BOOKS

THE OXFORD BOOK OF ENGLISH GHOST STORIES

Chosen by Michael Cox and R. A. Gilbert

This anthology includes some of the best and most frightening ghost stories ever written, including M. R. James's 'Oh Whistle, and I'll Come to You, My Lad', 'The Monkey's Paw' by W. W. Jacobs, and H. G. Wells's 'The Red Room'. The important contribution of women writers to the genre is represented by stories such as Amelia Edwards's 'The Phantom Coach', Edith Wharton's 'Mr Jones', and Elizabeth Bowen's 'Hand in Glove'.

As the editors stress in their informative introduction, a good ghost story, though it may raise many profound questions about life and death, entertains as much as it unsettles us, and the best writers are careful to satisfy what Virginia Woolf called 'the strange human craving for the pleasure of feeling afraid'. This anthology, the first to present the full range of classic English ghost fiction, similarly combines a serious literary purpose with the plain intention of arousing pleasing fear at the doings of the dead.

'an excellent cross-section of familiar and unfamiliar stories and guaranteed to delight' *New Statesman*

OPUS

General Editors: Walter Bodmer, Christopher Butler, Robert Evans, John Skorupski

CLASSICAL THOUGHT

Terence Irwin

Spanning over a thousand years from Homer to Saint Augustine, *Classical Thought* encompasses a vast range of material, in succinct style, while remaining clear and lucid even to those with no philosophical or Classical background.

The major philosophers and philosophical schools are examined—the Presocratics, Socrates, Plato, Aristotle, Stoicism, Epicureanism, Neoplatonism; but other important thinkers, such as Greek tragedians, historians, medical writers, and early Christian writers, are also discussed. The emphasis is naturally on questions of philosophical interest (although the literary and historical background to Classical philosophy is not ignored), and again the scope is broad—ethics, the theory of knowledge, philosophy of mind, philosophical theology. All this is presented in a fully integrated, highly readable text which covers many of the most important areas of ancient thought and in which stress is laid on the variety and continuity of philosophical thinking after Aristotle.

OXFORD BOOKS

THE NEW OXFORD BOOK OF
IRISH VERSE

Edited, with Translations, by Thomas Kinsella

Verse in Irish, especially from the early and med-
ieval periods, has long been felt to be the preserve of
linguists and specialists, while Anglo-Irish poetry is
usually seen as an adjunct to the English tradition.
This original anthology approaches the Irish poetic
tradition as a unity and presents a relationship
between two major bodies of poetry that reflects a
shared and painful history.

'the first coherent attempt to present the entire
range of Irish poetry in both languages to an Eng-
lish-speaking readership' *Irish Times*

'a very satisfying and moving introduction to Irish
poetry' *Listener*

OXFORD POETS

FLEUR ADCOCK

Time Zones

In this lively new collection, Fleur Adcock's subjects range from domestic matters—recalling the birth of her son some years back; remembering her father, the news of whose death in New Zealand reaches her, the expatriate, in England; working in her own London garden—to matters of contemporary concern, such as the Romanian bid for freedom in 1989, and support for Green causes, including the anti-nuclear stand.

'She is an eminently readable poet, whose quiet accuracy sometimes makes me laugh out loud.'
Wendy Cope, *Guardian*

THE OXFORD AUTHORS

General Editor: Frank Kermode

THE OXFORD AUTHORS is a series of authoritative editions of major English writers. Aimed at both students and general readers, each volume contains a generous selection of the best writings—poetry, prose, and letters—to give the essence of a writer's work and thinking. All the texts are complemented by essential notes, an introduction, chronology, and suggestions for further reading.

ANTHONY TROLLOPE IN THE
WORLD'S CLASSICS

THE THREE CLERKS

Anthony Trollope

Edited with an Introduction by
Graham Handley

The Three Clerks is Trollope's first important and incisive commentary on the contemporary scene. Set in the 1850s, it satirizes the recently instituted Civil Service examinations and financial corruption in dealings on the stock market.

The story of the three clerks and the three sisters who become their wives shows Trollope probing and exposing relationships with natural sympathy and insight before the fuller triumphs of Barchester, the political novels, and *The Way We Live* Now. The novel is imbued with autobiographical warmth and immediacy, the ironic appraisal of politics and society deftly balanced by romantic and domestic pathos and tribulation. The unscrupulous wheeling and dealing of Undy Scott is colourfully offset by the first appearance in Trollope's fiction of the bullying, eccentric, and compelling lawyer Mr Chaffanbrass.

The text is that of the single-volume edition of 1859, and an appendix gives the most important cuts that Trollope made for that edition.

WORLD'S CLASSICS SHAKESPEARE

'not simply a better text but a new conception of Shakespeare. This is a major achievement of twentieth-century scholarship.' Times Literary Supplement

Hamlet
Macbeth
The Merchant of Venice
As You Like It
Henry IV Part I
Henry V
Measure for Measure
The Tempest
Much Ado About Nothing
All's Well that Ends Well
Love's Labours Lost
The Merry Wives of Windsor
The Taming of the Shrew
Titus Andronicus
Troilus & Cressida
The Two Noble Kinsmen
King John
Julius Caesar
Coriolanus
Anthony & Cleopatra

WORLD'S CLASSICS SHAKESPEARE
MACBETH
Edited by Nicholas Brooke

Dark and violent, *Macbeth* is also the most theatrically spectacular of Shakepeare's tragedies. This fully annotated edition reconsiders textual and staging problems, appraises past and present critical views, and represents a major contribution to our understanding of the play.

In his introduction Nicholas Brooke relates *Macbeth*'s changing fortunes to changes within society and the theatre and investigates the sources of its enduring appeal. He examines its many layers of illusion and interprets its linguistic turns and echoes, arguing that the earliest surviving text is an adaptation, perhaps carried out by Shakespeare himself in collaboration with Thomas Middleton.

WORLD'S CLASSICS SHAKESPEARE
AS YOU LIKE IT
Edited by Alan Brissenden

As You Like It is Shakespeare's most light-hearted comedy, and its witty heroine Rosalind has his longest female role.

In this edition, Alan Brissenden reassesses both its textual and performance history, showing how interpretations have changed since the first recorded production in 1740. He examines Shakespeare's sources and elucidates the central themes of love, pastoral, and doubleness. Detailed annotations investigate the allusive and often bawdy language, enabling student, actor, and director to savour the humour and the seriousness of the play to the full.

Oxford Reference

The Oxford Reference series offers authoritative and up-to-date reference books in paperback across a wide range of topics.

Abbreviations
Art and Artists
Ballet
Biology
Botany
Business
Card Games
Chemistry
Christian Church
Classical Literature
Computing
Dates
Earth Sciences
Ecology
English Christian
    Names
English Etymology
English Language
English Literature
English Place-Names
Eponyms
Finance
Fly-Fishing
Fowler's Modern
    English Usage
Geography
Irish Mythology
King's English
Law
Literary Guide to Great
    Britain and Ireland
Literary Terms

Mathematics
Medical Dictionary
Modern Quotations
Modern Slang
Music
Nursing
Opera
Oxford English
Physics
Popes
Popular Music
Proverbs
Quotations
Sailing Terms
Saints
Science
Ships and the Sea
Sociology
Spelling
Superstitions
Theatre
Twentieth-Century Art
Twentieth-Century
    History
Twentieth-Century
    World Biography
Weather Facts
Word Games
World Mythology
Writer's Dictionary
Zoology

ILLUSTRATED HISTORIES IN OXFORD PAPERBACKS

THE OXFORD ILLUSTRATED HISTORY OF ENGLISH LITERATURE

Edited by Pat Rogers

Britain possesses a literary heritage which is almost unrivalled in the Western world. In this volume, the richness, diversity, and continuity of that tradition are explored by a group of Britain's foremost literary scholars.

Chapter by chapter the authors trace the history of English literature, from its first stirrings in Anglo-Saxon poetry to the present day. At its heart towers the figure of Shakespeare, who is accorded a special chapter to himself. Other major figures such as Chaucer, Milton, Donne, Wordsworth, Dickens, Eliot, and Auden are treated in depth, and the story is brought up to date with discussion of living authors such as Seamus Heaney and Edward Bond.

'[a] lovely volume . . . put in your thumb and pull out plums' Michael Foot

'scholarly and enthusiastic people have written inspiring essays that induce an eagerness in their readers to return to the writers they admire' *Economist*

OXFORD REFERENCE

THE CONCISE OXFORD COMPANION
TO ENGLISH LITERATURE

*Edited by Margaret Drabble and
Jenny Stringer*

Based on the immensely popular fifth edition of the
Oxford Companion to English Literature this is an
indispensable, compact guide to the central matter
of English literature.

There are more than 5,000 entries on the lives
and works of authors, poets, playwrights, essayists,
philosophers, and historians; plot summaries of
novels and plays; literary movements; fictional
characters; legends; theatres; periodicals; and much
more.

The book's sharpened focus on the English literature of the British Isles makes it especially convenient to use, but there is still generous coverage of
the literature of other countries and of other disci-
plines which have influenced or been influenced by
English literature.

From reviews of *The Oxford Companion to
English Literature*:

'a book which one turns to with constant pleasure
. . . a book with much style and little prejudice' Iain
Gilchrist, *TLS*

'it is quite difficult to imagine, in this genre, a more
useful publication' Frank Kermode, *London Review of Books*

'incarnates a living sense of tradition . . . sensitive
not to fashion merely but to the spirit of the age'
Christopher Ricks, *Sunday Times*

OXFORD POPULAR FICTION

THE ORIGINAL MILLION SELLERS!

This series boasts some of the most talked-about works of British and US fiction of the last 150 years—books that helped define the literary styles and genres of crime, historical fiction, romance, adventure, and social comedy, which modern readers enjoy.